CW01510194

CAPITAL CHRISTIE

ALSO BY AGATHA CHRISTIE

★ novelized by Charles Osborne

AGATHA CHRISTIE

CAPITAL CHRISTIE

TWELVE LONDON MYSTERIES

HarperCollins*Publishers*

HarperCollins*Publishers* Ltd
1 London Bridge Street,
London SE1 9GF
www.harpercollins.co.uk

HarperCollins*Publishers*
Macken House, 39/40 Mayor Street Upper
Dublin 1, D01 C9W8, Ireland

First published by HarperCollins*Publishers* 2025
1

Capital Christie © 2025 Agatha Christie Limited.
All rights reserved

WITNESS FOR THE PROSECUTION, AGATHA CHRISTIE,
POIROT, MARPLE, TOMMY AND TUPPENCE, the Agatha Christie
Signature and the AC Monogram Logo are registered trademarks of
Agatha Christie Limited in the UK and elsewhere. All rights reserved.
www.agathachristie.co.uk

A catalogue record for this book is available from the British Library

ISBN: 978-0-00-873800-6

Set in Bembo Std by HarperCollins*Publishers* India

Printed and bound in the UK using 100%
Renewable Electricity at CPI Group (UK) Ltd

All rights reserved. No part of this publication may be reproduced,
stored in a retrieval system, or transmitted, in any form or by any means,
electronic, mechanical, photocopying, recording or otherwise,
without the prior written permission of the publishers.

Without limiting the author's and publisher's exclusive rights, any unauthorised
use of this publication to train generative artificial intelligence (AI) technologies
is expressly prohibited. HarperCollins also exercise their rights under Article 4(3)
of the Digital Single Market Directive 2019/790 and expressly reserve
this publication from the text and data mining exception.

This book is produced from independently certified FSC™ paper
to ensure responsible forest management.

For more information visit: www.harpercollins.co.uk/green

CONTENTS

INTRODUCTION
London WWII

The war seemed to have shifted from our part of the world . . . I had decided that I would go to London and join Max, who was working there on Turkish Relief. I arrived in London, just after the raids, and Max, having met me at Paddington, drove me to a flat in Half Moon Street. 'I'm afraid,' he said apologetically, 'it is a pretty nasty one. We can look around for something else.'

What slightly put me off, when I arrived, was the fact that the house in question stood up like a tooth—the houses on either side of it were missing. They had apparently been hit by a bomb about ten days before, and for that reason the flat was available for rent, its owners having cleared out quickly. I can't say I felt very comfortable in that house. It smelt horribly of dirt and grease and cheap scent.

Max and I moved after a week into Park Place, off St. James's Street, which had once been rather an expensive service flat. We lived there for some little time, with noisy sessions of bombs going off all round us. I was particularly sorry for the waiters, who had to serve meals in the evening and then take themselves home through the air raids. Presently our tenants in Sheffield Terrace asked if they could give up the lease of our house, so we moved back in.

Then Max, to his great joy, got into the Air Force, helped by our friend Stephen Glanville, who was a Professor of Egyptology. He and Max were both at the Air Ministry, where they shared a room, both of them smoking—Max a pipe—without ceasing. The atmosphere was such that it was called by all their friends 'the small cat-house'.

Events happened in confusing order. I remember that Sheffield Terrace was bombed on a weekend when we were away from London. A landmine came down exactly opposite it, on the other side of the street, and completely destroyed three houses. The effect it had on 48 Sheffield Terrace was to blow up the basement, which might have been presumed the safest place, and to damage the roof and the top floor, leaving the ground and first floors almost unharmed. My Steinway was never quite the same afterwards. Since Max and I had always slept in our own bedroom, and never went down to the basement, we should not have suffered any personal damage even if we had been in the house. I myself never went down to any shelter during the war. I always had a horror of being trapped underground—so I slept in my own bed no matter where I was. I became used in the end to raids on London—so much so, that I hardly woke up. I would think, half drowsily, that I heard the siren, or bombs not too far away. 'Oh dear, there they are again!' I would mutter, and turn over.

One of the difficulties with the bombing of Sheffield Terrace was that by this time it was difficult to get storage space anywhere in London. As the house now was, it was difficult to get into it through the front door and one could only get access to it by ladder. In the end, I prevailed upon a firm to move me, and hit upon the idea of storing the furniture at Wallingford, in the squash court which we had built a year or two previously.

So everything was moved down there. I had builders in attendance ready to take out the squash court door and its framework if necessary—and this they had to do because the sofa and chairs would not go through the narrow doorway.

Max and I moved to a block of flats in Hampstead—Lawn Road Flats—and I started work at University College Hospital as a dispenser.

When Max broke to me what he had already known, I think, for some time, that he would have to go abroad to the Middle East, probably North Africa or Egypt, I was glad for him. I knew how he had been fretting to go, and it seemed right, too, that his knowledge of Arabic should be used. It was our first parting for ten years.

Agatha Christie

The Affair at the Victory Ball

Pure chance led my friend Hercule Poirot, formerly chief of the Belgian force, to be connected with the Styles Case. His success brought him notoriety, and he decided to devote himself to the solving of problems in crime. Having been wounded on the Somme and invalided out of the Army, I finally took up my quarters with him in London. Since I have a first-hand knowledge of most of his cases, it has been suggested to me that I select some of the most interesting and place them on record. In doing so, I feel that I cannot do better than begin with that strange tangle which aroused such widespread public interest at the time. I refer to the affair at the Victory Ball.

Although perhaps it is not so fully demonstrative of Poirot's peculiar methods as some of the more obscure cases, its sensational features, the well-known people involved, and the tremendous publicity given it by the Press, make it stand out as a *cause célèbre* and I have long felt that it is only fitting that Poirot's connection with the solution should be given to the world.

It was a fine morning in spring, and we were sitting in Poirot's rooms. My little friend, neat and dapper as ever, his egg-shaped head tilted on one side, was delicately applying a new pomade to his moustache. A certain harmless vanity was a characteristic of Poirot's and fell into line with his general love of order and method. The *Daily Newsmonger*, which I had been reading, had slipped to the floor, and I was deep in a brown study when Poirot's voice recalled me.

'Of what are you thinking so deeply, *mon ami*?'

'To tell you the truth,' I replied, 'I was puzzling over this unaccountable affair at the Victory Ball. The papers are full of it.' I tapped the sheet with my finger as I spoke.

'Yes?'

'The more one reads of it, the more shrouded in mystery the whole thing becomes!' I warmed to my subject. 'Who killed Lord Cronshaw? Was Coco Courtenay's death on the same night a mere coincidence? Was it an accident? Or did she deliberately take an overdose of cocaine?' I stopped, and then added dramatically: 'These are the questions I ask myself.'

Poirot, somewhat to my annoyance, did not play up. He was peering into the glass, and merely murmured: 'Decidedly, this new pomade, it is a marvel for the moustaches!' Catching my eye, however, he added hastily: 'Quite so—and how do you reply to your questions?'

But before I could answer, the door opened, and our landlady announced Inspector Japp.

The Scotland Yard man was an old friend of ours and we greeted him warmly.

'Ah, my good Japp,' cried Poirot, 'and what brings you to see us?'

'Well, Monsieur Poirot,' said Japp, seating himself and nodding to me, 'I'm on a case that strikes me as being very much in your line, and I came along to know whether you'd care to have a finger in the pie?'

Poirot had a good opinion of Japp's abilities, though deploring his lamentable lack of method, but I, for my part, considered that the detective's highest talent lay in the gentle art of seeking favours under the guise of conferring them!

'It's the Victory Ball,' said Japp persuasively. 'Come, now, you'd like to have a hand in that.'

Poirot smiled at me.

'My friend Hastings would, at all events. He was just holding forth on the subject, *n'est-ce pas, mon ami?*'

'Well, sir,' said Japp condescendingly, 'you shall be in it too. I can tell you, it's something of a feather in your cap to have inside knowledge of a case like this. Well, here's to business. You know the main facts of the case, I suppose, Monsieur Poirot?'

'From the papers only—and the imagination of the journalist is sometimes misleading. Recount the whole story to me.'

Japp crossed his legs comfortably and began.

'As all the world and his wife knows, on Tuesday last a grand Victory Ball was held. Every twopenny-halfpenny hop calls itself that nowadays, but this was the real thing, held at the Colossus Hall, and all London at it—including your Lord Cronshaw and his party.'

'His *dossier?*' interrupted Poirot. 'I should say his bioscope—no, how do you call it—biograph?'

'Viscount Cronshaw was fifth viscount, twenty-five years of age, rich, unmarried, and very fond of the

3

theatrical world. There were rumours of his being engaged to Miss Courtenay of the Albany Theatre, who was known to her friends as "Coco" and who was, by all accounts, a very fascinating young lady.'

'Good. *Continuez*!'

'Lord Cronshaw's party consisted of six people: he himself, his uncle, the Honourable Eustace Beltane, a pretty American widow, Mrs Mallaby, a young actor, Chris Davidson, his wife, and last but not least, Miss Coco Courtenay. It was a fancy dress ball, as you know, and the Cronshaw party represented the old Italian Comedy—whatever that may be.'

'The *Commedia dell' Arte*,' murmured Poirot. 'I know.'

'Anyway, the costumes were copied from a set of china figures forming part of Eustace Beltane's collection. Lord Cronshaw was Harlequin; Beltane was Punchinello; Mrs Mallaby matched him as Pulcinella; the Davidsons were Pierrot and Pierette; and Miss Courtenay, of course, was Columbine. Now, quite early in the evening it was apparent that there was something wrong. Lord Cronshaw was moody and strange in his manner. When the party met together for supper in a small private room engaged by the host, everyone noticed that he and Miss Courtenay were no longer on speaking terms. She had obviously been crying, and seemed on the verge of hysterics. The meal was an uncomfortable one, and as they all left the supper-room, she turned to Chris Davidson and requested him audibly to take her home, as she was "sick of the ball". The young actor hesitated, glancing at Lord Cronshaw, and finally drew them both back to the supper-room.

'But all his efforts to secure a reconciliation were unavailing, and he accordingly got a taxi and escorted the now weeping Miss Courtenay back to her flat. Although obviously very much upset, she did not confide in him, merely reiterating again and again that she would "make old Cronch sorry for this!" That is the only hint we have that her death might not have been accidental, and it's precious little to go upon. By the time Davidson had quieted her down somewhat, it was too late to return to the Colossus Hall, and Davidson accordingly went straight home to his flat in Chelsea, where his wife arrived shortly afterwards, bearing the news of the terrible tragedy that had occurred after his departure.

'Lord Cronshaw, it seems, became more and more moody as the ball went on. He kept away from his party, and they hardly saw him during the rest of the evening. It was about one-thirty a.m., just before the grand cotillion when everyone was to unmask, that Captain Digby, a brother officer who knew his disguise, noticed him standing in a box gazing down on the scene.

'"Hullo, Cronch!" he called. "Come down and be sociable! What are you moping about up there for like a boiled owl? Come along; there's a good old rag coming on now."

'"Right!" responded Cronshaw. "Wait for me, or I'll never find you in the crowd."

'He turned and left the box as he spoke. Captain Digby, who had Mrs Davidson with him, waited. The minutes passed, but Lord Cronshaw did not appear. Finally Digby grew impatient.

'"Does the fellow think we're going to wait all night for him?" he exclaimed.

'At that moment Mrs Mallaby joined them, and they explained the situation.

'"Say, now," cried the pretty widow vivaciously, "he's like a bear with a sore head tonight. Let's go right away and rout him out."

'The search commenced, but met with no success until it occurred to Mrs Mallaby that he might possibly be found in the room where they had supped an hour earlier. They made their way there. What a sight met their eyes! There was Harlequin, sure enough, but stretched on the ground with a table-knife in his heart!'

Japp stopped, and Poirot nodded, and said with the relish of the specialist: '*Une belle affaire*! And there was no clue as to the perpetrator of the deed? But how should there be!'

'Well,' continued the inspector, 'you know the rest. The tragedy was a double one. Next day there were headlines in all the papers, and a brief statement to the effect that Miss Courtenay, the popular actress, had been discovered dead in her bed, and that her death was due to an overdose of cocaine. Now, was it accident or suicide? Her maid, who was called upon to give evidence, admitted that Miss Courtenay was a confirmed taker of the drug, and a verdict of accidental death was returned. Nevertheless we can't leave the possibility of suicide out of account. Her death is particularly unfortunate, since it leaves us no clue now to the cause of the quarrel the preceding night. By the way, a small enamel box was found on the dead man. It had *Coco* written across it in diamonds, and was half full of cocaine. It was identified by Miss Courtenay's maid as belonging to her mistress, who nearly always carried it about with her, since it contained her supply of the drug to which she was fast becoming a slave.'

'Was Lord Cronshaw himself addicted to the drug?'

'Very far from it. He held unusually strong views on the subject of dope.'

Poirot nodded thoughtfully.

'But since the box was in his possession, he knew that Miss Courtenay took it. Suggestive, that, is it not, my good Japp?'

'Ah!' said Japp rather vaguely.

I smiled.

'Well,' said Japp, 'that's the case. What do you think of it?'

'You found no clue of any kind that has not been reported?'

'Yes, there was this.' Japp took a small object from his pocket and handed it over to Poirot. It was a small pompon of emerald green silk, with some ragged threads hanging from it, as though it had been wrenched violently away.

'We found it in the dead man's hand, which was tightly clenched over it,' explained the inspector.

Poirot handed it back without any comment and asked: 'Had Lord Cronshaw any enemies?'

'None that anyone knows of. He seemed a popular young fellow.'

'Who benefits by his death?'

'His uncle, the Honourable Eustace Beltane, comes into the title and estates. There are one or two suspicious facts against him. Several people declare that they heard a violent altercation going on in the little supper-room, and that Eustace Beltane was one of the disputants. You see, the table-knife being snatched up off the table would fit in with the murder being done in the heat of a quarrel.'

'What does Mr Beltane say about the matter?'

'Declares one of the waiters was the worse for liquor, and that he was giving him a dressing down. Also that it was nearer to one than half past. You see, Captain Digby's evidence fixes the time pretty accurately. Only about ten minutes elapsed between his speaking to Cronshaw and the finding of the body.'

'And in any case I suppose Mr Beltane, as Punchinello, was wearing a hump and a ruffle?'

'I don't know the exact details of the costumes,' said Japp, looking curiously at Poirot. 'And anyway, I don't quite see what that has got to do with it?'

'No?' There was a hint of mockery in Poirot's smile. He continued quietly, his eyes shining with the green light I had learned to recognize so well: 'There was a curtain in this little supper-room, was there not?'

'Yes, but—'

'With a space behind it sufficient to conceal a man?'

'Yes—in fact, there's a small recess, but how you knew about it—you haven't been to the place, have you, Monsieur Poirot?'

'No, my good Japp, I supplied the curtain from my brain. Without it, the drama is not reasonable. And always one must be reasonable. But tell me, did they not send for a doctor?'

'At once, of course. But there was nothing to be done. Death must have been instantaneous.'

Poirot nodded rather impatiently.

'Yes, yes, I understand. This doctor, now, he gave evidence at the inquest?'

'Yes.'

'Did he say nothing of any unusual symptom—was there nothing about the appearance of the body which struck him as being abnormal?'

Japp stared hard at the little man.

'Yes, Monsieur Poirot. I don't know what you're getting at, but he did mention that there was a tension and stiffness about the limbs which he was quite at a loss to account for.'

'Aha!' said Poirot. 'Aha! *Mon Dieu!* Japp, that gives one to think, does it not?'

I saw that it had certainly not given Japp to think.

'If you're thinking of poison, monsieur, who on earth would poison a man first and then stick a knife into him?'

'In truth that would be ridiculous,' agreed Poirot placidly.

'Now is there anything you want to see, monsieur? If you'd like to examine the room where the body was found—'

Poirot waved his hand.

'Not in the least. You have told me the only thing that interests me—Lord Cronshaw's views on the subject of drug-taking.'

'Then there's nothing you want to see?'

'Just one thing.'

'What is that?'

'The set of china figures from which the costumes were copied.'

Japp stared.

'Well, you're a funny one!'

'You can manage that for me?'

'Come round to Berkeley Square now if you like. Mr Beltane—or His Lordship, as I should say now—won't object.'

We set off at once in a taxi. The new Lord Cronshaw was not at home, but at Japp's request we were shown into the 'china room', where the gems of the collection were kept. Japp looked round him rather helplessly.

'I don't see how you'll ever find the ones you want, monsieur.'

But Poirot had already drawn a chair in front of the mantelpiece and was hopping up upon it like a nimble robin. Above the mirror, on a small shelf to themselves, stood six china figures. Poirot examined them minutely, making a few comments to us as he did so.

'*Les voilà*! The old Italian Comedy. Three pairs! Harlequin and Columbine, Pierrot and Pierrette—very dainty in white and green—and Punchinello and Pulcinella in mauve and yellow. Very elaborate, the costume of Punchinello—ruffles and frills, a hump, a high hat. Yes, as I thought, very elaborate.'

He replaced the figures carefully, and jumped down.

Japp looked unsatisfied, but as Poirot had clearly no intention of explaining anything, the detective put the best face he could upon the matter. As we were preparing to leave, the master of the house came in, and Japp performed the necessary introductions.

The sixth Viscount Cronshaw was a man of about fifty, suave in manner, with a handsome, dissolute face. Evidently an elderly roué, with the languid manner of a poseur. I took an instant dislike to him. He greeted us graciously enough, declaring he had heard great accounts of Poirot's skill, and placing himself at our disposal in every way.

'The police are doing all they can, I know,' Poirot said.

'But I much fear the mystery of my nephew's death will never be cleared up. The whole thing seems utterly mysterious.'

Poirot was watching him keenly. 'Your nephew had no enemies that you know of?'

'None whatever. I am sure of that.' He paused, and then went on: 'If there are any questions you would like to ask—'

'Only one.' Poirot's voice was serious. 'The costumes—they were reproduced *exactly* from your figurines?'

'To the smallest detail.'

'Thank you, milor'. That is all I wanted to be sure of. I wish you good day.'

'And what next?' inquired Japp as we hurried down the street. 'I've got to report at the Yard, you know.'

'*Bien*! I will not detain you. I have one other little matter to attend to, and then—'

'Yes?'

'The case will be complete.'

'What? You don't mean it! You know who killed Lord Cronshaw?'

'*Parfaitement.*'

'Who was it? Eustace Beltane?'

'Ah, *mon ami*, you know my little weakness! Always I have a desire to keep the threads in my own hands up to the last minute. But have no fear. I will reveal all when the time comes. I want no credit—the affair shall be yours, on the condition that you permit me to play out the *dénouement* my own way.'

'That's fair enough,' said Japp. 'That is, if the *dénouement* ever comes! But I say, you *are* an oyster, aren't you?'
Poirot smiled. 'Well, so long. I'm off to the Yard.'

He strode off down the steet, and Poirot hailed a passing taxi.

'Where are we going now?' I asked in lively curiosity.

'To Chelsea to see the Davidsons.'

He gave the address to the driver.

'What do you think of the new Lord Cronshaw?' I
asked.

'What says my good friend Hastings?'

'I distrust him instinctively.'

'You think he is the "wicked uncle" of the story-
books, eh?'

'Don't you?'

'Me, I think he was most amiable towards us,' said
Poirot noncommittally.

'Because he had his reasons!'

Poirot looked at me, shook his head sadly, and murmured something that sounded like: 'No method.'

The Davidsons lived on the third floor of a block of 'mansion' flats. Mr Davidson was out, we were told, but Mrs
Davidson was at home. We were ushered into a long, low
room with garish Oriental hangings. The air felt close
and oppressive, and there was an overpowering fragrance
of joss-sticks. Mrs Davidson came to us almost immediately, a small, fair creature whose fragility would have
seemed pathetic and appealing had it not been for the
rather shrewd and calculating gleam in her light blue eyes.

Poirot explained our connection with the case, and
she shook her head sadly.

'Poor Cronch—and poor Coco too! We were both so fond of her, and her death has been a terrible grief to us. What is it you want to ask me? Must I really go over all that dreadful evening again?'

'Oh, madame, believe me, I would not harass your feelings unnecessarily. Indeed, Inspector Japp has told me all that is needful. I only wish to see the constume you wore at the ball that night.'

The lady looked somewhat surprised, and Poirot continued smoothly: 'You comprehend, madame, that I work on the system of my country. There we always "reconstruct" the crime. It is possible that I may have an actual *représentation*, and if so, you understand, the costumes would be important.'

Mrs Davidson still looked a bit doubtful.

'I've heard of reconstructing a crime, of course,' she said. 'But I didn't know you were so particular about details. But I'll fetch the dress now.'

She left the room and returned almost immediately with a dainty wisp of white satin and green. Poirot took it from her and examined it, handing it back with a bow.

'*Merci, madame*! I see you have had the misfortune to lose one of your green pompons, the one on the shoulder here.'

'Yes, it got torn off at the ball. I picked it up and gave it to poor Lord Cronshaw to keep for me.'

'That was after supper?'

'Yes.'

'Not long before the tragedy, perhaps?'

A faint look of alarm came into Mrs Davidson's pale eyes, and she replied quickly: 'Oh no—long before that. Quite soon after supper, in fact.'

'I see. Well, that is all. I will not derange you further. *Bonjour, madame.*'

'Well,' I said as we emerged from the building, 'that explains the mystery of the green pompon.'

'I wonder.'

'Why, what do you mean?'

'You saw me examine the dress, Hastings?'

'Yes?'

'*Eh bien*, the pompon that was missing had not been wrenched off, as the lady said. On the contrary, it had been *cut* off, my friend, cut off with scissors. The threads were all quite even.'

'Dear me!' I exclaimed. 'This becomes more and more involved.'

'On the contrary,' replied Poirot placidly, 'it becomes more and more simple.'

'Poirot,' I cried, 'one day I shall murder you! Your habit of finding everything perfectly simple is aggravating to the last degree!'

'But when I explain, *mon ami*, is it not always perfectly simple?'

'Yes; that is the annoying part of it! I feel then that I could have done it myself.'

'And so you could, Hastings, so you could. If you would but take the trouble of arranging your ideas! Without method—'

'Yes, yes,' I said hastily, for I knew Poirot's eloquence when started on his favourite theme only too well. 'Tell me, what do we do next? Are you really going to reconstruct the crime?'

'Hardly that. Shall we say that the drama is over, but that I propose to add a—harlequinade?'

★ ★ ★

The following Tuesday was fixed upon by Poirot as the day for this mysterious performance. The preparations greatly intrigued me. A white screen was erected at one side of the room, flanked by heavy curtains at either side. A man with some lighting apparatus arrived next, and finally a group of members of the theatrical profession, who disappeared into Poirot's bedroom, which had been rigged up as a temporary dressing-room.

Shortly before eight, Japp arrived, in no very cheerful mood. I gathered that the official detective hardly approved of Poirot's plan.

'Bit melodramatic, like all his ideas. But there, it can do no harm, and as he says, it might save us a good bit of trouble. He's been very smart over the case. I was on the same scent myself, of course—' I felt instinctively that Japp was straining the truth here—'but there, I promised to let him play the thing out his own way. Ah! Here is the crowd.'

His Lordship arrived first, escorting Mrs Mallaby, whom I had not as yet seen. She was a pretty, dark-haired woman, and appeared perceptibly nervous. The Davidsons followed. Chris Davidson also I saw for the first time. He was handsome enough in a rather obvious style, tall and dark, with the easy grace of the actor.

Poirot had arranged seats for the party facing the screen. This was illuminated by a bright light. Poirot switched out the other lights so that the room was in darkness except for the screen. Poirot's voice rose out of the gloom.

'Messieurs, mesdames, a word of explanation. Six figures in turn will pass across the screen. They are familiar to you. Pierrot and his Pierrette; Punchinello the buffoon, and elegant Pulcinella; beautiful Columbine, lightly dancing, Harlequin, the sprite, invisible to man!'

With these words of introduction, the show began. In turn each figure that Poirot had mentioned bounded before the screen, stayed there a moment poised, and then vanished. The lights went up, and a sigh of relief went round. Everyone had been nervous, fearing they knew not what. It seemed to me that the proceedings had gone singularly flat. If the criminal was among us, and Poirot expected him to break down at the mere sight of a familiar figure the device had failed signally—as it was almost bound to do. Poirot, however, appeared not a whit discomposed. He stepped forward, beaming.

'Now, messieurs and mesdames, will you be so good as to tell me, one at a time, what it is that we have just seen? Will you begin, milor'?'

The gentleman looked rather puzzled. 'I'm afraid I don't quite understand.'

'Just tell me what we have been seeing.'

'I—er—well, I should say we have seen six figures passing in front of a screen and dressed to represent the personages in the old Italian Comedy, or—er—ourselves the other night.'

'Never mind the other night, milor',' broke in Poirot. 'The first part of your speech was what I wanted. Madame, you agree with Milor' Cronshaw?'

He had turned as he spoke to Mrs Mallaby.

'I—er—yes, of course.'

'You agree that you have seen six figures representing the Italian Comedy?'

'Why, certainly.'

'Monsieur Davidson? You too?'

'Yes.'

'Madame?'

'Yes.'

'Hastings? Japp? Yes? You are all in accord?'

He looked around upon us; his face grew rather pale, and his eyes were green as any cat's.

'And yet—*you are all wrong*! Your eyes have lied to you—as they lied to you on the night of the Victory Ball. To "see things with your eyes", as they say, is not always to see the truth. One must see with the eyes of the mind; one must employ the little cells of grey! Know, then, that tonight and on the night of the Victory Ball, you saw not *six* figures but *five*! See!'

The lights went out again. A figure bounded in front of the screen—Pierrot!

'Who is that?' demanded Poirot. 'Is it Pierrot?'

'Yes,' we all cried.

'Look again!'

With a swift movement the man divested himself of his loose Pierrot garb. There in the limelight stood glittering Harlequin! At the same moment there was a cry and an overturned chair.

'Curse you,' snarled Davidson's voice. 'Curse you! How did you guess?'

Then came the clink of handcuffs and Japp's calm official voice. 'I arrest you, Christopher Davidson—charge of murdering Viscount Cronshaw—anything you say will be used in evidence against you.'

It was a quarter of an hour later. A recherché little supper had appeared; and Poirot, beaming all over his face, was dispensing hospitality and answering our eager questions.

'It was all very simple. The circumstances in which the green pompon was found suggested at once that it had been torn from the costume of the murderer. I dismissed Pierrette from my mind (since it takes considerable strength to drive a table-knife home) and fixed upon Pierrot as the criminal. But Pierrot left the ball nearly two hours before the murder was committed. So he must either have returned to the ball later to kill Lord Cronshaw, or—*eh bien*, he must have killed him before he left! Was that impossible? Who had seen Lord Cronshaw after supper that evening? Only Mrs Davidson, whose statement, I suspected, was a deliberate fabrication uttered with the object of accounting for the missing pompon, which, of course, she cut from her own dress to replace the one missing on her husband's costume. But then, Harlequin, who was seen in the box at one-thirty, must have been an impersonation. For a moment, earlier, I had considered the possibility of Mr Beltane being the guilty party. But with his elaborate costume, it was clearly impossible that he could have doubled the roles of Punchinello and Harlequin. On the other hand, to Davidson, a young man of about the same height as the murdered man and an actor by profession, the thing was simplicity itself.

'But one thing worried me. Surely a doctor could not fail to perceive the difference between a man who had been dead two hours and one who had been dead ten minutes! *Eh bien*, the doctor *did* perceive it! But he was not taken to the body and asked, 'How long has this man been dead?' On the contrary, he was informed that the man had been seen alive ten minutes ago, and so he merely commented at the inquest on the abnormal stiffening of the limbs for which he was quite unable to account!

'All was now marching famously for my theory. Davidson had killed Lord Cronshaw immediately after supper, when, as you remember, he was seen to draw him back into the supper-room. Then he departed with Miss Courtenay, left her at the door of her flat (instead of going in and trying to pacify her as he affirmed) and returned post-haste to the Colossus—but as Harlequin, not Pierrot—a simple transformation effected by removing his outer costume.'

The uncle of the dead man leaned forward, his eyes perplexed.

'But if so, he must have come to the ball prepared to kill his victim. What earthly motive could he have had? The motive, that's what I can't get.'

'Ah! There we come to the second tragedy—that of Miss Courtenay. There was one simple point which everyone overlooked. Miss Courtenay died of cocaine poisoning—but her supply of the drug was in the enamel box which was found on Lord Cronshaw's body. Where, then, did she obtain the dose which killed her? Only one person could have supplied her with it—Davidson. And that explains everything. It accounts for her friendship with the Davidsons and her demand that Davidson should escort her home. Lord Cronshaw, who was almost fanatically opposed to drug-taking, discovered that she was addicted to cocaine, and suspected that Davidson supplied her with it. Davidson doubtless denied this, but Lord Cronshaw determined to get the truth from Miss Courtenay at the ball. He could forgive the wretched girl, but he would certainly have no mercy on the man who made a living by trafficking in drugs. Exposure and ruin confronted Davidson. He went to the ball determined that Cronshaw's silence must be obtained at any cost.'

'Was Coco's death an accident, then?'

'I suspect that it was an accident cleverly engineered by Davidson. She was furiously angry with Cronshaw, first for his reproaches, and secondly for taking her cocaine from her. Davidson supplied her with more, and probably suggested her augmenting the dose as a defiance to "old Cronch"!'

'One other thing,' I said. 'The recess and the curtain? How did you know about them?'

'Why, *mon ami*, that was the most simple of all. Waiters had been in and out of that little room, so, obviously, the body could not have been lying where it was found on the floor. There must be some place in the room where it could be hidden. I deduced a curtain and a recess behind it. Davidson dragged the body there, and later, after drawing attention to himself in the box, he dragged it out again before finally leaving the Hall. It was one of his best moves. He is a clever fellow!'

But in Poirot's green eyes I read unmistakably the unspoken remark: 'But not quite so clever as Hercule Poirot!'

The Tuesday Night Club

'Unsolved mysteries.'

Raymond West blew out a cloud of smoke and repeated the words with a kind of deliberate self-conscious pleasure.

'Unsolved mysteries.'

He looked round him with satisfaction. The room was an old one with broad black beams across the ceiling and it was furnished with good old furniture that belonged to it. Hence Raymond West's approving glance. By profession he was a writer and he liked the atmosphere to be flawless. His Aunt Jane's house always pleased him as the right setting for her personality. He looked across the hearth to where she sat erect in the big grandfather chair. Miss Marple wore a black brocade dress, very much pinched in round the waist. Mechlin lace was arranged in a cascade down the front of the bodice. She had on black lace mittens, and a black lace cap surmounted the piled-up masses of her snowy hair. She was knitting—something white and soft and fleecy. Her faded blue eyes, benignant and kindly, surveyed her nephew and her nephew's guests with gentle pleasure.

They rested first on Raymond himself, self-consciously debonair, then on Joyce Lemprière, the artist, with her close-cropped black head and queer hazel-green eyes, then on that well- groomed man of the world, Sir Henry Clithering. There were two other people in the room, Dr Pender, the elderly clergyman of the parish, and Mr Petherick, the solicitor, a dried-up little man with eye-glasses which he looked over and not through. Miss Marple gave a brief moment of attention to all these people and returned to her knitting with a gentle smile upon her lips.

Mr Petherick gave the dry little cough with which he usually prefaced his remarks.

'What is that you say, Raymond? Unsolved mysteries? Ha—and what about them?'

'Nothing about them,' said Joyce Lemprière. 'Raymond just likes the sound of the words and of himself saying them.'

Raymond West threw her a glance of reproach at which she threw back her head and laughed.

'He is a humbug, isn't he, Miss Marple?' she demanded. 'You know that, I am sure.'

Miss Marple smiled gently at her but made no reply.

'Life itself is an unsolved mystery,' said the clergyman gravely.

Raymond sat up in his chair and flung away his cigarette with an impulsive gesture.

'That's not what I mean. I was not talking philosophy,' he said. 'I was thinking of actual bare prosaic facts, things that have happened and that no one has ever explained.'

'I know just the sort of thing you mean, dear,' said Miss Marple. 'For instance Mrs Carruthers had a very strange experience yesterday morning. She bought two gills of picked shrimps at Elliot's. She called at two other shops and when she got home she found she had not got the shrimps with her. She went back to the two shops she had visited but these shrimps had completely disappeared. Now that seems to me very remarkable.'

'A very fishy story,' said Sir Henry Clithering gravely.

'There are, of course, all kinds of possible explanations,' said Miss Marple, her cheeks growing slightly pinker with excitement. 'For instance, somebody else—'

'My dear Aunt,' said Raymond West with some amusement, 'I didn't mean that sort of village incident. I was thinking of murders and disappearances—the kind of thing that Sir Henry could tell us about by the hour if he liked.'

'But I never talk shop,' said Sir Henry modestly. 'No, I never talk shop.'

Sir Henry Clithering had been until lately Commissioner of Scotland Yard.

'I suppose there are a lot of murders and things that never are solved by the police,' said Joyce Lemprière.

'That is an admitted fact, I believe,' said Mr Petherick.

'I wonder,' said Raymond West, 'what class of brain really succeeds best in unravelling a mystery? One always feels that the average police detective must be hampered by lack of imagination.'

'That is the layman's point of view,' said Sir Henry dryly.

'You really want a committee,' said Joyce, smiling. 'For psychology and imagination go to the writer—'

She made an ironical bow to Raymond but he remained serious.

'The art of writing gives one an insight into human nature,' he said gravely. 'One sees, perhaps, motives that the ordinary person would pass by.'

'I know, dear,' said Miss Marple, 'that your books are very clever. But do you think that people are really so unpleasant as you make them out to be?'

'My dear Aunt,' said Raymond gently, 'keep your beliefs. Heaven forbid that *I* should in any way shatter them.'

'I mean,' said Miss Marple, puckering her brow a little as she counted the stitches in her knitting, 'that so many people seem to me not to be either bad or good, but simply, you know, very silly.'

Mr Petherick gave his dry little cough again.

'Don't you think, Raymond,' he said, 'that you attach too much weight to imagination? Imagination is a very dangerous thing, as we lawyers know only too well. To be able to sift evidence impartially, to take the facts and look at them as facts—that seems to me the only logical method of arriving at the truth. I may add that in my experience it is the only one that succeeds.'

'Bah!' cried Joyce, flinging back her black head indignantly. 'I bet I could beat you all at this game. I am not only a woman—and say what you like, women have an intuition that is denied to men—I am an artist as well. I see things that you don't. And then, too, as an artist I have knocked about among all sorts and conditions of people. I know life as darling Miss Marple here cannot possibly know it.'

'I don't know about that, dear,' said Miss Marple. 'Very painful and distressing things happen in villages sometimes.'

'May I speak?' said Dr Pender smiling. 'It is the fashion nowadays to decry the clergy, I know, but we hear things, we know a side of human character which is a sealed book to the outside world.'

'Well,' said Joyce, 'it seems to me we are a pretty representative gathering. How would it be if we formed a Club? What is today? Tuesday? We will call it The Tuesday Night Club. It is to meet every week, and each member in turn has to propound a problem. Some mystery of which they have personal knowledge, and to which, of course, they know the answer. Let me see, how many are we? One, two, three, four, five. We ought really to be six.'

'You have forgotten me, dear,' said Miss Marple, smiling brightly.

Joyce was slightly taken aback, but she concealed the fact quickly.

'That would be lovely, Miss Marple,' she said. 'I didn't think you would care to play.'

'I think it would be very intersting,' said Miss Marple, 'especially with so many clever gentlemen present. I am afraid I am not clever myself, but living all these years in St Mary Mead does give one an insight into human nature.'

'I am sure your co-operation will be very valuable,' said Sir Henry, courteously.

'Who is going to start?' said Joyce.

'I think there is no doubt as to that,' said Dr Pender, 'when we have the great good fortune to have such a distinguished man as Sir Henry staying with us—'

He left his sentence unfinished, making a courtly bow in the direction of Sir Henry.

The latter was silent for a minute or two. At last he sighed and recrossed his legs and began:

'It is a little difficult for me to select just the kind of thing you want, but I think, as it happens, I know of an instance which fits these conditions very aptly. You may have seen some mention of the case in the papers of a year ago. It was laid aside at the time as an unsolved mystery, but, as it happens, the solution came into my hands not very many days ago.

'The facts are very simple. Three people sat down to a supper consisting, amongst other things, of tinned lobster. Later in the night, all three were taken ill, and a doctor was hastily summoned. Two of the people recovered, the third one died.'

'Ah!' said Raymond approvingly.

'As I say, the facts as such were very simple. Death was considered to be due to ptomaine poisoning, a certificate was given to that effect, and the victim was duly buried. But things did not rest at that.'

Miss Marple nodded her head.

'There was talk, I suppose,' she said, 'there usually is.'

'And now I must describe the actors in this little drama. I will call the husband and wife Mr and Mrs Jones, and the wife's companion Miss Clark. Mr Jones was a traveller for a firm of manufacturing chemists. He was a good-looking man in a kind of coarse, florid way, aged about fifty. His wife was a rather commonplace woman, of about forty-five. The companion, Miss Clark, was a woman of sixty, a stout cheery woman with a beaming rubicund face. None of them, you might say, very interesting.

'Now the beginning of the troubles arose in a very

curious way. Mr Jones had been staying the previous night at a small commercial hotel in Birmingham. It happened that the blotting paper in the blotting book had been put in fresh that day, and the chambermaid, having apparently nothing better to do, amused herself by studying the blotter in the mirror just after Mr Jones had been writing a letter there. A few days later there was a report in the papers of the death of Mrs Jones as the result of eating tinned lobster, and the chambermaid then imparted to her fellow servants the words that she had deciphered on the blotting pad. They were as follows: *Entirely dependent on my wife . . . when she is dead I will . . . hundreds and thousands . . .*

'You may remember that there had recently been a case of a wife being poisoned by her husband. It needed very little to fire the imagination of these maids. Mr Jones had planned to do away with his wife and inherit hundreds of thousands of pounds! As it happened one of the maids had relations living in the small market town where the Joneses resided. She wrote to them, and they in return wrote to her. Mr Jones, it seemed, had been very attentive to the local doctor's daughter, a good-looking young woman of thirty-three. Scandal began to hum. The Home Secretary was petitioned. Numerous anonymous letters poured into Scotland Yard all accusing Mr Jones of having murdered his wife. Now I may say that not for one moment did we think there was anything in it except idle village talk and gossip. Nevertheless, to quiet public opinion an exhumation order was granted. It was one of these cases of popular superstition based on nothing solid whatever, which proved to be so surprisingly justified. As a result of the autopsy sufficient arsenic was found to make it quite clear that the deceased lady had died of arsenical poisoning. It was for Scotland Yard working with the local authorities to prove how that arsenic had been administered, and by whom.'

'Ah!' said Joyce. 'I like this. This is the real stuff.'

'Suspicion naturally fell on the husband. He benefited by his wife's death. Not to the extent of the hundreds of thousands romantically imagined by the hotel chambermaid, but to the very solid amount of £8000. He had no money of his own apart from what he earned, and he was a man of somewhat extravagant habits with a partiality for the society of women. We investigated as delicately as possible the rumour of his attachment to the doctor's daughter; but while it seemed clear that there had been a strong friendship between them at one time, there had been a most abrupt break two months previously, and they did not appear to have seen each other since. The doctor himself, an elderly man of a straightforward and unsuspicious type, was dumbfounded at the result of the autopsy. He had been called in about midnight to find all three people suffering. He had realized immediately the serious condition of Mrs Jones, and had sent back to his dispensary for some opium pills, to allay the pain. In spite of all his efforts, however, she succumbed, but not for a moment did he suspect that anything was amiss. He was convinced that her death was due to a form of botulism. Supper that night had consisted of tinned lobster and salad, trifle and bread and cheese. Unfortunately none of the lobster remained—it had all been eaten and the tin thrown away. He had interrogated the young maid, Gladys Linch. She was terribly upset, very tearful and agitated, and he found it hard to get her to keep to the point, but she declared again and again that the tin had not been distended in any way and that the lobster had appeared to her in a perfectly good condition.

'Such were the facts we had to go upon. If Jones had feloniously administered arsenic to his wife, it seemed clear that it could not have been done in any of the things eaten at supper, as all three persons had partaken of the meal. Also—another point—Jones himself had returned from Birmingham just as supper was being brought in to table, so that he would have had no opportunity of doctoring any of the food beforehand.'

'What about the companion?' asked Joyce—'the stout woman with the good-humoured face.'

Sir Henry nodded.

'We did not neglect Miss Clark, I can assure you. But it seemed doubtful what motive she could have had for the crime. Mrs Jones left her no legacy of any kind and the net result of her employer's death was that she had to seek for another situation.'

'That seems to leave her out of it,' said Joyce thoughtfully.

'Now one of my inspectors soon discovered a significant fact,' went on Sir Henry. 'After supper on that evening Mr Jones had gone down to the kitchen and had demanded a bowl of cornflour for his wife who had complained of not feeling well. He had waited in the kitchen until Gladys Linch prepared it, and then carried it up to his wife's room himself. That, I admit, seemed to clinch the case.'

The lawyer nodded.

'Motive,' he said, ticking the points off on his fingers. 'Opportunity. As a traveller for a firm of druggists, easy access to the poison.'

'And a man of weak moral fibre,' said the clergyman.

Raymond West was staring at Sir Henry.

'There is a catch in this somewhere,' he said. 'Why did you not arrest him?'

Sir Henry smiled rather wryly.

'That is the unfortunate part of the case. So far all had gone swimmingly, but now we come to the snags. Jones was not arrested because on interrogating Miss Clark she told us that the whole of the bowl of cornflour was drunk not by Mrs Jones but by her.

'Yes, it seems that she went to Mrs Jones's room as was her custom. Mrs Jones was sitting up in bed and the bowl of cornflour was beside her.

'"I am not feeling a bit well, Milly," she said. "Serves me right, I suppose, for touching lobster at night. I asked Albert to get me a bowl of cornflour, but now that I have got it I don't seem to fancy it."

'"A pity," commented Miss Clark—"it is nicely made too, no lumps. Gladys is really quite a nice cook. Very few girls nowadays seem to be able to make a bowl of cornflour nicely. I declare I quite fancy it myself, I am that hungry."

'"I should think you were with your foolish ways," said Mrs Jones.

'I must explain,' broke off Sir Henry, 'that Miss Clark, alarmed at her increasing stoutness, was doing a course of what is popularly known as "banting".

'"It is not good for you, Milly, it really isn't," urged Mrs Jones. "If the Lord made you stout he meant you to

30

be stout. You drink up that bowl of cornflour. It will do you all the good in the world."

'And straight away Miss Clark set to and did in actual fact finish the bowl. So, you see, that knocked our case against the husband to pieces. Asked for an explanation of the words on the blotting book Jones gave one readily enough. The letter, he explained, was in answer to one written from his brother in Australia who had applied to him for money. He had written, pointing out that he was entirely dependent on his wife. When his wife was dead he would have control of money and would assist his brother if possible. He regretted his inability to help but pointed out that there were hundreds and thousands of people in the world in the same unfortunate plight.'

'And so the case fell to pieces?' said Dr Pender.

'And so the case fell to pieces,' said Sir Henry gravely. 'We could not take the risk of arresting Jones with nothing to go upon.'

There was a silence and then Joyce said, 'And that is all, is it?'

'That is the case as it has stood for the last year. The true solution is now in the hands of Scotland Yard, and in two or three days' time you will probably read of it in the newspapers.'

'The true solution,' said Joyce thoughtfully. 'I wonder. Let's all think for five minutes and then speak.'

Raymond West nodded and noted the time on his watch. When the five minutes were up he looked over at Dr Pender.

'Will you speak first?' he said.

The old man shook his head. 'I confess,' he said, 'that I am utterly baffled. I can but think that the husband in

31

some way must be the guilty party, but how he did it I cannot imagine. I can only suggest that he must have given her the poison in some way that has not yet been discovered, although how in that case it should have come to light after all this time I cannot imagine.'

'Joyce?'

'The companion!' said Joyce decidedly. 'The companion every time! How do we know what motive she may have had? Just because she was old and stout and ugly it doesn't follow that she wasn't in love with Jones herself. She may have hated the wife for some other reason. Think of being a companion—always having to be pleasant and agree and stifle yourself and bottle yourself up. One day she couldn't bear it any longer and then she killed her. She probably put the arsenic in the bowl of cornflour and all that story about eating it herself is a lie.'

'Mr Petherick?'

The lawyer joined the tips of his fingers together professionally. 'I should hardly like to say. On the facts I should hardly like to say.'

'But you have got to, Mr Petherick,' said Joyce. 'You can't reserve judgement and say "without prejudice", and be legal. You have got to play the game.'

'On the facts,' said Mr Petherick, 'there seems nothing to be said. It is my private opinion, having seen, alas, too many cases of this kind, that the husband was guilty. The only explanation that will cover the facts seems to be that Miss Clark for some reason or other deliberately sheltered him. There may have been some financial arrangement made between them. He might realize that he would be suspected, and she, seeing only a future of poverty before her, may have agreed to tell the story of drinking the cornflour in return for a substantial sum to be paid to her privately. If that was the case it was of course most irregular. Most irregular indeed.'

'I disagree with you all,' said Raymond. 'You have forgotten the one important factor in the case. *The doctor's daughter.* I will give you my reading of the case. The tinned lobster was bad. It accounted for the poisoning symptoms. The doctor was sent for. He finds Mrs Jones, who has eaten more lobster than the others, in great pain, and he sends, as you told us, for some opium pills. He does not go himself, he sends. Who will give the messenger the opium pills? Clearly his daughter. Very likely she dispenses his medicines for him. She is in love with Jones and at this moment all the worst instincts in her nature rise and she realizes that the means to procure his freedom are in her hands. The pills she sends contain pure white arsenic. That is my solution.'

'And now, Sir Henry, tell us,' said Joyce eagerly.

'One moment,' said Sir Henry. 'Miss Marple has not yet spoken.'

Miss Marple was shaking her head sadly.

'Dear, dear,' she said. 'I have dropped another stitch. I have been so interested in the story. A sad case, a very sad case. It reminds me of old Mr Hargraves who lived up at the Mount. His wife never had the least suspicion—until he died, leaving all his money to a woman he had been living with and by whom he had five children. She had at one time been their housemaid. Such a nice girl, Mrs Hargraves always said—thoroughly to be relied upon to turn the mattresses every day—except Fridays, of course. And there was old Hargraves keeping this woman in a house in the neighbouring town and continuing to be a Churchwarden and to hand round the plate every Sunday.'

'My dear Aunt Jane,' said Raymond with some impatience. 'What has dead and gone Hargraves got to do with the case?'

'This story made me think of him at once,' said Miss Marple. 'The facts are so very alike, aren't they? I suppose the poor girl has confessed now and that is how you know, Sir Henry.'

'What girl?' said Raymond. 'My dear Aunt, what *are* you talking about?'

'That poor girl, Gladys Linch, of course—the one who was so terribly agitated when the doctor spoke to her—and well she might be, poor thing. I hope that wicked Jones is hanged, I am sure, making that poor girl a murderess. I suppose they will hang her too, poor thing.'

'I think, Miss Marple, that you are under a slight misapprehension,' began Mr Petherick.

But Miss Marple shook her head obstinately and looked across at Sir Henry.

'I am right, am I not? It seems so clear to me. The hundreds and thousands—and the trifle—I mean, one cannot miss it.'

'What about the trifle and the hundreds and thousands?' cried Raymond.

His aunt turned to him.

'Cooks nearly always put hundreds and thousands on trifle, dear,' she said. 'Those little pink and white sugar things. Of course when I heard that they had trifle for supper and that the husband had been writing to someone about hundreds and thousands, I naturally connected the two things together. That is where the arsenic was—in the hundreds and thousands. He left it with the girl and told her to put it on the trifle.'

'But that is impossible,' said Joyce quickly. 'They all ate the trifle.'

'Oh, no,' said Miss Marple. 'The companion was banting, you remember. You never eat anything like trifle if you are banting; and I expect Jones just scraped the hundreds and thousands off his share and left them at the side of his plate. It was a clever idea, but a very wicked one.'

The eyes of the others were all fixed upon Sir Henry.

'It is a very curious thing,' he said slowly, 'but Miss Marple happens to have hit upon the truth. Jones had got Gladys Linch into trouble, as the saying goes. She was nearly desperate. He wanted his wife out of the way and promised to marry Gladys when his wife was dead. He doctored the hundreds and thousands and gave them to her with instructions how to use them. Gladys Linch died a week ago. Her child died at birth and Jones had deserted her for another woman. When she was dying she confessed the truth.'

There was a few moments' silence and then Raymond said:

'Well, Aunt Jane, this is one up to you. I can't think how on earth you managed to hit upon the truth. I should never have thought of the little maid in the kitchen being connected with the case.'

'No, dear,' said Miss Marple, 'but you don't know as much of life as I do. A man of that Jones's type—coarse and jovial. As soon as I heard there was a pretty young girl in the house I felt sure that he would not have left her alone. It is all very distressing and painful, and not a very nice thing to talk about. I can't tell you the shock it was to Mrs Hargraves, and a nine days' wonder in the village.'

The Case of the Discontented Soldier

Major Wilbraham hesitated outside the door of Mr Parker Pyne's office to read, not for the first time, the advertisement from the morning paper which had brought him there. It was simple enough:

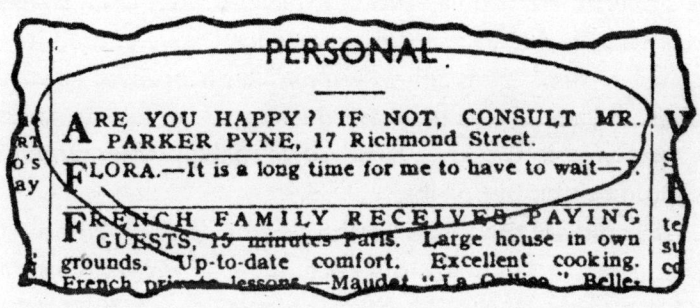

PERSONAL

ARE YOU HAPPY? IF NOT, CONSULT MR. PARKER PYNE, 17 Richmond Street.

FLORA.—It is a long time for me to have to wait—J.

FRENCH FAMILY RECEIVES PAYING GUESTS, 15 minutes Paris. Large house in own grounds. Up-to-date comfort. Excellent cooking. French private lessons.—Maudet "La Colline," Belle.

The major took a deep breath and abruptly plunged through the swing door leading to the outer office. A plain young woman looked up from her typewriter and glanced at him inquiringly.

'Mr Parker Pyne?' said Major Wilbraham, blushing.

'Come this way, please.'

He followed her into an inner office—into the presence of the bland Mr Parker Pyne.

'Good-morning,' said Mr Pyne. 'Sit down, won't you? And now tell me what I can do for you.'

'My name is Wilbraham—' began the other.

'Major? Colonel?' said Mr Pyne.

'Major.'

'Ah! And recently returned from abroad? India? East Africa?'

'East Africa.'

'A fine country, I believe. Well, so you are home again—and you don't like it. Is that the trouble?'

'You're absolutely right. Though how you knew—'

Mr Parker Pyne waved an impressive hand. 'It is my business to know. You see, for thirty-five years of my life I have been engaged in the compiling of statistics in a government office. Now I have retired and it has occurred to me to use the experience I have gained in a novel fashion. It is all so simple. Unhappiness can be classified under five main heads—no more, I assure you. Once you know the cause of a malady, the remedy should not be impossible.

'I stand in the place of the doctor. The doctor first diagnoses the patient's disorder, then he recommends a course of treatment. There are cases where no treatment can be of any avail. If that is so, I say quite frankly that I can do nothing about it. But if I undertake a case, the cure is practically guaranteed.

'I can assure you, Major Wilbraham, that ninety-six per cent of retired empire builders—as I call them—are unhappy. They exchange an active life, a life full of responsibility, a life of possible danger, for—what?

Straitened means, a dismal climate and a general feeling of being a fish out of water.'

'All you've said is true,' said the major. 'It's the boredom I object to. The boredom and the endless tittle-tattle about petty village matters. But what can I do about it? I've got a little money besides my pension. I've a nice cottage near Cobham. I can't afford to hunt or shoot or fish. I'm not married. My neighbours are all pleasant folk, but they've no ideas beyond this island.'

'The long and short of the matter is that you find life tame,' said Mr Parker Pyne.

'Damned tame.'

'You would like excitement, possibly danger?' asked Mr Pyne.

The soldier shrugged. 'There's no such thing in this tinpot country.'

'I beg your pardon,' said Mr Pyne seriously. 'There you are wrong. There is plenty of danger, plenty of excitement, here in London if you know where to go for it. You have seen only the surface of our English life, calm, pleasant. But there is another side. If you wish it, I can show you that other side.'

Major Wilbraham regarded him thoughtfully. There was something reassuring about Mr Pyne. He was large, not to say fat; he had a bald head of noble proportions, strong glasses and little twinkling eyes. And he had an aura—an aura of dependability.

'I should warn you, however,' continued Mr Pyne, 'that there is an element of risk.'

The soldier's eye brightened. 'That's all right,' he said. Then, abruptly: 'And—your fees?'

'My fee,' said Mr Pyne, 'is fifty pounds, payable in

advance. If in a month's time you are still in the same state of boredom, I will refund your money.'

Wilbraham considered. 'Fair enough,' he said at last. 'I agree. I'll give you a cheque now.'

The transaction was completed. Mr Parker Pyne pressed a buzzer on his desk.

'It is now one o'clock,' he said. 'I am going to ask you to take a young lady out to lunch.' The door opened. 'Ah, Madeleine, my dear, let me introduce Major Wilbraham, who is going to take you out to lunch.'

Wilbraham blinked slightly, which was hardly to be wondered at. The girl who entered the room was dark, languorous, with wonderful eyes and long black lashes, a perfect complexion and a voluptuous scarlet mouth. Her exquisite clothes set off the swaying grace of her figure. From head to foot she was perfect.

'Er—delighted,' said Major Wilbraham.

'Miss de Sara,' said Mr Parker Pyne.

'How very kind of you,' murmured Madeleine de Sara. 'I have your address here,' announced Mr Parker Pyne. 'Tomorrow morning you will receive my further instructions.'

Major Wilbraham and the lovely Madeleine departed.

It was three o'clock when Madeleine returned.

Mr Parker Pyne looked up. 'Well?' he demanded.

Madeleine shook her head. 'Scared of me,' she said. 'Thinks I'm a vamp.'

'I thought as much,' said Mr Parker Pyne. 'You carried out my instructions?'

'Yes. We discussed the occupants of the other tables freely. The type he likes is fair-haired, blue-eyed, slightly anaemic, not too tall.'

'That should be easy,' said Mr Pyne. 'Get me Schedule B and let me see what we have in stock at present.' He ran his finger down a list, finally stopping at a name. 'Freda Clegg. Yes, I think Freda Clegg will do excellently. I had better see Mrs Oliver about it.'

The next day Major Wilbraham received a note, which read:

> On Monday morning next at eleven o'clock go to Eaglemont, Friars Lane, Hampstead, and ask for Mr Jones. You will represent yourself as coming from the Guava Shipping Company.

Obediently on the following Monday (which happened to be Bank Holiday), Major Wilbraham set out for Eaglemont, Friars Lane. He set out, I say, but he never got there. For before he got there, something happened.

All the world and his wife seemed to be on their way to Hampstead. Major Wilbraham got entangled in crowds, suffocated in the tube and found it hard to discover the whereabouts of Friars Lane.

Friars Lane was a cul-de-sac, a neglected road full of ruts, with houses on either side standing back from the road. They were largish houses which had seen better days and had been allowed to fall into disrepair.

Wilbraham walked along peering at the half-erased names on the gate-posts, when suddenly he heard something that made him stiffen to attention. It was a kind of gurgling, half-choked cry.

It came again and this time it was faintly recognizable as the word 'Help!' It came from inside the wall of the house he was passing.

Without a moment's hesitation, Major Wilbraham pushed open the rickety gate and sprinted noiselessly up the weed-covered drive. There in the shrubbery was a girl struggling in the grasp of two enormous men. She was putting up a brave fight, twisting and turning and kicking. One man held his hand over her mouth in spite of her furious efforts to get her head free.

Intent on their struggle with the girl, neither of the men had noticed Wilbraham's approach. The first they knew of it was when a violent punch on the jaw sent the man who was covering the girl's mouth reeling backwards. Taken by surprise, the other man relinquished his hold of the girl and turned. Wilbraham was ready for him. Once again his fist shot out, and the man reeled backwards and fell. Wilbraham turned on the other man, who was closing in behind him.

But the two men had had enough. The second one rolled over, sat up; then, rising, he made a dash for the gate. His companion followed suit. Wilbraham started after them, but changed his mind and turned towards the girl, who was leaning against a tree, panting.

'Oh, thank you!' she gasped. 'It was terrible.'

Major Wilbraham saw for the first time who it was he had rescued so opportunely. She was a girl of about twenty-one or two, fair-haired and blue-eyed, pretty in a rather colourless way.

'If you hadn't come!' she gasped.

'There, there,' said Wilbraham soothingly. 'It's all right now. I think, though, that we'd better get away from here. It's possible those fellows might come back.'

A faint smile came to the girl's lips. 'I don't think they

will—not after the way you hit them. Oh, it was splendid of you!'

Major Wilbraham blushed under the warmth of her glance of admiration. 'Nothin' at all,' he said indistinctly. 'All in day's work. Lady being annoyed. Look here, if you take my arm, can you walk? It's been a nasty shock, I know.'

'I'm all right now,' said the girl. However, she took the proffered arm. She was still rather shaky. She glanced behind her at the house as they emerged through the gate. 'I can't understand it,' she murmured. 'That's clearly an empty house.'

'It's empty, right enough,' agreed the major, looking up at the shuttered windows and general air of decay.

'And yet it *is* Whitefriars.' She pointed to a half-obliterated name on the gate. 'And Whitefriars was the place I was to go.'

'Don't worry about anything now,' said Wilbraham. 'In a minute or two we'll be able to get a taxi. Then we'll drive somewhere and have a cup of coffee.'

At the end of the lane they came out into a more frequented street, and by good fortune a taxi had just set down a fare at one of the houses. Wilbraham hailed it, gave an address to the driver and they got in.

'Don't try to talk,' he admonished his companion. 'Just lie back. You've had a nasty experience.'

She smiled at him gratefully.

'By the way—er—my name is Wilbraham.'

'Mine is Clegg—Freda Clegg.'

Ten minutes later, Freda was sipping hot coffee and looking gratefully across a small table at her rescuer.

'It seems like a dream,' she said. 'A bad dream.' She

43

shuddered. 'And only a short while ago I was wishing for something to happen—anything! Oh, I don't like adventures.'

'Tell me how it happened.'

'Well, to tell you properly I shall have to talk a lot about myself, I'm afraid.'

'An excellent subject,' said Wilbraham, with a bow.

'I am an orphan. My father—he was a sea captain—died when I was eight. My mother died three years ago. I work in the city. I am with the Vacuum Gas Company—a clerk. One evening last week I found a gentleman waiting to see me when I returned to my lodgings. He was a lawyer, a Mr Reid from Melbourne.

'He was very polite and asked me several questions about my family. He explained that he had known my father many years ago. In fact, he had transacted some legal business for him. Then he told me the object of his visit. "Miss Clegg," he said, "I have reason to suppose that you might benefit as the result of a financial transaction entered into by your father several years before he died." I was very much surprised, of course.

'"It is unlikely that you would ever have heard anything of the matter," he explained. "John Clegg never took the affair seriously, I fancy. However, it has materialized unexpectedly, but I am afraid any claim you might put in would depend on your ownership of certain papers. These papers would be part of your father's estate, and of course it is possible that they have been destroyed as worthless. Have you kept any of your father's papers?"

'I explained that my mother had kept various things of my father's in an old sea chest. I had looked through it cursorily, but had discovered nothing of interest.

44

'"You would hardly be likely to recognize the importance of these documents, perhaps," he said, smiling.

'Well, I went to the chest, took out the few papers it contained and brought them to him. He looked at them, but said it was impossible to say off-hand what might or might not be connected with the matter in question. He would take them away with him and would communicate with me if anything turned up.

'By the last post on Saturday I received a letter from him in which he suggested that I come to his house to discuss the matter. He gave me the address: Whitefriars, Friars Lane, Hampstead. I was to be there at a quarter to eleven this morning.

'I was a little late finding the place. I hurried through the gate and up towards the house, when suddenly those two dreadful men sprang at me from the bushes. I hadn't time to cry out. One man put his hand over my mouth. I wrenched my head free and screamed for help. Luckily you heard me. If it hadn't been for you—' She stopped. Her looks were more eloquent than further words.

'Very glad I happened to be on the spot. By Gad, I'd like to get hold of those two brutes. You'd never seen them before, I suppose?'

She shook her head. 'What do you think it means?'

'Difficult to say. But one thing seems pretty sure. There's something someone wants among your father's papers. This man Reid told you a cock-and-bull story so as to get the opportunity of looking through them. Evidently what he wanted wasn't there.'

'Oh!' said Freda. 'I wonder. When I got home on Saturday I thought my things had been tampered with. To tell you the truth, I suspected my landlady of having pried about in my room out of curiosity. But now—'

'Depend upon it, that's it. Someone gained admission to your room and searched it, without finding what he was after. He suspected that you knew the value of this paper, whatever it was, and that you carried it about on your person. So he planned this ambush. If you had it with you, it would have been taken from you. If not, you would have been held prisoner while he tried to make you tell where it was hidden.'

'But what can it possibly *be*?' cried Freda.

'I don't know. But it must be something pretty good for him to go to this length.'

'It doesn't seem possible.'

'Oh, I don't know. Your father was a sailor. He went to out-of-the-way places. He might have come across something the value of which he never knew.'

'Do you really think so?' A pink flush of excitement showed in the girl's pale cheeks.

'I do indeed. The question is, what shall we do next? You don't want to go to the police, I suppose?'

'Oh, no, please.'

'I'm glad you say that. I don't see what good the police could do, and it would only mean unpleasantness for you. Now I suggest that you allow me to give you lunch somewhere and that I then accompany you back to your lodgings, so as to be sure you reach them safely. And then, we might have a look for the paper. Because, you know, it must be somewhere.'

'Father may have destroyed it himself.'

'He may, of course, but the other side evidently doesn't think so, and that looks hopeful for us.'

'What do you think it can be? Hidden treasure?'

'By jove, it might be!' exclaimed Major Wilbraham, all the boy in him rising joyfully to the suggestion. 'But now, Miss Clegg, lunch!'

They had a pleasant meal together. Wilbraham told Freda all about his life in East Africa. He described elephant hunts, and the girl was thrilled. When they had finished, he insisted on taking her home in a taxi.

Her lodgings were near Notting Hill Gate. On arriving there, Freda had a brief conversation with her landlady. She returned to Wilbraham and took him up to the second floor, where she had a tiny bedroom and sitting-room.

'It's exactly as we thought,' she said. 'A man came on Saturday morning to see about laying a new electric cable; he told her there was a fault in the wiring in my room. He was there some time.'

'Show me this chest of your father's,' said Wilbraham.

Freda showed him a brass-bound box. 'You see,' she said, raising the lid, 'it's empty.'

The soldier nodded thoughtfully. 'And there are no papers anywhere else?'

'I'm sure there aren't. Mother kept everything in here.'

Wilbraham examined the inside of the chest. Suddenly he uttered an exclamation. 'Here's a slit in the lining.'

Carefully he inserted his hand, feeling about. A slight crackle rewarded him. 'Something's slipped down behind.'

In another minute he had drawn out his find. A piece of dirty paper folded several times. He smoothed it out on the table; Freda was looking over his shoulder. She uttered an exclamation of disappointment.

'It's just a lot of queer marks.'

'Why, the thing's in Swahili. *Swahili*, of all things!' cried Major Wilbraham. 'East African native dialect, you know.'

'How extraordinary!' said Freda. 'Can you read it, then?'

'Rather. But what an amazing thing.' He took the paper to the window.

'Is it anything?' asked Freda tremulously. Wilbraham read the thing through twice, and then came back to the girl. 'Well,' he said, with a chuckle, 'here's your hidden treasure, all right.'

'Hidden treasure? Not *really*? You mean Spanish gold—a sunken galleon—that sort of thing?'

'Not quite so romantic as that, perhaps. But it comes to the same thing. This paper gives the hiding-place of a cache of ivory.'

'Ivory?' said the girl, astonished.

'Yes. Elephants, you know. There's a law about the number you're allowed to shoot. Some hunter got away with breaking that law on a grand scale. They were on his trail and he cached the stuff. There's a thundering lot of it—and this gives fairly clear directions how to find it. Look here, we'll have to go after this, you and I.'

'You mean there's really a lot of money in it?'

'Quite a nice little fortune for you.'

'But how did that paper come to be among my father's things?'

Wilbraham shrugged. 'Maybe the Johnny was dying or something. He may have written the thing down in Swahili for protection and given it to your father, who possibly had befriended him in some way. Your father, not being able to read it, attached no importance to it. That's only a guess on my part, but I dare say it's not far wrong.'

Freda gave a sigh. 'How frightfully exciting!'

'The thing is—what to do with the precious document,' said Wilbraham. 'I don't like leaving it here. They might come and have another look. I suppose you wouldn't entrust it to me?'

'Of course I would. But—mightn't it be dangerous for you?' she faltered.

'I'm a tough nut,' said Wilbraham grimly. 'You needn't worry about me.' He folded up the paper and put it in his pocket-book. 'May I come to see you tomorrow evening?' he asked. 'I'll have worked out a plan by then, and I'll look up the places on my map. What time do you get back from the city?'

'I get back about half-past six.'

'Capital. We'll have a powwow and then perhaps you'll let me take you out to dinner. We ought to celebrate. So long, then. Tomorrow at half-past six.'

Major Wilbraham arrived punctually on the following day. He rang the bell and enquired for Miss Clegg. A maid-servant had answered the door.

'Miss Clegg? She's out.'

'Oh!' Wilbraham did not like to suggest that he come in and wait. 'I'll call back presently,' he said.

He hung about in the street opposite, expecting every minute to see Freda tripping towards him. The minutes passed. Quarter to seven. Seven. Quarter-past seven. Still no Freda. A feeling of uneasiness swept over him. He went back to the house and rang the bell again.

'Look here,' he said, 'I had an appointment with Miss

Clegg at half-past six. Are you sure she isn't in or hasn't—er—left any message?'

'Are you Major Wilbraham?' asked the servant.

'Yes.'

'Then there's a note for you. It come by hand.'

Dear Major Wilbraham,—Something rather strange has happened. I won't write more now, but will you meet me at Whitefriars? Go there as soon as you get this.

Yours sincerely, Freda Clegg

Wilbraham drew his brows together as he thought rapidly. His hand drew a letter absent-mindedly from his pocket. It was to his tailor. 'I wonder,' he said to the maidservant, 'if you could let me have a stamp.'

'I expect Mrs Parkins could oblige you.'

She returned in a moment with the stamp. It was paid for with a shilling. In another minute Wilbraham was walking towards the tube station, dropping the envelope in a box as he passed.

Freda's letter had made him most uneasy. What could have taken the girl, alone, to the scene of yesterday's sinister encounter?

He shook his head. Of all the foolish things to do! Had Reid appeared? Had he somehow or other prevailed upon the girl to trust him? What had taken her to Hampstead?

He looked at his watch. Nearly half-past seven. She would have counted on his starting at half-past six. An hour late. Too much. If only she had had the sense to give him some hint.

The letter puzzled him. Somehow its independent tone was not characteristic of Freda Clegg.

It was ten minutes to eight when he reached Friars Lane. It was getting dark. He looked sharply about him; there was no one in sight. Gently he pushed the rickety gate so that it swung noiselessly on its hinges. The drive was deserted. The house was dark. He went up the path cautiously, keeping a look out from side to side. He did not intend to be caught by surprise.

Suddenly he stopped. Just for a minute a chink of light had shone through one of the shutters. The house was not empty. There was someone inside.

Softly Wilbraham slipped into the bushes and worked his way round to the back of the house. At last he found what he was looking for. One of the windows on the ground floor was unfastened. It was the window of a kind of scullery. He raised the sash, flashed a torch (he had bought it at a shop on the way over) around the deserted interior and climbed in.

Carefully he opened the scullery door. There was no sound. He flashed the torch once more. A kitchen— empty. Outside the kitchen were half a dozen steps and a door evidently leading to the front part of the house.

He pushed open the door and listened. Nothing. He slipped through. He was now in the front hall. Still there was no sound. There was a door to the right and a door to the left. He chose the right-hand door, listened for a time, then turned the handle. It gave. Inch by inch he opened the door and stepped inside.

Again he flashed the torch. The room was unfurnished and bare.

Just at that moment he heard a sound behind him,

whirled round—too late. Something came down on his head and he pitched forward into unconsciousness . . .

How much time elapsed before he regained consciousness Wilbraham had no idea. He returned painfully to life, his head aching. He tried to move and found it impossible. He was bound with ropes.

His wits came back to him suddenly. He remembered now. He had been hit on the head.

A faint light from a gas jet high up on the wall showed him that he was in a small cellar. He looked around and his heart gave a leap. A few feet away lay Freda, bound like himself. Her eyes were closed, but even as he watched her anxiously, she sighed and they opened. Her bewildered gaze fell on him and joyous recognition leaped into them.

'You, too!' she said. 'What has happened?'

'I've let you down badly,' said Wilbraham. 'Tumbled headlong into the trap. Tell me, did you send me a note asking me to meet you here?'

The girl's eyes opened in astonishment. '*I*? But you sent *me* one.'

'Oh, I sent you one, did I?'

'Yes. I got it at the office. It asked me to meet you here instead of at home.'

'Same method for both of us,' he groaned, and he explained the situation.

'I see,' said Freda. 'Then the idea was—?'

'To get the paper. We must have been followed yesterday. That's how they got on to me.'

'And—have they got it?' asked Freda.

'Unfortunately, I can't feel and see,' said the soldier, regarding his bound hands ruefully.

And then they both started. For a voice spoke, a voice that seemed to come from the empty air.

'Yes, thank you,' it said. 'I've got it, all right. No mistake about that.'

The unseen voice made them both shiver.

'Mr Reid,' murmured Freda.

'Mr Reid is one of my names, my dear young lady,' said the voice. 'But only one of them. I have a great many. Now, I am sorry to say that you two have interfered with my plans—a thing I never allow. Your discovery of this house is a serious matter. You have not told the police about it yet, but you might do so in the future.

'I very much fear that I cannot trust you in the matter. You might promise—but promises are seldom kept. And, you see, this house is very useful to me. It is, you might say, my clearing house. The house from which there is no return. From here you pass on—elsewhere. You, I am sorry to say, are so passing on. Regrettable—but necessary.'

The voice paused for a brief second, then resumed: 'No bloodshed. I abhor bloodshed. My method is much simpler. And really not too painful, so I understand. Well, I must be getting along. Good-evening to you both.'

'Look here!' It was Wilbraham who spoke. 'Do what you like to me, but this young lady has done nothing—nothing. It can't hurt you to let her go.'

But there was no answer.

At that moment there came a cry from Freda. 'The water—the water!'

Wilbraham twisted himself painfully and followed

53

the direction of her eyes. From a hole up near the ceiling a steady trickle of water was pouring in.

Freda gave a hysterical cry. 'They're going to drown us!'

The perspiration broke out on Wilbraham's brow. 'We're not done yet,' he said. 'We'll shout for help. Surely somebody will hear us. Now, both together.'

They yelled and shouted at the tops of their voices. Not until they were hoarse did they stop.

'No use, I'm afraid,' said Wilbraham sadly. 'We're too far underground and I expect the doors are muffled. After all, if we could be heard, I've no doubt that brute would have gagged us.'

'Oh,' cried Freda. 'And it's all my fault. I got you into this.'

'Don't worry about that, little girl. It's you I'm thinking about. I've been in tight corners before now and got out of them. Don't you lose heart. I'll get you out of this. We've plenty of time. At the rate that water's flowing in, it will be hours before the worst happens.'

'How wonderful you are!' said Freda. 'I've never met anybody like you—except in books.'

'Nonsense—just common sense. Now, I've got to loosen those infernal ropes.'

At the end of a quarter of an hour, by dint of straining and twisting, Wilbraham had the satisfaction of feeling that his bonds were appreciably loosened. He managed to bend his head down and his wrists up till he was able to attack the knots with his teeth.

Once his hands were free, the rest was only a matter of time. Cramped, stiff, but free, he bent over the girl. A minute later she was also free.

So far the water was only up to their ankles.

'And now,' said the soldier, 'to get out of here.'

The door of the cellar was up a few stairs. Major Wilbraham examined it.

'No difficulty here,' he said. 'Flimsy stuff. It will soon give at the hinges.' He set his shoulders to it and heaved.

There was a cracking of wood—a crash, and the door burst from its hinges.

Outside was a flight of stairs. At the top was another door—a very different affair—of solid wood, barred with iron.

'A bit more difficult, this,' said Wilbraham. 'Hallo, here's a piece of luck. It's unlocked.'

He pushed it open, peered round it, then beckoned the girl to come on. They emerged into a passage behind the kitchen. In another moment they were standing under the stars in Friars Lane.

'Oh!' Freda gave a little sob. 'Oh, how dreadful it's been!'

'My poor darling.' He caught her in his arms. 'You've been so wonderfully brave. Freda—darling angel—could you ever—I mean, would you—I love you, Freda. Will you marry me?'

After a suitable interval, highly satisfactory to both parties, Major Wilbraham said, with a chuckle:

'And what's more, we've still got the secret of the ivory cache.'

'But they took it from you!'

The major chuckled again. 'That's just what they didn't do! You see, I wrote out a spoof copy, and before joining you here tonight, I put the real thing in a letter I was sending to my tailor and posted it. They've got the spoof copy—and I wish them joy of it! Do you know

55

what we'll do, sweetheart! We'll go to East Africa for our honeymoon and hunt out the cache.'

Mr Parker Pyne left his office and climbed two flights of stairs. Here in a room at the top of the house sat Mrs Oliver, the sensational novelist, now a member of Mr Pyne's staff.

Mr Parker Pyne tapped at the door and entered. Mrs Oliver sat at a table on which were a typewriter, several notebooks, a general confusion of loose manuscripts and a large bag of apples.

'A very good story, Mrs Oliver,' said Mr Parker Pyne genially.

'It went off well?' said Mrs Oliver. 'I'm glad.'

'That water-in-the-cellar business,' said Mr Parker Pyne. 'You don't think, on a future occasion, that something more original—perhaps?' He made the suggestion with proper diffidence.

Mrs Oliver shook her head and took an apple from her bag. 'I think not, Mr Pyne. You see, people are used to reading about such things. Water rising in a cellar, poison gas, et cetera. Knowing about it beforehand gives it an extra thrill when it happens to oneself. The public is conservative, Mr Pyne; it likes the old well-worn gadgets.'

'Well, you should know,' admitted Mr Parker Pyne, mindful of the authoress's forty-six successful works of fiction, all best sellers in England and America, and freely translated into French, German, Italian, Hungarian, Finnish, Japanese and Abyssinian. 'How about expenses?'

Mrs Oliver drew a paper towards her. 'Very moderate, on the whole. The two hired assailants, Percy and

Jerry, wanted very little. Young Lorrimer, the actor, was willing to enact the part of Mr Reid for five guineas. The cellar speech was a phonograph record, of course.'

'Whitefriars has been extremely useful to me,' said Mr Pyne. 'I bought it for a song and it has already been the scene of eleven exciting dramas.'

'Oh, I forgot,' said Mrs Oliver. 'Johnny's wages. Five shillings.'

'Johnny?'

'Yes. The boy who poured the water from the watering cans through the hole in the wall.'

'Ah yes. By the way, Mrs Oliver, how did you happen to know Swahili?'

'I didn't.'

'I see. The British Museum perhaps?'

'No. Delfridge's Information Bureau.'

'How marvellous are the resources of modern commerce!' he murmured.

'The only thing that worries me,' said Mrs Oliver, 'is that those two young people won't find any cache when they get there.'

'One cannot have everything in this world,' said Mr Parker Pyne. 'They will have had a honeymoon.'

Mrs Wilbraham was sitting in a deck-chair. Her husband was writing a letter. 'What's the date, Freda?'

'The sixteenth.'

'The sixteenth. By jove!'

'What is it, dear?'

'Nothing. I just remembered a chap named Jones.'

However happily married, there are some things one never tells.

'Dash it all,' thought Major Wilbraham. 'I ought to have called at that place and got my money back.' And then, being a fair-minded man, he looked at the other side of the question. 'After all, it was I who broke the bargain. I suppose if I'd gone to see Jones something would have happened. And, anyway, as it turns out, if I hadn't been going to see Jones, I should never have heard Freda cry for help, and we might never have met. So, indirectly, perhaps they have a right to the fifty pounds!'

Mrs Wilbraham was also following out a train of thought. 'What a silly little fool I was to believe in that advertisement and pay those people three guineas. Of course, they never did anything for it and nothing ever happened. If I'd only known what was coming—first Mr Reid, and then the queer, romantic way that Charlie came into my life. And to think that *but for pure chance* I might never have met him!'

She turned and smiled adoringly at her husband.

The Adventure of the Clapham Cook

At the time that I was sharing rooms with my friend Hercule Poirot, it was my custom to read aloud to him the headlines in the morning newspaper, the *Daily Blare*.

The *Daily Blare* was a paper that made the most of any opportunity for sensationalism. Robberies and murders did not lurk obscurely in its back pages. Instead they hit you in the eye in large type on the front page.

ABSCONDING BANK CLERK
DISAPPEARS WITH FIFTY THOUSAND
POUNDS' WORTH OF NEGOTIABLE
SECURITIES.
HUSBAND PUTS HIS HEAD IN
GAS-OVEN. UNHAPPY HOME LIFE.
MISSING TYPIST. PRETTY GIRL OF
TWENTY-ONE. WHERE IS EDNA FIELD?

'There you are, Poirot, plenty to choose from. An absconding bank clerk, a mysterious suicide, a missing typist—which will you have?'

My friend was in a placid mood. He quietly shook his head.

'I am not greatly attracted to any of them, *mon ami*. Today I feel inclined for the life of ease. It would have to be a very interesting problem to tempt me from my chair. See you, I have affairs of importance of my own to attend to.'

'Such as?'

'My wardrobe, Hastings. If I mistake not, there is on my new grey suit the spot of grease—only the unique spot, but it is sufficient to trouble me. Then there is my winter overcoat—I must lay him aside in the powder of Keatings. And I think—yes, I think—the moment is ripe for the trimmings of my moustaches—and afterwards I must apply the pomade.'

'Well,' I said, strolling to the window, 'I doubt if you'll be able to carry out this delirious programme. That was a ring at the bell. You have a client.'

'Unless the affair is one of national importance, I touch it not,' declared Poirot with dignity.

A moment later our privacy was invaded by a stout red-faced lady who panted audibly as a result of her rapid ascent of the stairs.

'You're M. Poirot?' she demanded, as she sank into a chair.

'I am Hercule Poirot, yes, madame.'

'You're not a bit like what I thought you'd be,' said the lady, eyeing him with some disfavour. 'Did you pay for the bit in the paper saying what a clever detective you were, or did they put it in themselves?'

'Madame!' said Poirot, drawing himself up.

'I'm sorry, I'm sure, but you know what these papers are nowadays. You begin reading a nice article: "What a bride said to her plain unmarried friend", and it's all about a simple thing you buy at the chemist's and shampoo your hair with. Nothing but puff. But no offence taken, I hope? I'll tell you what I want you to do for me. I want you to find my cook.'

Poirot stared at her; for once his ready tongue failed him. I turned aside to hide the broadening smile I could not control.

'It's all this wicked dole,' continued the lady. 'Putting ideas into servants' heads, wanting to be typists and what nots. Stop the dole, that's what I say. I'd like to know what *my* servants have to complain of—afternoon and evening off a week, alternate Sundays, washing put out, same food as we have—and never a bit of margarine in the house, nothing but the very best butter.'

She paused for want of breath and Poirot seized his opportunity. He spoke in his haughtiest manner, rising to his feet as he did so.

'I fear you are making a mistake, madame. I am not holding an inquiry into the conditions of domestic service. I am a private detective.'

'I know that,' said our visitor. 'Didn't I tell you I wanted you to find my cook for me? Walked out of the house on Wednesday, without so much as a word to me, and never came back.'

'I am sorry, madame, but I do not touch this particular kind of business. I wish you good morning.'

Our visitor snorted with indignation.

'That's it, is it, my fine fellow? Too proud, eh? Only deal with Government secrets and countesses' jewels? Let me tell you a servant's every bit as important as a tiara to a woman in my position. We can't all be fine ladies going out in our motors with our diamonds and our pearls. A good cook's a good cook—and when you lose her, it's as much to you as her pearls are to some fine lady.'

For a moment or two it appeared to be a toss up between Poirot's dignity and his sense of humour. Finally he laughed and sat down again.

'Madame, you are in the right, and I am in the wrong. Your remarks are just and intelligent. This case will be a novelty. Never yet have I hunted a missing domestic. Truly here is the problem of national importance that I was demanding of fate just before your arrival. *En avant*! You say this jewel of a cook went out on Wednesday and did not return. That is the day before yesterday.'

'Yes, it was her day out.'

'But probably, madame, she has met with some accident. Have you inquired at any of the hospitals?'

'That's exactly what I thought yesterday, but this morning, if you please, she sent for her box. And not so much as a line to me! If I'd been at home, I'd not have let it go—treating me like that! But I'd just stepped out to the butcher.'

'Will you describe her to me?'

'She was middle-aged, stout, black hair turning grey—most respectable. She'd been ten years in her last place. Eliza Dunn, her name was.'

'And you had had—no disagreement with her on the Wednesday?'

'None whatever. That's what makes it all so queer.'

'How many servants do you keep, madame?'

'Two. The house-parlourmaid, Annie, is a very nice girl. A bit forgetful and her head full of young men, but a good servant if you keep her up to her work.'

'Did she and the cook get on well together?'

'They had their ups and downs, of course—but on the whole, very well.'

'And the girl can throw no light on the mystery?'

'She says not—but you know what servants are—they all hang together.'

'Well, well, we must look into this. Where did you say you resided, madame?'

'At Clapham; 88 Prince Albert Road.'

'*Bien*, madame, I will wish you good morning, and you may count upon seeing me at your residence during the course of the day.'

Mrs Todd, for such was our new friend's name, then took her departure. Poirot looked at me somewhat ruefully.

'Well, well, Hastings, this is a novel affair that we have here. The Disappearance of the Clapham Cook! Never, *never*, must our friend Inspector Japp get to hear of this!'

He then proceeded to heat an iron and carefully removed the grease spot from his grey suit by means of a piece of blotting-paper. His moustaches he regretfully postponed to another day, and we set out for Clapham.

Prince Albert Road proved to be a street of small prim houses, all exactly alike, with neat lace curtains veiling the windows, and well-polished brass knockers on the doors.

We rang the bell at No. 88, and the door was opened by a neat maid with a pretty face. Mrs Todd came out in the hall to greet us.

'Don't go, Annie,' she cried. 'This gentleman's a detective and he'll want to ask you some questions.'

Annie's face displayed a struggle between alarm and a pleasurable excitement.

'I thank you, madame,' said Poirot bowing. 'I would like to question your maid now—and to see her alone, if I may.' We were shown into a small drawing-room, and when Mrs Todd, with obvious reluctance, had left the room, Poirot commenced his cross-examination.

'*Voyons, Mademoiselle Annie,* all that you shall tell us will be of the greatest importance. You alone can shed any light on the case. Without your assistance I can do nothing.' The alarm vanished from the girl's face and the pleasurable excitement became more strongly marked.

'I'm sure, sir,' she said, 'I'll tell you anything I can.'

'That is good.' Poirot beamed approval on her. 'Now, first of all what is your own idea? You are a girl of remarkable intelligence. That can be seen at once! What is your own explanation of Eliza's disappearance?'

Thus encouraged, Annie fairly flowed into excited speech.

'White slavers, sir, I've said so all along! Cook was always warning me against them. "Don't you sniff no scent, or eat any sweets—no matter how gentlemanly the fellow!" Those were her words to me. And now they've got her! I'm sure of it. As likely as not, she's been shipped to Turkey or one of them Eastern places where I've heard they like them fat!'

Poirot preserved an admirable gravity.

'But in that case—and it is indeed an idea!—would she have sent for her trunk?'

'Well, I don't know, sir. She'd want her things—even in those foreign places.'

'Who came for the trunk—a man?' 'It was Carter Paterson, sir.'

'Did you pack it?'

'No, sir, it was already packed and corded.'

'Ah! That's interesting. That shows that when she left the house on Wednesday, she had already determined not to return. You see that, do you not?'

'Yes, sir.' Annie looked slightly taken aback. 'I hadn't thought of that. But it might still have been white slavers, mightn't it, sir? she added wistfully.

'Undoubtedly!' said Poirot gravely. He went on: 'Did you both occupy the same bedroom?'

'No, sir, we had separate rooms.'

'And had Eliza expressed any dissatisfaction with her present post to you at all? Were you both happy here?'

'She'd never mentioned leaving. The place is all right—' The girl hesitated.

'Speak freely,' said Poirot kindly. 'I shall not tell your mistress.'

'Well, of course, sir, she's a caution, Missus is. But the food's good. Plenty of it, and no stinting. Something hot for supper, good outings, and as much frying-fat as you like. And anyway, if Eliza did want to make a change, she'd never have gone off this way, I'm sure. She'd have stayed her month. Why, Missus could have a month's wages out of her for doing this!'

65

'And the work, it is not too hard?'

'Well, she's particular—always poking round in corners and looking for dust. And then there's the lodger, or paying guest as he's always called. But that's only breakfast and dinner, same as Master. They're out all day in the City.'

'You like your master?'

'He's all right—very quiet and a bit on the stingy side.'

'You can't remember, I suppose, the last thing Eliza said before she went out?'

'Yes, I can. "If there's any stewed peaches over from the dining-room," she says, "we'll have them for supper, and a bit of bacon and some fried potatoes." Mad over stewed peaches, she was. I shouldn't wonder if they didn't get her that way.'

'Was Wednesday her regular day out?'

'Yes, she had Wednesdays and I had Thursdays.'

Poirot asked a few more questions, then declared himself satisfied. Annie departed, and Mrs Todd hurried in, her face alight with curiosity. She had, I felt certain, bitterly resented her exclusion from the room during our conversation with Annie. Poirot, however, was careful to soothe her feelings tactfully.

'It is difficult,' he explained, 'for a woman of exceptional intelligence such as yourself, madame, to bear patiently the roundabout methods we poor detectives are forced to use. To have patience with stupidity is difficult for the quick-witted.'

Having thus charmed away any little resentment on Mrs Todd's part, he brought the conversation round to her husband and elicited the information that he worked with a firm in the City and would not be home until after six.

'Doubtless he is very disturbed and worried by this unaccountable business, eh? It is not so?'

'He's never worried,' declared Mrs Todd. '"Well, well, get another, my dear." That's all *he* said! He's so calm that it drives me to distraction sometimes. "An ungrateful woman," he said. "We are well rid of her."'

'What about the other inmates of the house, madame?'

'You mean Mr Simpson, our paying guest? Well, as long as he gets his breakfast and his evening meal all right, *he* doesn't worry.'

'What is his profession, madame?'

'He works in a bank.' She mentioned its name, and I started slightly, remembering my perusal of the *Daily Blare*.

'A young man?'

'Twenty-eight, I believe. Nice quiet young fellow.'

'I should like to have a few words with him, and also with your husband, if I may. I will return for that purpose this evening. I venture to suggest that you should repose yourself a little, madame, you look fatigued.'

'I should just think I am! First the worry about Eliza, and then I was at the sales practically all yesterday, and you know what *that* is, M. Poirot, and what with one thing and another and a lot to do in the house, because of course Annie can't do it all—and very likely she'll give notice anyway, being unsettled in this way—well, what with it all, I'm tired out!'

Poirot murmured sympathetically, and we took our leave.

'It's a curious coincidence,' I said, 'but that absconding clerk, Davis, was from the same bank as Simpson. Can there be any connection, do you think?'

Poirot smiled.

'At the one end, a defaulting clerk, at the other a vanishing cook. It is hard to see any relation between the two, unless possibly Davis visited Simpson, fell in love with the cook, and persuaded her to accompany him on his flight!'

I laughed. But Poirot remained grave.

'He might have done worse,' he said reprovingly. 'Remember, Hastings, if you are going into exile, a good cook may be of more comfort than a pretty face!' He paused for a moment and then went on. 'It is a curious case, full of contradictory features. I am interested— yes, I am distinctly interested.'

That evening we returned to 88 Prince Albert Road and interviewed both Todd and Simpson. The former was a melancholy lantern-jawed man of forty-odd.

'Oh! Yes, yes,' he said vaguely. 'Eliza. Yes. A good cook, I believe. And economical. I make a strong point of economy.'

'Can you imagine any reason for her leaving you so suddenly?'

'Oh, well,' said Mr Todd vaguely. 'Servants, you know. My wife worries too much. Worn out from always worrying. The whole problem's quite simple really. "Get another, my dear," I say. "Get another." That's all there is to it. No good crying over spilt milk.'

Mr Simpson was equally unhelpful. He was a quiet inconspicuous young man with spectacles.

'I must have seen her, I suppose,' he said. 'Elderly woman, wasn't she? Of course, it's the other one I see always, Annie. Nice girl. Very obliging.'

'Were those two on good terms with each other?'

Mr Simpson said he couldn't say, he was sure. He supposed so.

'Well, we get nothing of interest there, *mon ami*,' said Poirot as we left the house. Our departure had been delayed by a burst of vociferous repetition from Mrs Todd, who repeated everything she had said that morning at rather greater length.

'Are you disappointed?' I asked. 'Did you expect to hear something?'

Poirot shook his head.

'There was a possibility, of course,' he said. 'But I hardly thought it likely.'

The next development was a letter which Poirot received on the following morning. He read it, turned purple with indignation, and handed it to me.

Mrs Todd regrets that after all she will not avail herself of Mr Poirot's services. After talking the matter over with her husband she sees that it is foolish to call in a detective about a purely domestic affair. Mrs Todd encloses a guinea for consultation fee.

'Aha!' cried Poirot angrily. 'And they think to get rid of Hercule Poirot like that! As a favour—a great favour—I consent to investigate their miserable little twopenny-halfpenny affair—and they dismiss me *comme ça*! Here, I mistake not, is the hand of Mr Todd. But I say no!—thirty-six times no! I will spend my own guineas, thirty-six hundred of them if need be, but I will get to the bottom of this matter!'

'Yes,' I said. 'But how?'

Poirot calmed down a little.

'*D'abord*,' he said, 'we will advertise in the papers. Let me see—yes—something like this: "If Eliza Dunn will communicate with this address, she will hear of something to her advantage." Put it in all the papers you can think of, Hastings. Then I will make some little inquiries of my own. Go, go—all must be done as quickly as possible!'

I did not see him again until the evening, when he condescended to tell me what he had been doing.

'I have made inquiries at the firm of Mr Todd. He was not absent on Wednesday, and he bears a good character—so much for him. Then Simpson, on Thursday he was ill and did not come to the bank, but he was there on Wednesday. He was moderately friendly with Davis. Nothing out of the common. There does not seem to be anything there. No. We must place our reliance on the advertisement.'

The advertisement duly appeared in all the principal daily papers. By Poirot's orders it was to be continued every day for a week. His eagerness over this uninteresting matter of a defaulting cook was extraordinary, but I realized that he considered it a point of honour to persevere until he finally succeeded. Several extremely interesting cases were brought to him about this time, but he declined them all. Every morning he would rush at his letters, scrutinize them earnestly and then lay them down with a sigh.

But our patience was rewarded at last. On the

Wednesday following Mrs Todd's visit, our landlady informed us that a person of the name of Eliza Dunn had called.

'*Enfin*!' cried Poirot. 'But make her mount then! At once. Immediately.'

Thus admonished, our landlady hurried out and returned a moment or two later, ushering in Miss Dunn. Our quarry was much as described: tall, stout, and eminently respectable.

'I came in answer to the advertisement,' she explained. 'I thought there must be some muddle or other, and that perhaps you didn't know I'd already got my legacy.'

Poirot was studying her attentively. He drew forward a chair with a flourish.

'The truth of the matter is,' he explained, 'that your late mistress, Mrs Todd, was much concerned about you. She feared some accident might have befallen you.'

Eliza Dunn seemed very much surprised.

'Didn't she get my letter then?'

'She got no word of any kind.' He paused, and then said persuasively: 'Recount to me the whole story, will you not?'

Eliza Dunn needed no encouragement. She plunged at once into a lengthy narrative.

'I was just coming home on Wednesday night and had nearly got to the house, when a gentleman stopped me. A tall gentleman he was, with a beard and a big hat. "Miss Eliza Dunn?" he said. "Yes," I said. "I've been inquiring for you at No. 88," he said. "They told me I might meet you coming along here. Miss Dunn, I have come from Australia specially to find you. Do you happen to know the maiden name of your maternal

71

grandmother?" "Jane Emmott," I said. "Exactly," he said. "Now, Miss Dunn, although you may never have heard of the fact, your grandmother had a great friend, Eliza Leech. This friend went to Australia where she married a very wealthy settler. Her two children died in infancy, and she inherited all her husband's property. She died a few months ago, and by her will you inherit a house in this country and a considerable sum of money."

'You could have knocked me down with a feather,' continued Miss Dunn. 'For a minute, I was suspicious, and he must have seen it, for he smiled. "Quite right to be on your guard, Miss Dunn," he said. "Here are my credentials." He handed me a letter from some lawyers in Melbourne, Hurst and Crotchet, and a card. He was Mr Crotchet. "There are one or two conditions," he said. "Our client was a little eccentric, you know. The bequest is conditional on your taking possession of the house (it is in Cumberland) before twelve o'clock tomorrow. The other condition is of no importance—it is merely a stipulation that you should not be in domestic service." My face fell. "Oh, Mr Crotchet," I said. "I'm a cook. Didn't they tell you at the house?" "Dear, dear," he said. "I had no idea of such a thing. I thought you might possibly be a companion or governess there. This is very unfortunate—very unfortunate indeed."

"'Shall I have to lose all the money?" I said, anxious like. He thought for a minute or two. "There are always ways of getting round the law, Miss Dunn," he said at last. "We lawyers know that. The way out here is for you to have left your employment this afternoon." "But my month?" I said. "My dear Miss Dunn," he said with a smile. "You can leave an employer any minute by forfeiting a month's wages. Your mistress will understand in view of the circumstances. The difficulty is *time*! It is imperative that you should catch the 11.05 from King's Cross to the north. I can advance you ten pounds or so for the fare, and you can write a note at the station to your employer. I will take it to her myself and explain the whole circumstances." I agreed, of course, and an hour later I was in the train, so flustered that I didn't know whether I was on my head or heels. Indeed by the time I got to Carlisle, I was half inclined to think the whole thing was one of those confidence tricks you read about. But I went to the address he had given me—solicitors they were, and it was all right. A nice little house, and an income of three hundred a year. These lawyers knew very little, they'd just got a letter from a gentleman in London instructing them to hand over the house to me and £150 for the first six months. Mr Crotchet sent up my things to me, but there was no word from Missus. I supposed she was angry and grudged me my bit of luck. She kept back my box too, and sent my clothes in paper parcels. But there, of course if she never had my letter, she might think it a bit cool of me.'

Poirot had listened attentively to this long history. Now he nodded his head as though completely satisfied.

'Thank you, mademoiselle. There had been, as you say, a little muddle. Permit me to recompense you for your trouble.' He handed her an envelope. 'You return to Cumberland immediately? A little word in your ear. *Do not forget how to cook*. It is always useful to have some-thing to fall back upon in case things go wrong.'

'Credulous,' he murmured, as our visitor departed,

'but perhaps not more than most of her class.' His face grew grave. 'Come, Hastings, there is no time to be lost. Get a taxi while I write a note to Japp.'

Poirot was waiting on the doorstep when I returned with the taxi.

'Where are we going?' I asked anxiously.

'First, to despatch this note by special messenger.'

This was done, and re-entering the taxi Poirot gave the address to the driver.

'Eighty-eight Prince Albert Road, Clapham.'

'So we are going there?'

'*Mais oui*. Though frankly I fear we shall be too late. Our bird will have flown, Hastings.'

'Who is our bird?'

Poirot smiled.

'The inconspicuous Mr Simpson.'

'What?' I exclaimed.

'Oh, come now, Hastings, do not tell me that all is not clear to you now!'

'The cook was got out of the way, I realize that,' I said, slightly piqued. 'But why? *Why* should Simpson wish to get her out of the house? Did she know something about him?'

'Nothing whatever.'

'Well, then—'

'But he wanted something that she had.'

'Money? The Australian legacy?'

'No, my friend—something quite different.' He paused a moment and then said gravely: '*A battered tin trunk . . .*'

I looked sideways at him. His statement seemed so fantastic that I suspected him of pulling my leg, but he was perfectly grave and serious.

'Surely he could buy a trunk if he wanted one,' I cried.

'He did not want a new trunk. He wanted a trunk of pedigree. A trunk of assured respectability.'

'Look here, Poirot,' I cried, 'this really is a bit thick. You're pulling my leg.'

He looked at me.

'You lack the brains and the imagination of Mr Simpson, Hastings. See here: On Wednesday evening, Simpson decoys away the cook. A printed card and a printed sheet of notepaper are simple matters to obtain, and he is willing to pay £150 and a year's house rent to assure the success of his plan. Miss Dunn does not recognize him—the beard and the hat and the slight colonial accent completely deceive her. That is the end of Wednesday—except for the trifling fact that Simpson has helped himself to fifty thousand pounds' worth of negotiable securities.'

'*Simpson*—but it was *Davis*—'

'If you will kindly permit me to continue, Hastings! Simpson knows that the theft will be discovered on Thursday afternoon. He does not go to the bank on Thursday, but he lies in wait for Davis when he comes out to lunch. Perhaps he admits the theft and tells Davis he will return the securities to him—anyhow he succeeds in getting Davis to come to Clapham with him. It is the maid's day out, and Mrs Todd was at the sales, so there is no one in the house. When the theft is discovered and Davis is missing, the implication will be overwhelming. Davis is the thief! Mr Simpson will be perfectly safe, and can return to work on the morrow like the honest clerk they think him.'

'And Davis?'

Poirot made an expressive gesture, and slowly shook his head.

'It seems too cold-blooded to be believed, and yet what other explanation can there be, *mon ami*. The one difficulty for a murderer is the disposal of the body—and Simpson had planned that out beforehand. I was struck at once by the fact that although Eliza Dunn obviously meant to return that night when she went out (witness her remark about the stewed peaches) *yet her trunk was all ready packed when they came for it*. It was Simpson who sent word to Carter Paterson to call on Friday and it was Simpson who corded up the box on Thursday afternoon. What suspicion could possibly arise? A maid leaves and sends for her box, it is labelled and addressed ready in her name, probably to a railway station within easy reach of London. On Saturday afternoon, Simpson, in his Australian disguise, claims it, he affixes a new label and address and redespatches it somewhere else, again "to be left till called for". When the authorities get suspicious, for excellent reasons, and open it, all that can be elicited will be that a bearded colonial despatched it from some junction near London. There will be nothing to connect it with 88 Prince Albert Road. Ah! Here we are.'

Poirot's prognostications had been correct. Simpson had left days previously. But he was not to escape the consequences of his crime. By the aid of wireless, he was discovered on the *Olympia*, en route to America.

A tin trunk, addressed to Mr Henry Wintergreen, attracted the attention of railway officials at Glasgow. It was opened and found to contain the body of the unfortunate Davis.

Mrs Todd's cheque for a guinea was never cashed. Instead Poirot had it framed and hung on the all of our sitting-room.

'It is to me a little reminder, Hastings. Never to despise the trivial—the undignified. A disappearing domestic at one end—a cold-blooded murder at the other. To me, one of the most interesting of my cases.'

Traitor Hands

Also published as
The Witness for the Prosecution

Mr Mayherne adjusted his pince-nez and cleared his throat with a little dry-as-dust cough that was wholly typical of him. Then he looked again at the man opposite him, the man charged with wilful murder.

Mr Mayherne was a small man precise in manner, neatly, not to say foppishly dressed, with a pair of very shrewd and piercing grey eyes. By no means a fool. Indeed, as a solicitor, Mr Mayherne's reputation stood very high. His voice, when he spoke to his client, was dry but not unsympathetic.

'I must impress upon you again that you are in very grave danger, and that the utmost frankness is necessary.'

Leonard Vole, who had been staring in a dazed fashion at the blank wall in front of him, transferred his glance to the solicitor.

'I know,' he said hopelessly. 'You keep telling me so. But I can't seem to realize yet that I'm charged with murder—*murder*. And such a dastardly crime too.'

Mr Mayherne was practical, not emotional. He

coughed again, took off his pince-nez, polished them carefully, and replaced them on his nose. Then he said:

'Yes, yes, yes. Now, my dear Mr Vole, we're going to make a determined effort to get you off—and we shall succeed—we shall succeed. But I must have all the facts. I must know just how damaging the case against you is likely to be. Then we can fix upon the best line of defence.'

Still the young man looked at him in the same dazed, hopeless fashion. To Mr Mayherne the case had seemed black enough, and the guilt of the prisoner assured. Now, for the first time, he felt a doubt.

'You think I'm guilty,' said Leonard Vole, in a low voice. 'But, by God, I swear I'm not! It looks pretty black against me, I know that. I'm like a man caught in a net—the meshes of it all round me, entangling me whichever way I turn. But I didn't do it, Mr Mayherne, I didn't do it!'

In such a position a man was bound to protest his innocence. Mr Mayherne knew that. Yet, in spite of himself, he was impressed. It might be, after all, that Leonard Vole was innocent.

'You are right, Mr Vole,' he said gravely. 'The case does look very black against you. Nevertheless, I accept your assurance. Now, let us get to facts. I want you to tell me in your own words exactly how you came to make the acquaintance of Miss Emily French.'

'It was one day in Oxford Street. I saw an elderly lady crossing the road. She was carrying a lot of parcels. In the middle of the street she dropped them, tried to recover them, found a bus was almost on top of her and just managed to reach the kerb safely, dazed and bewildered by people having shouted at her. I recovered the parcels, wiped the mud off them as best I could, re-tied the string of one, and returned them to her.'

'There was no question of your having saved her life?'

'Oh! dear me, no. All I did was to perform a common act of courtesy. She was extremely grateful, thanked me warmly, and said something about my manners not being those of most of the younger generation—I can't remember the exact words. Then I lifted my hat and went on. I never expected to see her again. But life is full of coincidences. That very evening I came across her at a party at a friend's house. She recognized me at once and asked that I should be introduced to her. I then found out that she was a Miss Emily French and that she lived at Cricklewood. I talked to her for some time. She was, I imagine, an old lady who took sudden violent fancies to people. She took one to me on the strength of a perfectly simple action which anyone might have performed. On leaving, she shook me warmly by the hand, and asked me to come and see her. I replied, of course, that I should be very pleased to do so, and she then urged me to name a day. I did not want particularly to go, but it would have seemed churlish to refuse, so I fixed on the following Saturday. After she had gone, I learned something about her from my friends. That she was rich, eccentric, lived alone with one maid and owned no less than eight cats.'

'I see,' said Mr Mayherne. 'The question of her being well off came up as early as that?'

'If you mean that I inquired—' began Leonard Vole hotly, but Mr Mayherne stilled him with a gesture.

'I have to look at the case as it will be presented by the other side. An ordinary observer would not have supposed Miss French to be a lady of means. She lived poorly, almost humbly. Unless you had been told the contrary, you would in all probability have considered her to be in poor circumstances—at any rate to begin with. Who was it exactly who told you that she was well off?'

'My friend, George Harvey, at whose house the party took place.'

'Is he likely to remember having done so?'

'I really don't know. Of course it is some time ago now.'

'Quite so, Mr Vole. You see, the first aim of the prosecution will be to establish that you were in low water financially—that is true, is it not?'

Leonard Vole flushed.

'Yes,' he said, in a low voice. 'I'd been having a run of infernal bad luck just then.'

'Quite so,' said Mr Mayherne again. 'That being, as I say, in low water financially, you met this rich old lady and cultivated her acquaintance assiduously. Now if we are in a position to say that you had no idea she was well off, and that you visited her out of pure kindness of heart—'

'Which is the case.'

'I dare say. I am not disputing the point. I am looking at it from the outside point of view. A great deal depends on the memory of Mr Harvey. Is he likely to remember that conversation or is he not? Could he be confused by counsel into believing that it took place later?'

Leonard Vole reflected for some minutes. Then he said steadily enough, but with a rather paler face:

'I do not think that that line would be successful, Mr Mayherne. Several of those present heard his remark, and one or two of them chaffed me about my conquest of a rich old lady.'

The solicitor endeavoured to hide his disappointment with a wave of the hand.

'Unfortunately,' he said. 'But I congratulate you upon your plain speaking, Mr Vole. It is to you I look to guide me. Your judgement is quite right. To persist in the line I spoke of would have been disastrous. We must leave that point. You made the acquaintance of Miss French, you called upon her, the acquaintanceship progressed. We want a clear reason for all this. Why did you, a young man of thirty-three, good-looking, fond of sport, popular with your friends, devote so much time to an elderly woman with whom you could hardly have anything in common?'

Leonard Vole flung out his hands in a nervous gesture.

'I can't tell you—I really can't tell you. After the first visit, she pressed me to come again, spoke of being lonely and unhappy. She made it difficult for me to refuse. She showed so plainly her fondness and affection for me that I was placed in an awkward position. You see, Mr Mayherne, I've got a weak nature—I drift—I'm one of those people who can't say "No." And believe me or not, as you like, after the third or fourth visit I paid her I found myself getting genuinely fond of the old thing. My mother died when I was young, an aunt brought me up, and she too died before I was fifteen. If I told you that I genuinely enjoyed being mothered and pampered, I dare say you'd only laugh.'

Mr Mayherne did not laugh. Instead he took off his pince-nez again and polished them, always a sign with him that he was thinking deeply.

'I accept your explanation, Mr Vole,' he said at last. 'I believe it to be psychologically probable. Whether a jury would take that view of it is another matter. Please continue your narrative. When was it that Miss French first asked you to look into her business affairs?'

'After my third or fourth visit to her. She understood very little of money matters, and was worried about some investments.'

Mr Mayherne looked up sharply.

'Be careful, Mr Vole. The maid, Janet Mackenzie, declares that her mistress was a good woman of business and transacted all her own affairs, and this is borne out by the testimony of her bankers.'

'I can't help that,' said Vole earnestly. 'That's what she said to me.'

Mr Mayherne looked at him for a moment or two in silence. Though he had no intention of saying so, his belief in Leonard Vole's innocence was at that moment strengthened. He knew something of the mentality of elderly ladies. He saw Miss French, infatuated with the good-looking young man, hunting about for pretexts that should bring him to the house. What more likely than that she would plead ignorance of business, and beg him to help her with her money affairs? She was enough of a woman of the world to realize that any man is slightly flattered by such an admission of his superiority. Leonard Vole had been flattered. Perhaps, too, she had not been averse to letting this young man know that she was wealthy. Emily French had been a strong-willed old woman, willing to pay her price for what she wanted. All this passed rapidly through Mr Mayherne's mind, but he gave no indication of it, and asked instead a further question.

'And you did handle her affairs for her at her request?'

'I did.'

'Mr Vole,' said the solicitor, 'I am going to ask you a very serious question, and one to which it is vital I should have a truthful answer. You were in low water financially. You had the handling of an old lady's affairs—an old lady who according to her own statement, knew little or nothing of business. Did you at any time, or in any manner, convert to your own use the securities which you handled? Did you engage in any transaction for your own pecuniary advantage which will not bear the light of day?' He quelled the other's response. 'Wait a minute before you answer. There are two courses open to us. Either we can make a feature of your probity and honesty in conducting her affairs whilst pointing out how unlikely it is that you would commit murder to obtain money which you might have obtained by such infinitely easier means. If, on the other hand, there is anything in your dealings which the prosecution will get hold of—if, to put it baldly, it can be proved that you swindled the old lady in any way, we must take the line that you had no motive for the murder, since she was already a profitable source of income to you. You perceive the distinction. Now, I beg of you, take your time before you reply.'

But Leonard Vole took no time at all.

'My dealings with Miss French's affairs are all perfectly fair and above board. I acted for her interests to the very best of my ability, as anyone will find who looks into the matter.'

'Thank you,' said Mr Mayherne. 'You relieve my mind very much. I pay you the compliment of believing that you are far too clever to lie to me over such an important matter.'

'Surely,' said Vole eagerly, 'the strongest point in my favour is the lack of motive. Granted that I cultivated the acquaintanceship of a rich old lady in the hope of getting money out of her—that, I gather, is the substance of what you have been saying—surely her death frustrates all my hopes?'

The solicitor looked at him steadily. Then, very deliberately, he repeated his unconscious trick with his pince-nez. It was not until they were firmly replaced on his nose that he spoke.

'Are you not aware, Mr Vole, Miss French left a will under which you are the principal beneficiary?'

'What?' The prisoner sprang to his feet. His dismay was obvious and unforced. 'My God! What are you saying? She left her money to me?'

Mr Mayherne nodded slowly. Vole sank down again, his head in his hands.

'You pretend you know nothing of this will?'

'Pretend? There's no pretence about it. I knew nothing about it.'

'What would you say if I told you that the maid, Janet Mackenzie, swears that you *did* know? That her mistress told her distinctly that she had consulted you in the matter, and told you of her intentions?'

'Say? That she's lying! No, I go too fast. Janet is an elderly woman. She was a faithful watchdog to her mistress, and she didn't like me. She was jealous and suspicious. I should say that Miss French confided her intentions to Janet, and that Janet either mistook something she said, or else was convinced in her own mind that I had persuaded the old lady into doing it. I dare say that she believes herself now that Miss French actually told her so.'

'You don't think she dislikes you enough to lie deliberately about the matter?'

Leonard Vole looked shocked and startled.

'No, indeed! Why should she?'

'I don't know,' said Mr Mayherne thoughtfully. 'But she's very bitter against you.'

The wretched young man groaned again.

'I'm beginning to see,' he muttered. 'It's frightful. I made up to her, that's what they'll say, I got her to make a will leaving her money to me, and then I go there that night, and there's nobody in the house—they find her the next day—oh! my God, it's awful!'

'You are wrong about there being nobody in the house,' said Mr Mayherne. 'Janet, as you remember, was to go out for the evening. She went, but about half past nine she returned to fetch the pattern of a blouse sleeve which she had promised to a friend. She let herself in by the back door, went upstairs and fetched it, and went out again. She heard voices in the sitting-room, though she could not distinguish what they said, but she will swear that one of them was Miss French's and one was a man's.'

'At half past nine,' said Leonard Vole. 'At half past nine . . .' He sprang to his feet. 'But then I'm saved—saved—'

'What do you mean, saved?' cried Mr Mayherne, astonished.

'*By half past nine I was at home again!* My wife can prove that. I left Miss French about five minutes to nine. I arrived home about twenty past nine. My wife was

87

there waiting for me. Oh! thank God—thank God! And bless Janet Mackenzie's sleeve pattern.'

In his exuberance, he hardly noticed that the grave expression of the solicitor's face had not altered. But the latter's words brought him down to earth with a bump.

'Who, then, in your opinion, murdered Miss French?'

'Why, a burglar, of course, as was thought at first. The window was forced, you remember. She was killed with a heavy blow from a crowbar, and the crowbar was found lying on the floor beside the body. And several articles were missing. But for Janet's absurd suspicions and dislike of me, the police would never have swerved from the right track.'

'That will hardly do, Mr Vole,' said the solicitor. 'The things that were missing were mere trifles of no value, taken as a blind. And the marks on the window were not all conclusive. Besides, think for yourself. You say you were no longer in the house by half past nine. Who, then, was the man Janet heard talking to Miss French in the sitting-room? She would hardly be having an amicable conversation with a burglar?'

'No,' said Vole. 'No—' He looked puzzled and discouraged. 'But anyway,' he added with reviving spirit, 'it lets me out. I've got an *alibi*. You must see Romaine—my wife—at once.'

'Certainly,' acquiesced the lawyer. 'I should already have seen Mrs Vole but for her being absent when you were arrested. I wired to Scotland at once, and I understand that she arrives back tonight. I am going to call upon her immediately I leave here.'

Vole nodded, a great expression of satisfaction settling down over his face.

'Yes, Romaine will tell you. My God! it's a lucky chance that.'

'Excuse me, Mr Vole, but you are very fond of your wife?'

'Of course.'

'And she of you?'

'Romaine is devoted to me. She'd do anything in the world for me.'

He spoke enthusiastically, but the solicitor's heart sank a little lower. The testimony of a devoted wife—would it gain credence?

'Was there anyone else who saw you return at nine-twenty? A maid, for instance?'

'We have no maid.'

'Did you meet anyone in the street on the way back?'

'Nobody I knew. I rode part of the way in a bus. The conductor might remember.'

Mr Mayherne shook his head doubtfully.

'There is no one, then, who can confirm your wife's testimony?'

'No. But it isn't necessary, surely?'

'I dare say not. I dare say not,' said Mr Mayherne hastily. 'Now there's just one thing more. Did Miss French know that you were a married man?'

'Oh, yes.'

'Yet you never took your wife to see her. Why was that?'

For the first time, Leonard Vole's answer came halting and uncertain.

'Well—I don't know.'

'Are you aware that Janet Mackenzie says her mistress believed you to be single, and contemplated marrying you in the future?'

Vole laughed.

'Absurd! There was forty years difference in age between us.'

'It has been done,' said the solicitor drily. 'The fact remains. Your wife never met Miss French?'

'No—' Again the constraint.

'You will permit me to say,' said the lawyer, 'that I hardly understand your attitude in the matter.'

Vole flushed, hesitated, and then spoke.

'I'll make a clean breast of it. I was hard up, as you know. I hoped that Miss French might lend me some money. She was fond of me, but she wasn't at all interested in the struggles of a young couple. Early on, I found that she had taken it for granted that my wife and I didn't get on—were living apart. Mr Mayherne—I wanted the money—for Romaine's sake. I said nothing, and allowed the old lady to think what she chose. She spoke of my being an adopted son for her. There was never any question of marriage—that must be just Janet's imagination.'

'And that is all?'

'Yes—that is all.'

Was there just a shade of hesitation in the words? The lawyer fancied so. He rose and held out his hand.

'Goodbye, Mr Vole.' He looked into the haggard young face and spoke with an unusual impulse. 'I believe in your innocence in spite of the multitude of facts arrayed against you. I hope to prove it and vindicate you completely.'

Vole smiled back at him.

'You'll find the alibi is all right,' he said cheerfully.

Again he hardly noticed that the other did not respond.

'The whole thing hinges a good deal on the testimony of Janet Mackenzie,' said Mr Mayherne. 'She hates you. That much is clear.'

'She can hardly hate me,' protested the young man.

The solicitor shook his head as he went out.

'Now for Mrs Vole,' he said to himself.

He was seriously disturbed by the way the thing was shaping.

The Voles lived in a small shabby house near Paddington Green. It was to this house that Mr Mayherne went.

In answer to his ring, a big slatternly woman, obviously a charwoman, answered the door.

'Mrs Vole? Has she returned yet?'

'Got back an hour ago. But I dunno if you can see her.'

'If you will take my card to her,' said Mr Mayherne quietly, 'I am quite sure that she will do so.'

The woman looked at him doubtfully, wiped her hand on her apron and took the card. Then she closed the door in his face and left him on the step outside.

In a few minutes, however, she returned with a slightly altered manner.

'Come inside, please.'

She ushered him into a tiny drawing-room. Mr Mayherne, examining a drawing on the wall, started up suddenly to face a tall pale woman who had entered so quietly that he had not heard her.

'Mr Mayherne? You are my husband's solicitor, are you not? You have come from him? Will you please sit down?'

Until she spoke he had not realized that she was not English. Now, observing her more closely, he noticed the high cheek-bones, the dense blue-black of the hair, and an occasional very slight movement of the hands that was distinctly foreign. A strange woman, very quiet. So quiet as to make one uneasy. From the very first Mr Mayherne was conscious that he was up against something that he did not understand.

'Now, my dear Mrs Vole,' he began, 'you must not give way—'

He stopped. It was so very obvious that Romaine Vole had not the slightest intention of giving way. She was perfectly calm and composed.

'Will you please tell me all about it?' she said. 'I must know everything. Do not think to spare me. I want to know the worst.' She hesitated, then repeated in a lower tone, with a curious emphasis which the lawyer did not understand: 'I want to know the worst.'

Mr Mayherne went over his interview with Leonard Vole. She listened attentively, nodding her head now and then.

'I see,' she said, when he had finished. 'He wants me to say that he came in at twenty minutes past nine that night?'

'He did come in at that time?' said Mr Mayherne sharply.

'That is not the point,' she said coldly. 'Will my saying so acquit him? Will they believe me?'

Mr Mayherne was taken aback. She had gone so quickly to the core of the matter.

'That is what I want to know,' she said. 'Will it be enough? Is there anyone else who can support my evidence?'

There was a suppressed eagerness in her manner that made him vaguely uneasy.

'So far there is no one else,' he said reluctantly.

'I see,' said Romaine Vole.

She sat for a minute or two perfectly still. A little smile played over her lips.

The lawyer's feeling of alarm grew stronger and stronger.

'Mrs Vole—' he began. 'I know what you must feel—'

'Do you?' she said. 'I wonder.'

'In the circumstances—'

'In the circumstances—I intend to play a lone hand.'

He looked at her in dismay.

'But, my dear Mrs Vole—you are overwrought. Being so devoted to your husband—'

'I beg your pardon?'

The sharpness of her voice made him start. He repeated in a hesitating manner:

'Being so devoted to your husband—'

Romaine Vole nodded slowly, the same strange smile on her lips.

'Did he tell you that I was devoted to him?' she asked softly. 'Ah! yes, I can see he did. How stupid men are! Stupid—stupid—stupid—'

She rose suddenly to her feet. All the intense emotion that the lawyer had been conscious of in the atmosphere was now concentrated in her tone.

'I hate him, I tell you! I hate him. I hate him, I hate him! I would like to see him hanged by the neck till he is dead.'

The lawyer recoiled before her and the smouldering passion in her eyes.

She advanced a step nearer, and continued vehemently:

'Perhaps I *shall* see it. Supposing I tell you that he did not come in that night at twenty past nine, but at twenty past *ten?* You say that he tells you he knew nothing about the money coming to him. Supposing I tell you he knew all about it, and counted on it, and committed murder to get it? Supposing I tell you that he admitted to me that night when he came in what he had done? That there was blood on his coat? What then? Supposing that I stand up in court and say all these things?'

Her eyes seemed to challenge him. With an effort, he concealed his growing dismay, and endeavoured to speak in a rational tone.

'You cannot be asked to give evidence against your husband—'

'He is not my husband!'

The words came out so quickly that he fancied he had misunderstood her.

'I beg your pardon? I—'

'He is not my husband.'

The silence was so intense that you could have heard a pin drop.

'I was an actress in Vienna. My husband is alive but in a madhouse. So we could not marry. I am glad now.'

She nodded defiantly.

'I should like you to tell me one thing,' said Mr Mayherne. He contrived to appear as cool and unemotional as ever. 'Why are you so bitter against Leonard Vole?'

She shook her head, smiling a little.

'Yes, you would like to know. But I shall not tell you. I will keep my secret . . .'

Mr Mayherne gave his dry little cough and rose.

'There seems no point in prolonging this interview,' he remarked. 'You will hear from me again after I have communicated with my client.'

She came closer to him, looking into his eyes with her own wonderful dark ones.

'Tell me,' she said, 'did you believe—honestly—that he was innocent when you came here today?'

'I did,' said Mr Mayherne.

'You poor little man,' she laughed.

'And I believe so still,' finished the lawyer. 'Good evening, madam.'

He went out of the room, taking with him the memory of her startled face.

'This is going to be the devil of a business,' said Mr Mayherne to himself as he strode along the street.

Extraordinary, the whole thing. An extraordinary woman. A very dangerous woman. Women were the devil when they got their knife into you.

What was to be done? That wretched young man hadn't a leg to stand upon. Of course, possibly he did commit the crime . . .

'No,' said Mr Mayherne to himself. 'No—there's almost too much evidence against him. I don't believe this woman. She was trumping up the whole story. But she'll never bring it into court.'

He wished he felt more conviction on the point.

The police court proceedings were brief and dramatic. The principal witnesses for the prosecution were Janet Mackenzie, maid to the dead woman, and Romaine Heilger, Austrian subject, the mistress of the prisoner.

Mr Mayherne sat in the court and listened to the damning story that the latter told. It was on the lines she had indicated to him in their interview.

The prisoner reserved his defence and was committed for trial.

Mr Mayherne was at his wits' end. The case against Leonard Vole was black beyond words. Even the famous KC who was engaged for the defence held out little hope.

'If we can shake that Austrian woman's testimony, we might do something,' he said dubiously. 'But it's a bad business.'

Mr Mayherne had concentrated his energies on one single point. Assuming Leonard Vole to be speaking the truth, and to have left the murdered woman's house at nine o'clock, who was the man whom Janet heard talking to Miss French at half past nine?

The only ray of light was in the shape of a scapegrace nephew who had in bygone days cajoled and threatened his aunt out of various sums of money. Janet Mackenzie, the solicitor learned, had always been attached to this young man, and had never ceased urging his claims upon her mistress. It certainly seemed possible that it was this nephew who had been with Miss French after Leonard Vole left, especially as he was not to be found in any of his old haunts.

In all other directions, the lawyer's researches had been negative in their result. No one had seen Leonard Vole entering his own house, or leaving that of Miss French. No one had seen any other man enter or leave the house in Cricklewood. All inquiries drew blank.

It was the eve of the trial when Mr Mayherne received the letter which was to lead his thoughts in an entirely new direction.

It came by the six o'clock post. An illiterate scrawl,

written on common paper and enclosed in a dirty envelope with the stamp stuck on crooked.

Mr Mayherne read it through once or twice before he grasped its meaning.

Dear Mister:

Youre the lawyer chap wot acks for the young feller. if you want that painted foreign hussy showd up for wot she is an her pack of lies you come to 16 Shaw's Rents Stepney tonight. It ull cawst you 2 hundred quid Arsk for Missis Mogson.

The solicitor read and re-read this strange epistle. It might, of course, be a hoax, but when he thought it over, he became increasingly convinced that it was genuine, and also convinced that it was the one hope for the prisoner. The evidence of Romaine Heilger damned him completely, and the line the defence meant to pursue, the line that the evidence of a woman who had admittedly lived an immoral life was not to be trusted, was at best a weak one.

Mr Mayherne's mind was made up. It was his duty to save his client at all costs. He must go to Shaw's Rents.

He had some difficulty in finding the place, a ramshackle building in an evil-smelling slum, but at last he did so, and on inquiry for Mrs Mogson was sent up to a room on the third floor. On this door he knocked and getting no answer, knocked again.

At this second knock, he heard a shuffling sound inside, and presently the door was opened cautiously half an inch and a bent figure peered out.

Suddenly the woman, for it was a woman, gave a chuckle and opened the door wider.

'So it's you, dearie,' she said, in a wheezy voice. 'Nobody with you, is there? No playing tricks? That's right. You can come in—you can come in.'

With some reluctance the lawyer stepped across the threshold into the small dirty room, with its flickering gas jet. There was an untidy unmade bed in a corner, a plain deal table and two rickety chairs. For the first time Mr Mayherne had a full view of the tenant of this unsavoury apartment. She was a woman of middle age, bent in figure, with a mass of untidy grey hair and a scarf wound tightly round her face. She saw him looking at this and laughed again, the same curious toneless chuckle.

'Wondering why I hide my beauty, dear? He, he, he. Afraid it may tempt you, eh? But you shall see—you shall see.'

She drew aside the scarf and the lawyer recoiled involuntarily before the almost formless blur of scarlet. She replaced the scarf again.

'So you're not wanting to kiss me, dearie? He, he, I don't wonder. And yet I was a pretty girl once—not so long ago as you'd think, either. Vitriol, dearie, vitriol—that's what did that. Ah! but I'll be even with 'em—'

She burst into a hideous torrent of profanity which Mr Mayherne tried vainly to quell. She fell silent at last, her hands clenching and unclenching themselves nervously.

'Enough of that,' said the lawyer sternly. 'I've come here because I have reason to believe you can give me information which will clear my client, Leonard Vole. Is that the case?'

Her eyes leered at him cunningly.

'What about the money, dearie?' she wheezed. 'Two hundred quid, you remember.'

'It is your duty to give evidence, and you can be called upon to do so.'

'That won't do, dearie. I'm an old woman, and I know nothing. But you give me two hundred quid, and perhaps I can give you a hint or two. See?'

'What kind of hint?'

'What should you say to a letter? A letter from *her*. Never mind now how I got hold of it. That's my business. It'll do the trick. But I want my two hundred quid.'

Mr Mayherne looked at her coldly, and made up his mind.

'I'll give you ten pounds, nothing more. And only that if this letter is what you say it is.'

'Ten pounds?' She screamed and raved at him.

'Twenty,' said Mr Mayherne, 'and that's my last word.'

He rose as if to go. Then, watching her closely, he drew out a pocket book, and counted out twenty one-pound notes.

'You see,' he said. 'That is all I have with me. You can take it or leave it.'

But already he knew that the sight of the money was too much for her. She cursed and raved impotently, but at last she gave in. Going over to the bed, she drew something out from beneath the tattered mattress.

'Here you are, damn you!' she snarled. 'It's the top one you want.'

It was a bundle of letters that she threw to him, and Mr Mayherne untied them and scanned them in his usual cool, methodical manner. The woman, watching him eagerly, could gain no clue from his impassive face.

He read each letter through, then returned again to the top one and read it a second time. Then he tied the whole bundle up again carefully.

They were love letters, written by Romaine Heilger, and the man they were written to was not Leonard Vole. The top letter was dated the day of the latter's arrest.

'I spoke true, dearie, didn't I?' whined the woman. 'It'll do for her, that letter?'

Mr Mayherne put the letters in his pocket, then he asked a question.

'How did you get hold of this correspondence?'

'That's telling,' she said with a leer. 'But I know something more. I heard in court what that hussy said. Find out where *she* was at twenty past ten, the time she says she was at home. Ask at the Lion Road Cinema. They'll remember—a fine upstanding girl like that— curse her!'

'Who is the man?' asked Mr Mayherne. 'There's only a Christian name here.'

The other's voice grew thick and hoarse, her hands clenched and unclenched. Finally she lifted one to her face.

'He's the man that did this to me. Many years ago now. She took him away from me—a chit of a girl she was then. And when I went after him—and went for him too—he threw the cursed stuff at me! And she laughed—damn her! I've had it in for her for years. Followed her, I have, spied upon her. And now I've got her! She'll suffer for this, won't she, Mr Lawyer? She'll suffer?'

'She will probably be sentenced to a term of imprisonment for perjury,' said Mr Mayherne quietly.

'Shut away—that's what I want. You're going, are you? Where's my money? Where's that good money?'

Without a word, Mr Mayherne put down the notes on the table. Then, drawing a deep breath, he turned and left the squalid room. Looking back, he saw the old woman crooning over the money.

He wasted no time. He found the cinema in Lion Road easily enough, and, shown a photograph of Romaine Heilger, the commissionaire recognized her at once. She had arrived at the cinema with a man some time after ten o'clock on the evening in question. He had not noticed her escort particularly, but he remembered the lady who had spoken to him about the picture that was showing. They stayed until the end, about an hour later.

Mr Mayherne was satisfied. Romaine Heilger's evidence was a tissue of lies from beginning to end. She had evolved it out of her passionate hatred. The lawyer wondered whether he would ever know what lay behind that hatred. What had Leonard Vole done to her? He had seemed dumbfounded when the solicitor had reported her attitude to him. He had declared earnestly that such a thing was incredible—yet it had seemed to Mr Mayherne that after the first astonishment his protests had lacked sincerity.

He *did* know. Mr Mayherne was convinced of it. He knew, but had no intention of revealing the fact. The secret between those two remained a secret. Mr Mayherne wondered if some day he should come to learn what it was.

The solicitor glanced at his watch. It was late, but time was everything. He hailed a taxi and gave an address.

'Sir Charles must know of this at once,' he murmured to himself as he got in.

The trial of Leonard Vole for the murder of Emily French aroused widespread interest. In the first place the prisoner was young and good-looking, then he was accused of a particularly dastardly crime, and there was the further interest of Romaine Heilger, the principal witness for the prosecution. There had been pictures of her in many papers, and several fictitious stories as to her origin and history.

The proceedings opened quietly enough. Various technical evidence came first. Then Janet Mackenzie was called. She told substantially the same story as before. In cross-examination counsel for the defence succeeded in getting her to contradict herself once or twice over her account of Vole's association with Miss French. He emphasized the fact that though she had heard a man's voice in the sitting-room that night, there was nothing to show that it was Vole who was there, and he managed to drive home a feeling that jealousy and dislike of the prisoner were at the bottom of a good deal of her evidence.

Then the next witness was called.

'Your name is Romaine Heilger?'

'Yes.'

'You are an Austrian subject?'

'Yes.'

'For the last three years you have lived with the prisoner and passed yourself off as his wife?'

Just for a moment Romaine Heilger's eye met those of the man in the dock. Her expression held something curious and unfathomable.

'Yes.'

The questions went on. Word by word the damning facts came out. On the night in question the prisoner had taken out a crowbar with him. He had returned at twenty minutes past ten, and had confessed to having killed the old lady. His cuffs had been stained with blood, and he had burned them in the kitchen stove. He had terrorized her into silence by means of threats.

As the story proceeded, the feeling of the court which had, to begin with, been slightly favourable to the prisoner, now set dead against him. He himself sat with downcast head and moody air, as though he knew he were doomed.

Yet it might have been noted that her own counsel sought to restrain Romaine's animosity. He would have preferred her to be a more unbiased witness.

Formidable and ponderous, counsel for the defence arose.

He put it to her that her story was a malicious fabrication from start to finish, that she had not even been in her own house at the time in question, that she was in love with another man and was deliberately seeking to send Vole to his death for a crime he did not commit.

Romaine denied these allegations with superb insolence.

Then came the surprising denouement, the production of the letter. It was read aloud in court in the midst of a breathless stillness.

Max, beloved, the Fates have delivered him into our hands! He has been arrested for murder—but, yes, the murder of an old lady! Leonard who would not hurt a

103

fly! At last I shall have my revenge. The poor chicken! I shall say that he came in that night with blood upon him—that he confessed to me. I shall hang him, Max—and when he hangs he will know and realize that it was Romaine who sent him to his death. And then—happiness, Beloved! Happiness at last!

There were experts present ready to swear that the hand-writing was that of Romaine Heilger, but they were not needed. Confronted with the letter, Romaine broke down utterly and confessed everything. Leonard Vole had returned to the house at the time he said, twenty past nine. She had invented the whole story to ruin him.

With the collapse of Romaine Heilger, the case for the Crown collapsed also. Sir Charles called his few wit-nesses, the prisoner himself went into the box and told his story in a manly straightforward manner, unshaken by cross-examination.

The prosecution endeavoured to rally, but without great success. The judge's summing up was not wholly favourable to the prisoner, but a reaction had set in and the jury needed little time to consider their verdict.

'We find the prisoner not guilty.'

Leonard Vole was free!

Little Mr Mayherne hurried from his seat. He must congratulate his client.

He found himself polishing his pince-nez vigorously, and checked himself. His wife had told him only the night before that he was getting a habit of it. Curious things habits. People themselves never knew they had them.

An interesting case—a very interesting case. That woman, now, Romaine Heilger.

The case was dominated for him still by the exotic figure of Romaine Heilger. She had seemed a pale quiet woman in the house at Paddington, but in court she had flamed out against the sober background. She had flaunted herself like a tropical flower.

If he closed his eyes he could see her now, tall and vehement, her exquisite body bent forward a little, her right hand clenching and unclenching itself unconsciously all the time.

Curious things, habits. That gesture of hers with the hand was her habit, he supposed. Yet he had seen someone else do it quite lately. Who was it now? Quite lately—

He drew in his breath with a gasp as it came back to him. *The woman in Shaw's Rents . . .*

He stood still, his head whirling. It was impossible—impossible—Yet, Romaine Heilger was an actress.

The KC came up behind him and clapped him on the shoulder.

'Congratulated our man yet? He's had a narrow shave, you know. Come along and see him.'

But the little lawyer shook off the other's hand.

He wanted one thing only—to see Romaine Heilger face to face.

He did not see her until some time later, and the place of their meeting is not relevant.

'So you guessed,' she said, when he had told her all that was in his mind. 'The face? Oh! that was easy enough, and the light of that gas jet was too bad for you to see the make-up.'

'But why—why—'

'Why did I play a lone hand?' She smiled a little, remembering the last time she had used the words.

'Such an elaborate comedy!'

'My friend—I had to save him. The evidence of a woman devoted to him would not have been enough—you hinted as much yourself. But I know something of the psychology of crowds. Let my evidence be wrung from me, as an admission, damning me in the eyes of the law, and a reaction in favour of the prisoner would immediately set in.'

'And the bundle of letters?'

'One alone, the vital one, might have seemed like a—what do you call it?—put-up job.'

'Then the man called Max?'

'Never existed, my friend.'

'I still think,' said little Mr Mayherne, in an aggrieved manner, 'that we could have got him off by the—er—normal procedure.'

'I dared not risk it. You see, you *thought* he was innocent—'

'And you *knew* it? I see,' said little Mr Mayherne.

'My dear Mr Mayherne,' said Romaine, 'you do not see at all. I knew—he was guilty!'

A Fairy in the Flat

Mrs Thomas Beresford shifted her position on the divan and looked gloomily out of the window of the flat. The prospect was not an extended one, consisting solely of a small block of flats on the other side of the road. Mrs Beresford sighed and then yawned.

'I wish,' she said, 'something would happen.'

Her husband looked up reprovingly.

'Be careful, Tuppence, this craving for vulgar sensation alarms me.'

Tuppence sighed and closed her eyes dreamily.

'So Tommy and Tuppence were married,' she chanted, 'and lived happily ever afterwards. And six years later they were still living together happily ever afterwards. It is extraordinary,' she said, 'how different everything always is from what you think it is going to be.'

'A very profound statement, Tuppence. But not original. Eminent poets and still more eminent divines have said it before—and if you will excuse me saying so, have said it better.'

'Six years ago,' continued Tuppence, 'I would have

sworn that with sufficient money to buy things with, and with you for a husband, all life would have been one grand sweet song, as one of the poets you seem to know so much about puts it.'

'Is it me or the money that palls upon you?' inquired Tommy coldly.

'Palls isn't exactly the word,' said Tuppence kindly. 'I'm used to my blessings, that's all. Just as one never thinks what a boon it is to be able to breathe through one's nose until one has a cold in the head.'

'Shall I neglect you a little?' suggested Tommy. 'Take other women about to night clubs. That sort of thing.'

'Useless,' said Tuppence. 'You would only meet me there with other men. And I should know perfectly well that you didn't care for the other women, whereas you would never be quite sure that I didn't care for the other men. Women are so much more thorough.'

'It's only in modesty that men score top marks,' murmured her husband. 'But what is the matter with you, Tuppence? Why this yearning discontent?'

'I don't know. I want things to happen. Exciting things. Wouldn't you like to go chasing German spies again, Tommy? Think of the wild days of peril we went through once. Of course I know you're more or less in the Secret Service now, but it's pure office work.'

'You mean you'd like them to send me into darkest Russia disguised as a Bolshevik bootlegger, or something of that sort?'

'That wouldn't be any good,' said Tuppence. 'They wouldn't let me go with you and I'm the person who wants something to do so badly. Something to do. That is what I keep saying all day long.'

'Women's sphere,' suggested Tommy, waving his hand.

'Twenty minutes' work after breakfast every morning keeps the flag going to perfection. You have nothing to complain of, have you?'

'Your housekeeping is so perfect, Tuppence, as to be almost monotonous.'

'I do like gratitude,' said Tuppence.

'You, of course, have got your work,' she continued, 'but tell me, Tommy, don't you ever have a secret yearning for excitement, for things to *happen*?'

'No,' said Tommy, 'at least I don't think so. It is all very well to want things to happen—they might not be pleasant things.'

'How prudent men are,' sighed Tuppence. 'Don't you ever have a wild secret yearning for romance—adventure—life?'

'What *have* you been reading, Tuppence?' asked Tommy.

'Think how exciting it would be,' went on Tuppence, 'if we heard a wild rapping at the door and went to open it and in staggered a dead man.'

'If he was dead he couldn't stagger,' said Tommy critically.

'You know what I mean,' said Tuppence. 'They always stagger in just before they die and fall at your feet, just gasping out a few enigmatic words. "The Spotted Leopard", or something like that.'

'I advise a course of Schopenhauer or Emmanuel Kant,' said Tommy.

'That sort of thing would be good for you,' said Tuppence. 'You are getting fat and comfortable.'

'I am not,' said Tommy indignantly. 'Anyway you do slimming exercises yourself.'

'Everybody does,' said Tuppence. 'When I said you were getting fat I was really speaking metaphorically, you are getting prosperous and sleek and comfortable.'

'I don't know what has come over you,' said her husband.

'The spirit of adventure,' murmured Tuppence. 'It is better than a longing for romance anyway. I have that sometimes too. I think of meeting a man, a really handsome man—'

'You have met me,' said Tommy. 'Isn't that enough for you?'

'A brown, lean man, terrifically strong, the kind of man who can ride anything and lassoes wild horses—'

'Complete with sheepskin trousers and a cowboy hat,' interpolated Tommy sarcastically.

'—and has lived in the Wilds,' continued Tuppence. 'I should like him to fall simply madly in love with me. I should, of course, rebuff him virtuously and be true to my marriage vows, but my heart would secretly go out to him.'

'Well,' said Tommy, 'I often wish that I may meet a really beautiful girl. A girl with corn coloured hair who will fall desperately in love with me. Only I don't think I rebuff her—in fact I am quite sure I don't.'

'That,' said Tuppence, 'is naughty temper.'

'What,' said Tommy, 'is really the matter with you, Tuppence? You have never talked like this before.'

'No, but I have been boiling up inside for a long time,' said Tuppence. 'You see it is very dangerous to have everything you want—including enough money to buy things. Of course there are always hats.'

'You have got about forty hats already,' said Tommy, 'and they all look alike.'

'Hats are like that,' said Tuppence. 'They are not really alike. There are *nuances* in them. I saw rather a nice one in Violette's this morning.'

'If you haven't anything better to do than going on buying hats you don't need—'

'That's it,' said Tuppence, 'that's exactly it. If I had something better to do. I suppose I ought to take up good works. Oh, Tommy, I do wish something exciting would happen. I feel—I really do feel it would be good for us. If we could find a fairy—'

'Ah!' said Tommy. 'It is curious your saying that.'

He got up and crossed the room. Opening a drawer of the writing table he took out a small snapshot print and brought it to Tuppence.

'Oh!' said Tuppence, 'so you have got them developed. Which is this, the one you took of this room or the one I took?'

'The one I took. Yours didn't come out. You under exposed it. You always do.'

'It is nice for you,' said Tuppence, 'to think that there is one thing you can do better than me.'

'A foolish remark,' said Tommy, 'but I will let it pass for the moment. What I wanted to show you was this.'

He pointed to a small white speck on the photograph.

'That is a scratch on the film,' said Tuppence.

'Not at all,' said Tommy. 'That, Tuppence, is a fairy.'

'Tommy, you idiot.'

'Look for yourself.'

He handed her a magnifying glass. Tuppence studied the print attentively through it. Seen thus by a slight stretch of fancy the scratch on the film could be imagined to represent a small winged creature on the fender.

'It has got wings,' cried Tuppence. 'What fun, a real live fairy in our flat. Shall we write to Conan Doyle about it? Oh, Tommy. Do you think she'll give us wishes?'

'You will soon know,' said Tommy. 'You have been wishing hard enough for something to happen all the afternoon.'

At that minute the door opened, and a tall lad of fifteen who seemed undecided as to whether he was a butler or a page boy inquired in a truly magnificent manner.

'Are you at home, madam? The front-door bell has just rung.'

'I wish Albert wouldn't go to the Pictures,' sighed Tuppence, after she had signified her assent, and Albert had withdrawn. 'He's copying a Long Island butler now. Thank goodness I've cured him of asking for people's cards and bringing them to me on a salver.'

The door opened again, and Albert announced: 'Mr Carter,' much as though it were a Royal title.

'The Chief,' muttered Tommy, in great surprise.

Tuppence jumped up with a glad exclamation, and greeted a tall grey-haired man with piercing eyes and a tired smile.

'Mr Carter, I *am* glad to see you.'

'That's good, Mrs Tommy. Now answer me a question. How's life generally?'

'Satisfactory, but dull,' replied Tuppence with a twinkle.

'Better and better,' said Mr Carter. 'I'm evidently going to find you in the right mood.'

'This,' said Tuppence, 'sounds exciting.'

Albert, still copying the Long Island butler, brought in tea. When this operation was completed without mishap and the door had closed behind him Tuppence burst out once more.

'You did mean something, didn't you, Mr Carter? Are you going to send us on a mission into darkest Russia?'

'Not exactly that,' said Mr Carter.

'But there is something.'

'Yes—there is something. I don't think you are the kind who shrinks from risks, are you, Mrs Tommy?'

Tuppence's eyes sparkled with excitement.

'There is certain work to be done for the Department—and I fancied—I just fancied—that it might suit you two.'

'Go on,' said Tuppence.

'I see that you take the *Daily Leader*,' continued Mr Carter, picking up that journal from the table.

He turned to the advertisement column and indicating a certain advertisement with his finger pushed the paper across to Tommy.

'Read that out,' he said.

Tommy complied.

'The International Detective Agency, Theodore Blunt, Manager. Private Inquiries. Large staff of confidential and highly skilled Inquiry Agents. Utmost discretion. Consultations free. 118 Haleham St, W.C.'

He looked inquiringly at Mr Carter. The latter nodded.
'That detective agency has been on its last legs for some

time,' he murmured. 'Friend of mine acquired it for a mere song. We're thinking of setting it going again—say, for a six months' trial. And during that time, of course, it will have to have a manager.'

'What about Mr Theodore Blunt?' asked Tommy.

'Mr Blunt has been rather indiscreet, I'm afraid. In fact, Scotland Yard have had to interfere. Mr Blunt is being detained at Her Majesty's expense, and he won't tell us half of what we'd like to know.'

'I see, sir,' said Tommy. 'At least, I think I see.'

'I suggest that you have six months leave from the office. Ill health. And, of course, if you like to run a Detective Agency under the name of Theodore Blunt, it's nothing to do with me.'

Tommy eyed his Chief steadily.

'Any instructions, sir?'

'Mr Blunt did some foreign business, I believe. Look out for blue letters with a Russian stamp on them. From a ham merchant anxious to find his wife who came as a refugee to this country some years ago. Moisten the stamp and you'll find the number 16 written underneath. Make a copy of these letters and send the originals on to me. Also if any one comes to the office and makes a reference to the number 16, inform me immediately.'

'I understand, sir,' said Tommy. 'And apart from these instructions?'

Mr Carter picked up his gloves from the table and prepared to depart.

'You can run the Agency as you please. I fancied'—his eyes twinkled a little—'that it might amuse Mrs Tommy to try her hand at a little detective work.'

Mr and Mrs Beresford took possession of the offices of the International Detective Agency a few days later. They were on the second floor of a somewhat dilapidated building in Bloomsbury. In the small outer office, Albert relinquished the role of a Long Island butler, and took up that of office boy, a part which he played to perfection. A paper bag of sweets, inky hands, and a tousled head was his conception of the character.

From the outer office, two doors led into inner offices. On one door was painted the legend 'Clerks'. On the other 'Private'. Behind the latter was a small comfortable room furnished with an immense business-like desk, a lot of artistically labelled files, all empty, and some solid leather-seated chairs. Behind the desk sat the pseudo Mr Blunt trying to look as though he had run a Detective Agency all his life. A telephone, of course, stood at his elbow. Tuppence and he had rehearsed several good telephone effects, and Albert also had his instructions.

In the adjoining room was Tuppence, a typewriter, the necessary tables and chairs of an inferior type to those in the room of the great Chief, and a gas ring for making tea.

Nothing was wanting, in fact, save clients.

Tuppence, in the first ecstasies of initiation, had a few bright hopes.

'It will be too marvellous,' she declared. 'We will hunt down murderers, and discover the missing family jewels, and find people who've disappeared and detect embezzlers.'

At this point Tommy felt it his duty to strike a more discouraging note.

'Calm yourself, Tuppence, and try to forget the cheap fiction you are in the habit of reading. Our clientèle, if we have any clientèle at all—will consist solely of husbands who want their wives shadowed, and wives who want their husbands shadowed. Evidence for divorce is the sole prop of private inquiry agents.'

'Ugh!' said Tuppence, wrinkling a fastidious nose. 'We shan't touch divorce cases. We must raise the tone of our new profession.'

'Ye-es,' said Tommy doubtfully.

And now a week after installation they compared notes rather ruefully.

'Three idiotic women whose husbands go away for weekends,' sighed Tommy. 'Anyone come whilst I was out at lunch?'

'A fat old man with a flighty wife,' sighed Tuppence sadly. 'I've read in the papers for years that the divorce evil was growing, but somehow I never seemed to realise it until this last week. I'm sick and tired of saying, "We don't undertake divorce cases."'

'We've put it in the advertisements now,' Tommy reminded her. 'So it won't be so bad.'

'I'm sure we advertise in the most tempting way too,' said Tuppence in a melancholy voice. 'All the same, I'm not going to be beaten. If necessary, I shall commit a crime myself, and you will detect it.'

'And what good would that do? Think of my feelings when I bid you a tender farewell at Bow Street—or is it Vine Street?'

'You are thinking of your bachelor days,' said Tuppence pointedly.

'The Old Bailey, that is what I mean,' said Tommy.

'Well,' said Tuppence, 'something has got to be done about it. Here we are bursting with talent and no chance of exercising it.'

'I always like your cheery optimism, Tuppence. You seem to have no doubt whatever that you have talent to exercise.'

'Of course,' said Tuppence, opening her eyes very wide.

'And yet you have no expert knowledge whatever.'

'Well, I have read every detective novel that has been published in the last ten years.'

'So have I,' said Tommy, 'but I have a sort of feeling that that wouldn't really help us much.'

'You always were a pessimist, Tommy. Belief in oneself—that is the great thing.'

'Well, you have got it all right,' said her husband.

'Of course it is easy in detective stories,' said Tuppence thoughtfully, 'because one works backwards. I mean if one knows the solution one can arrange the clues. I wonder now—'

She paused wrinkling her brows.

'Yes?' said Tommy inquiringly.

'I have got a sort of idea,' said Tuppence. 'It hasn't quite come yet, but it's coming.' She rose resolutely. 'I think I shall go and buy that hat I told you about.'

'Oh, God!' said Tommy, 'another hat!'

'It's a very nice one,' said Tuppence with dignity.

She went out with a resolute look on her face.

Once or twice in the following days Tommy inquired curiously about the idea. Tuppence merely shook her head and told him to give her time.

And then, one glorious morning, the first client arrived, and all else was forgotten.

There was a knock on the outer door of the office and Albert, who had just placed an acid drop between his lips, roared out an indistinct 'Come in.' He then swallowed the acid drop whole in his surprise and delight. For this looked like the Real Thing.

A tall young man, exquisitely and beautifully dressed, stood hesitating in the doorway.

'A toff, if ever there was one,' said Albert to himself. His judgement in such matters was good.

The young man was about twenty-four years of age, had beautifully slicked back hair, a tendency to pink rims round the eyes, and practically no chin to speak of.

In an ecstasy, Albert pressed a button under his desk and almost immediately a perfect fusilade of typing broke out from the direction of 'Clerks'. Tuppence had rushed to the post of duty. The effect of this hum of industry was to overawe the young man still further.

'I say,' he remarked. 'Is this the whatnot—detective agency—Blunt's Brilliant Detectives? All that sort of stuff, you know? Eh?'

'Did you want, sir, to speak to Mr Blunt himself?' inquired Albert, with an air of doubt as to whether such a thing could be managed.

'Well—yes, laddie, that was the jolly old idea. Can it be done?'

'You haven't an appointment, I suppose?'

The visitor became more and more apologetic.

'Afraid I haven't.'

'It's always wise, sir, to ring up on the phone first. Mr Blunt is so terribly busy. He's engaged on the telephone at the moment. Called into consultation by Scotland Yard.'

The young man seemed suitably impressed.

Albert lowered his voice, and imparted information in a friendly fashion.

'Important theft of documents from a Government Office. They want Mr Blunt to take up the case.'

'Oh! really. I say. He must be no end of a fellow.'

'The Boss, sir,' said Albert, 'is It.'

The young man sat down on a hard chair, completely unconscious of the fact that he was being subjected to keen scrutiny by two pairs of eyes looking through cunningly contrived peep-holes—those of Tuppence, in the intervals of frenzied typing, and those of Tommy awaiting the suitable moment.

Presently a bell rang with violence on Albert's desk.

'The Boss is free now. I will find out whether he can see you,' said Albert, and disappeared through the door marked 'Private'.

He reappeared immediately.

'Will you come this way, sir?'

The visitor was ushered into the private office, and a pleasant faced young man with red hair and an air of brisk capability rose to greet him.

'Sit down. You wish to consult me? I am Mr Blunt.'

'Oh! Really. I say, you're awfully young, aren't you?'

'The day of the Old Men is over,' said Tommy, waving his hand. 'Who caused the war? The Old Men. Who is responsible for the present state of unemployment? The Old Men. Who is responsible for every single rotten thing that has happened? Again I say, the Old Men!'

'I expect you are right,' said the client, 'I know a fellow who is a poet—at least he says he is a poet—and he always talks like that.'

'Let me tell you this, sir, not a person on my highly trained staff is a day over twenty-five. That is the truth.'

Since the highly trained staff consisted of Tuppence and Albert, the statement was truth itself.

'And now—the facts,' said Mr Blunt.

'I want you to find someone that's missing,' blurted out the young man.

'Quite so. Will you give me the details?'

'Well, you see, it's rather difficult. I mean, it's a frightfully delicate business and all that. She might be frightfully waxy about it. I mean—well, it's so dashed difficult to explain.' He looked helplessly at Tommy. Tommy felt annoyed.

He had been on the point of going out to lunch, but he foresaw that getting the facts out of this client would be a long and tedious business.

'Did she disappear of her own free will, or do you suspect abduction?' he demanded crisply.

'I don't know,' said the young man. 'I don't know anything.'

Tommy reached for a pad and pencil.

'First of all,' he said, 'will you give me your name? My office boy is trained never to ask names. In that way consultations can remain completely confidential.'

'Oh! rather,' said the young man. 'Jolly good idea. My name—er—my name's Smith.'

'Oh! no,' said Tommy. 'The real one, please.'

His visitor looked at him in awe.

'Er—St Vincent,' he said. 'Lawrence St Vincent.'

'It's a curious thing,' said Tommy, 'how very few people there are whose real name is Smith. Personally, I don't know anyone called Smith. But nine men out of ten who wish to conceal their real name give that of Smith. I am writing a monograph upon the subject.'

At that moment a buzzer purred discreetly on his desk. That meant that Tuppence was requesting to take hold. Tommy, who wanted his lunch, and who felt profoundly unsympathetic towards Mr St Vincent, was only too pleased to relinquish the helm.

'Excuse me,' he said, and picked up the telephone.

Across his face there shot rapid changes—surprise, consternation, slight elation.

'You don't say so,' he said into the phone. 'The Prime Minister himself? Of course, in that case, I will come round at once.'

He replaced the receiver on the hook, and turned to his client.

'My dear sir, I must ask you to excuse me. A most urgent summons. If you will give the facts of the case to my confidential secretary, she will deal with them.'

He strode to the adjoining door.

'Miss Robinson.'

Tuppence, very neat and demure with smooth black head and dainty collars and cuffs, tripped in. Tommy made the necessary introductions and departed.

'A lady you take an interest in has disappeared, I understand, Mr St Vincent,' said Tuppence, in her soft voice, as she sat down and took up Mr Blunt's pad and pencil. 'A young lady?'

'Oh! rather,' said St Vincent. 'Young—and—and—awfully good-looking and all that sort of thing.'

Tuppence's face grew grave.

'Dear me,' she murmured. 'I hope that—'

'You don't think anything's really happened to her?' demanded Mr St Vincent, in lively concern.

'Oh! we must hope for the best,' said Tuppence, with a kind of false cheerfulness which depressed Mr St Vincent horribly.

'Oh! look here, Miss Robinson. I say, you must do something. Spare no expense. I wouldn't have anything happen to her for the world. You seem awfully sympathetic, and I don't mind telling you in confidence that I simply worship the ground that girl walks on. She's a topper, an absolute topper.'

'Please tell me her name and all about her.'

'Her name's Jeanette—I don't know her second name. She works in a hat shop—Madame Violette's in Brook Street—but she's as straight as they make them. Has ticked me off no end of times—I went round there yesterday—waiting for her to come out—all the others came, but not her. Then I found that she'd never turned up that morning to work at all—sent no message either—old Madame was furious about it. I got the address of her lodgings, and I went round there. She hadn't come home the night before, and they didn't know where she was. I was simply frantic. I thought of going to the police. But I knew that Jeanette would be absolutely furious with me for doing that if she were really all right and had gone off on her own. Then I remembered that she herself had pointed out your advertisement to me one day in the paper and told me that one of the women who'd been in buying hats had simply raved about your ability and discretion and all that sort of thing. So I toddled along here right away.'

'I see,' said Tuppence. 'What is the address of her lodgings?'

The young man gave it to her.

'That's all, I think,' said Tuppence reflectively. 'That is to say—am I to understand that you are engaged to this young lady?'

Mr St Vincent turned a brick red.

'Well, no—not exactly. I never said anything. But I can tell you this, I mean to ask her to marry me as soon as ever I see her—if I ever do see her again.'

Tuppence laid aside her pad.

'Do you wish for our special twenty-four hour service?' she asked in business-like tones.

'What's that?'

'The fees are doubled, but we put all our available staff on to the case. Mr St Vincent, if the lady is alive, I shall be able to tell you where she is by this time tomorrow.'

'What? I say, that's wonderful.'

'We only employ experts—and we guarantee results,' said Tuppence crisply.

'But I say, you know. You must have the most topping staff.'

'Oh! we have,' said Tuppence. 'By the way, you haven't given me a description of the young lady.'

'She's got the most marvellous hair—sort of golden but very deep, like a jolly old sunset—that's it, a jolly old sunset. You know, I never noticed things like sunsets until lately. Poetry too, there's a lot more in poetry than I ever thought.'

'Red hair,' said Tuppence unemotionally, writing it down. 'What height should you say the lady was?'

'Oh! tallish, and she's got ripping eyes, dark blue, I think. And a sort of decided manner with her—takes a fellow up short sometimes.'

Tuppence wrote down a few words more, then closed her notebook and rose.

'If you will call here tomorrow at two o'clock, I think we shall have news of some kind for you,' she said. 'Good morning, Mr St Vincent.'

When Tommy returned Tuppence was just consulting a page of Debrett.

'I've got all the details,' she said succinctly. 'Lawrence St Vincent is the nephew and heir of the Earl of Cheriton. If we pull this through we shall get publicity in the highest places.'

Tommy read through the notes on the pad.

'What do you really think has happened to the girl?' he asked.

'I think,' said Tuppence, 'that she has fled at the dictates of her heart, feeling that she loves this young man too well for her peace of mind.'

Tommy looked at her doubtfully.

'I know they do it in books,' he said, 'but I've never known any girl who did it in real life.'

'No?' said Tuppence. 'Well, perhaps you're right. But I dare say Lawrence St Vincent will swallow that sort of slush. He's full of romantic notions just now. By the way, I guaranteed results in twenty-four hours—our special service.'

'Tuppence—you congenital idiot, what made you do that?'

'The idea just came into my head. I thought it sounded rather well. Don't you worry. Leave it to mother. Mother knows best.'

She went out leaving Tommy profoundly dissatisfied.

Presently he rose, sighed, and went out to do what could be done, cursing Tuppence's over-fervent imagination.

When he returned weary and jaded at half-past four, he found Tuppence extracting a bag of biscuits from their place of concealment in one of the files.

'You look hot and bothered,' she remarked. 'What have you been doing?'

Tommy groaned.

'Making a round of the hospitals with that girl's description.'

'Didn't I tell you to leave it to me?' demanded Tuppence.

'You can't find that girl single-handed before two o'clock tomorrow.'

'I can—and what's more, I have!'

'You have? What do you mean?'

'A simple problem, Watson, very simple indeed.'

'Where is she now?'

Tuppence pointed a hand over her shoulder.

'She's in my office next door.'

'What is she doing there?'

Tuppence began to laugh.

'Well,' she said, 'early training will tell, and with a kettle, a gas ring, and half a pound of tea staring her in the face, the result is a foregone conclusion.

'You see,' continued Tuppence gently. 'Madame Violette's is where I go for my hats, and the other day I ran across an old pal of hospital days amongst the girls there. She gave up nursing after the war and started a hat shop, failed, and took this job at Madame Violette's. We fixed

125

up the whole thing between us. She was to rub the advertisement well into young St Vincent, and then disappear. Wonderful efficiency of Blunt's Brilliant Detectives. Publicity for us, and the necessary fillip to young St Vincent to bring him to the point of proposing. Janet was in despair about it.'

'Tuppence,' said Tommy. 'You take my breath away! The whole thing is the most immoral business I ever heard of. You aid and abet this young man to marry out of his class—'

'Stuff,' said Tuppence. 'Janet is a splendid girl—and the queer thing is that she really adores that weak-kneed young man. You can see with half a glance what *his* family needs. Some good red blood in it. Janet will be the making of him. She'll look after him like a mother, ease down the cocktails and the night clubs and make him lead a good healthy country gentleman's life. Come and meet her.'

Tuppence opened the door of the adjoining office and Tommy followed her.

A tall girl with lovely auburn hair, and a pleasant face, put down the steaming kettle in her hand, and turned with a smile that disclosed an even row of white teeth.

'I hope you'll forgive me, Nurse Cowley—Mrs Beresford, I mean. I thought that very likely you'd be quite ready for a cup of tea yourself. Many's the pot of tea you've made for me in the hospital at three o'clock in the morning.'

'Tommy,' said Tuppence. 'Let me introduce you to my old friend, Nurse Smith.'

'Smith, did you say? How curious!' said Tommy shaking hands. 'Eh? Oh! nothing—a little monograph that I was thinking of writing.'

'Pull yourself together, Tommy,' said Tuppence.

She poured him out a cup of tea.

'Now, then, let's drink together. Here's to the success of the International Detective Agency. Blunt's Brilliant Detectives! May they never know failure!'

The Kidnapped Prime Minister

Now that war and the problems of war are things of the past, I think I may safely venture to reveal to the world the part which my friend Poirot played in a moment of national crisis. The secret has been well guarded. Not a whisper of it reached the Press. But, now that the need for secrecy has gone by, I feel it is only just that England should know the debt it owes to my quaint little friend, whose marvellous brain so ably averted a great catastrophe.

One evening after dinner—I will not particularize the date; it suffices to say that it was at the time when 'Peace by negotiation' was the parrot-cry of England's enemies—my friend and I were sitting in his rooms. After being invalided out of the Army I had been given a recruiting job, and it had become my custom to drop in on Poirot in the evenings after dinner and talk with him of any cases of interest that he might have had on hand.

I was attempting to discuss with him the sensational news of the day—no less than an attempted assassination of Mr David MacAdam, England's Prime Minister. The account in the papers had evidently been carefully censored. No details were given, save that the Prime Minister had had a marvellous escape, the bullet just grazing his cheek.

I considered that our police must have been shamefully careless for such an outrage to be possible. I could well understand that the German agents in England would be willing to risk much for such an achievement. 'Fighting Mac', as his own party had nicknamed him, had strenuously and unequivocally combated the Pacifist influence which was becoming so prevalent.

He was more than England's Prime Minister—he *was* England; and to have removed him from his sphere of influence would have been a crushing and paralysing blow to Britain. Poirot was busy mopping a grey suit with a minute sponge.

Never was there a dandy such as Hercule Poirot. Neatness and order were his passion. Now, with the odour of benzine filling the air, he was quite unable to give me his full attention.

'In a little minute I am with you, my friend. I have all but finished. The spot of grease—he is not good—I remove him—so!' He waved his sponge.

I smiled as I lit another cigarette.

'Anything interesting on?' I inquired, after a minute or two.

'I assist a—how do you call it?—"charlady" to find her husband. A difficult affair, needing the tact. For I have a little idea that when he is found he will not be pleased. What would you? For my part, I sympathize with him. He was a man of discrimination to lose himself.'

I laughed.

'At last! The spot of grease, he is gone! I am at your disposal.' 'I was asking you what you thought of this attempt to assassinate MacAdam?'

'*Enfantillage!*' replied Poirot promptly. 'One can hardly take it seriously. To fire with the rifle—never does it succeed. It is a device of the past.'

'It was very near succeeding this time,' I reminded him.

Poirot shook his head impatiently. He was about to reply when the landlady thrust her head round the door and informed him that there were two gentlemen below who wanted to see him.

'They won't give their names, sir, but they says as it's very important.'

'Let them mount,' said Poirot, carefully folding his grey trousers.

In a few minutes the two visitors were ushered in, and my heart gave a leap as in the foremost I recognized no less a personage than Lord Estair, Leader of the House of Commons; whilst his companion, Mr Bernard Dodge, was also a member of the War Cabinet, and, as I knew, a close personal friend of the Prime Minister.

'Monsieur Poirot?' said Lord Estair interrogatively. My friend bowed. The great man looked at me and hesitated. 'My business is private.'

'You may speak freely before Captain Hastings,' said my friend, nodding to me to remain. 'He has not all the gifts, no! But I answer for his discretion.'

Lord Estair still hesitated, but Mr Dodge broke in abruptly:

'Oh, come on—don't let's beat about the bush! As far

as I can see, the whole of England will know the hole we're in soon enough. Time's everything.'

'Pray be seated, messieurs,' said Poirot politely. 'Will you take the big chair, *milord*?'

Lord Estair started slightly. 'You know me?'

Poirot smiled. 'Certainly. I read the little papers with the pictures. How should I not know you?'

'Monsieur Poirot, I have come to consult you upon a matter of the most vital urgency. I must ask for absolute secrecy.'

'You have the word of Hercule Poirot—I can say no more!' said my friend grandiloquently.

'It concerns the Prime Minister. We are in grave trouble.'

'We're up a tree!' interposed Mr Dodge.

'The injury is serious then?' I asked.

'What injury?'

'The bullet wound.'

'Oh, that!' cried Mr Dodge contemptuously. 'That's old history.'

'As my colleague says,' continued Lord Estair, 'that affair is over and done with. Luckily, it failed. I wish I could say as much for the second attempt.'

'There has been a second attempt, then?'

'Yes, though not of the same nature, Monsieur Poirot, the Prime Minister has disappeared.'

'What?'

'He has been kidnapped!'

'Impossible!' I cried, stupefied.

Poirot threw a withering glance at me, which I knew enjoined me to keep my mouth shut.

'Unfortunately, impossible as it seems, it is only too true,' continued his lordship.

Poirot looked at Mr Dodge. 'You said just now, monsieur, that time was everything. What did you mean by that?'

The two men exchanged glances, and then Lord Estair said:

'You have heard, Monsieur Poirot, of the approaching Allied Conference?'

'My friend nodded.

'For obvious reasons, no details have been given of when and where it is to take place. But, although it has been kept out of the newspapers, the date is, of course, widely known in diplomatic circles. The Conference is to be held tomorrow—Thursday—evening at Versailles. Now you perceive the terrible gravity of the situation. I will not conceal from you that the Prime Minister's presence at the Conference is a vital necessity. The Pacifist propaganda, started and maintained by the German agents in our midst, has been very active. It is the universal opinion that the turning-point of the Conference will be the strong personality of the Prime Minister. His absence may have the most serious results—possibly a premature and disastrous peace. And we have no one who can be sent in his place. He alone can represent England.'

Poirot's face had grown very grave. 'Then you regard the kidnapping of the Prime Minister as a direct attempt to prevent his being present at the Conference?'

'Most certainly I do. He was actually on his way to France at the time.'

'And the Conference is to be held?'

'At nine o'clock tomorrow night.'

Poirot drew an enormous watch from his pocket.

'It is now a quarter to nine.'

'Twenty-four hours,' said Mr Dodge thoughtfully.

'And a quarter,' amended Poirot. 'Do not forget the quarter, monsieur—it may come in useful. Now for the details—the abduction, did it take place in England or in France?'

'In France. Mr MacAdam crossed to France this morning. He was to stay tonight as the guest of the Commander-in-Chief, proceeding tomorrow to Paris. He was conveyed across the Channel by destroyer. At Boulogne he was met by a car from General Headquarters and one of the Commander-in-Chief's ADCs.'

'*Eh bien?*'

'Well, they started from Boulogne—but they never arrived.'

'What?'

'Monsieur Poirot, it was a bogus car and a bogus ADC. The real car was found in a side road, with the chauffeur and the ADC neatly gagged and bound.'

'And the bogus car?'

'Is still at large.'

Poirot made a gesture of impatience. 'Incredible! Surely it cannot escape attention for long?'

'So we thought. It seemed merely a question of searching thoroughly. That part of France is under Military Law. We were convinced that the car could not go long unnoticed. The French police and our own Scotland Yard men and the military are straining every nerve. It is, as you say, incredible—but nothing has been discovered!'

At that moment a tap came at the door, and a young officer entered with a heavily sealed envelope which he handed to Lord Estair.

'Just through from France, sir. I brought it on here, as you directed.'

The Minister tore it open eagerly, and uttered an exclamation. The officer withdrew.

'Here is news at last! This telegram has just been decoded. They have found the second car, also the secretary, Daniels, chloroformed, gagged, and bound, in an abandoned farm near C—. He remembers nothing, except something being pressed against his mouth and nose from behind, and struggling to free himself. The police are satisfied as to the genuineness of his statement.'

'And they have found nothing else?'

'No.'

'Not the Prime Minister's dead body? Then, there is hope. But it is strange. Why, after trying to shoot him this morning, are they now taking so much trouble to keep him alive?'

Dodge shook his head. 'One thing's quite certain. They're determined at all costs to prevent his attending the Conference.'

'If it is humanly possible, the Prime Minister shall be there. God grant it is not too late. Now, messieurs, recount to me everything—from the beginning. I must know about this shooting affair as well.'

'Last night, the Prime Minister, accompanied by one of his secretaries, Captain Daniels—'

'The same who accompanied him to France?'

'Yes. As I was saying, they motored down to Windsor, where the Prime Minister was granted an Audience. Early this morning he returned to town, and it was on the way that the attempted assassination took place.'

135

'One moment, if you please. Who is this Captain Daniels? You have his dossier?'

Lord Estair smiled. 'I thought you would ask me that. We do not know very much of him. He is of no particular family. He has served in the English Army, and is an extremely able secretary, being an exceptionally fine linguist. I believe he speaks seven languages. It is for that reason that the Prime Minister chose him to accompany him to France.'

'Has he any relatives in England?'

'Two aunts. A Mrs Everard, who lives at Hampstead, and a Miss Daniels, who lives near Ascot.'

'Ascot? That is near to Windsor, is it not?'

'That point has not been overlooked. But it has led to nothing.'

'You regard the Capitaine Daniels, then, as above suspicion?'

A shade of bitterness crept into Lord Estair's voice, as he replied:

'No, Monsieur Poirot. In these days, I should hesitate before I pronounced *anyone* above suspicion.'

'*Très bien.* Now I understand, *milord*, that the Prime Minister would, as a matter of course, be under vigilant police protection, which ought to render any assault upon him an impossibility?'

Lord Estair bowed his head. 'That is so. The Prime Minister's car was closely followed by another car containing detectives in plain clothes. Mr MacAdam knew nothing of these precautions. He is personally a most fearless man, and would be inclined to sweep them away arbitrarily. But, naturally, the police make their own arrangements. In fact, the Premier's chauffeur, O'Murphy, is a CID man.'

'O'Murphy? That is a name of Ireland, is it not so?'

'Yes, he is an Irishman.'

'From what part of Ireland?'

'County Clare, I believe.'

'*Tiens*! But proceed, *milord*.'

'The Premier started for London. The car was a closed one. He and Captain Daniels sat inside. The second car followed as usual. But, unluckily, for some unknown reason, the Prime Minister's car deviated from the main road—'

'At a point where the road curves?' interrupted Poirot.

'Yes—but how did you know?'

'Oh, *c'est évident!* Continue!'

'For some unknown reason,' continued Lord Estair, 'the Premier's car left the main road. The police car, unaware of the deviation, continued to keep to the high road. At a short distance down the unfrequented lane, the Prime Minister's car was suddenly held up by a band of masked men. The chauffeur—'

'That brave O'Murphy!' murmured Poirot thoughtfully.

'The chauffeur, momentarily taken aback, jammed on the brakes. The Prime Minister put his head out of the window. Instantly a shot rang out—then another. The first one grazed his cheek, the second, fortunately, went wide. The chauffeur, now realizing the danger, instantly forged straight ahead, scattering the band of men.'

'A near escape,' I ejaculated, with a shiver.

'Mr MacAdam refused to make any fuss over the slight wound he had received. He declared it was only a scratch. He stopped at a local cottage hospital, where it was dressed and bound up—he did not, of course, reveal his identity. He then drove, as per schedule, straight to Charing Cross, where a special train for Dover was awaiting him, and, after a brief account of what had happened had been given to the anxious police by Captain Daniels, he duly departed for France. At Dover, he went on board the waiting destroyer. At Boulogne, as you know, the bogus car was waiting for him, carrying the Union Jack, and correct in every detail.'

'That is all you have to tell me?'

'Yes.'

'There is no other circumstance that you have omitted, *milord*?'

'Well, there is one rather peculiar thing.'

'Yes?'

'The Prime Minister's car did not return home after leaving the Prime Minister at Charing Cross. The police were anxious to interview O'Murphy, so a search was instituted at once. The car was discovered standing outside a certain unsavoury little restaurant in Soho, which is well known as a meeting-place of German agents.'

'And the chauffeur?'

'The chauffeur was nowhere to be found. He, too, had disappeared.'

'So,' said Poirot thoughtfully, 'there are two disappearances: the Prime Minister in France, and O'Murphy in London.'

He looked keenly at Lord Estair, who made a gesture of despair.

'I can only tell you, Monsieur Poirot, that, if anyone had suggested to me yesterday that O'Murphy was a traitor, I should have laughed in his face.'

'And today?'

'Today I do not know what to think.'

Poirot nodded gravely. He looked at his turnip of a watch again.

'I understand that I have *carte blanche*, messieurs—in every way, I mean? I must be able to go where I choose, and how I choose.'

'Perfectly. There is a special train leaving for Dover in an hour's time, with a further contingent from Scotland Yard. You shall be accompanied by a Military officer and a CID man, who will hold themselves at your disposal in every way. Is that satisfactory?'

'Quite. One more question before you leave, messieurs. What made you come to me? I am unknown, obscure in this great London of yours.'

'We sought you out on the express recommendation and wish of a very great man of your own country.'

'*Comment*? My old friend the *Préfet*—?'

Lord Estair shook his head.

'One higher than the *Préfet*. One whose word was once law in Belgium—and shall be again! That England has sworn!'

Poirot's hand flew swiftly to a dramatic salute. 'Amen to that! Ah, but my Master does not forget… Messieurs, I, Hercule Poirot, will serve you faithfully. Heaven only send that it will be in time. But this is dark—dark . . . I cannot see.'

'Well, Poirot,' I cried impatiently, as the door closed behind the Ministers, 'what do you think?'

My friend was busy packing a minute suitcase, with quick, deft movements. He shook his head thoughtfully.

'I don't know what to think. My brains desert me.'

'Why, as you said, kidnap him, when a knock on the head would do as well?' I mused.

'Pardon me, *mon ami*, but I did not quite say that. It is undoubtedly far more their affair to kidnap him.'

'But why?'

'Because uncertainty creates panic. That is one reason. Were the Prime Minister dead, it would be a terrible calamity, but the situation would have to be faced. But now you have paralysis. Will the Prime Minister reappear, or will he not? Is he dead or alive? Nobody knows, and until they know nothing definite can be done. And, as I tell you, uncertainty breeds panic, which is what *les Boches* are playing for. Then, again, if the kidnappers are holding him secretly somewhere, they have the advantage of being able to make terms with both sides. The German Government is not a liberal paymaster, as a rule, but no doubt they can be made to disgorge substantial remittances in such a case as this. Thirdly, they run no risk of the hangman's rope. Oh, decidedly, kidnapping is their affair.'

'Then, if that is so, why should they first try to shoot him?' Poirot made a gesture of anger. 'Ah, that is just what I do not understand! It is inexplicable—stupid! They have all their arrangements made (and very good arrangements too!) for the abduction, and yet they imperil the whole affair by a melodramatic attack, worthy of a cinema, and quite as unreal. It is almost impossible to believe in it, with its band of masked men, not twenty miles from London!'

'Perhaps they were two quite separate attempts which happened irrespective of each other,' I suggested.

'Ah, no, that would be too much of a coincidence!

Then, further—who is the traitor? There must have been a traitor—in the first affair, anyway. But who was it—Daniels or O'Murphy? It must have been one of the two, or why did the car leave the main road? We cannot suppose that the Prime Minister connived at his own assassination! Did O'Murphy take that turning of his own accord, or was it Daniels who told him to do so?'

'Surely it must have been O'Murphy's doing.'

'Yes, because if it was Daniels' the Prime Minister would have heard the order, and would have asked the reason. But there are altogether too many "whys" in this affair, and they contradict each other. If O'Murphy is an honest man, *why* did he leave the main road? But if he was a dishonest man, *why* did he start the car again when only two shots had been fired—thereby, in all probability, saving the Prime Minister's life? And, again, if he was honest, why did he, immediately on leaving Charing Cross, drive to a well-known rendezvous of German spies?'

'It looks bad,' I said.

'Let us look at the case with method. What have we for and against these two men? Take O'Murphy first. Against: that his conduct in leaving the main road was suspicious; that he is an Irishman from County Clare; that he has disappeared in a highly suggestive manner. For: that his promptness in restarting the car saved the Premier's life; that he is a Scotland Yard man, and, obviously, from the post allotted to him, a trusted detective. Now for Daniels. There is not much against him, except the fact that nothing is known of his antecedents, and that he speaks too many languages for a good Englishman! (Pardon me, *mon ami*, but, as linguists, you are deplorable!) Now *for* him, we have the fact that he was found gagged, bound, and chloroformed—which does not look as though he had anything to do with the matter.'

'He might have gagged and bound himself, to divert suspicion.'

Poirot shook his head. 'The French police would make no mistake of that kind. Besides, once he had attained his object, and the Prime Minister was safely abducted, there would not be much point in his remaining behind. His accomplices *could* have gagged and chloroformed him, of course, but I fail to see what object they hoped to accomplish by it. He can be of little use to them now, for, until the circumstances concerning the Prime Minister have been cleared up, he is bound to be closely watched.'

'Perhaps he hoped to start the police on a false scent?'

'Then why did he not do so? He merely says that something was pressed over his nose and mouth, and that he remembers nothing more. There is no false scent there. It sounds remarkably like the truth.'

'Well,' I said, glancing at the clock, 'I suppose we'd better start for the station. You may find more clues in France.'

'Possibly, *mon ami*, but I doubt it. It is still incredible to me that the Prime Minister has not been discovered in that limited area, where the difficulty of concealing him must be tremendous. If the military and the police of two countries have not found him, how shall I?'

At Charing Cross we were met by Mr Dodge.

'This is Detective Barnes, of Scotland Yard, and Major Norman. They will hold themselves entirely at your disposal. Good luck to you. It's a bad business, but I've not given up hope. Must be off now.' And the Minister strode rapidly away.

We chatted in a desultory fashion with Major Norman. In the centre of the little group of men on the platform I recognized a little ferret-faced fellow talking to a tall, fair man. He was an old acquaintance of Poirot's—Detective-Inspector Japp, supposed to be one of the smartest of Scotland Yard's officers. He came over and greeted my friend cheerfully.

'I heard you were on this job too. Smart bit of work. So far they've got away with the goods all right. But I can't believe they can keep him hidden long. Our people are going through France with a toothcomb. So are the French. I can't help feeling it's only a matter of hours now.'

'That is, if he's still alive,' remarked the tall detective gloomily.

Japp's face fell. 'Yes . . . but somehow I've got the feeling he's still alive all right.'

Poirot nodded. 'Yes, yes; he's alive. But can he be found in time? I, like you, did not believe he could be hidden so long.'

The whistle blew, and we all trooped up into the Pullman car. Then, with a slow, unwilling jerk, the train drew out of the station.

It was a curious journey. The Scotland Yard men crowded together. Maps of Northern France were spread out, and eager forefingers traced the lines of roads and villages. Each man had his own pet theory. Poirot showed none of his usual loquacity, but sat staring in front of him, with an expression on his face that reminded me of a puzzled child. I talked to Norman, whom I found quite an amusing fellow. On arriving at Dover Poirot's behaviour moved me to intense amusement. The little man, as he went on board the boat, clutched desperately at my arm. The wind was blowing lustily.

'*Mon Dieu!*' he murmured. 'This is terrible!'

'Have courage, Poirot,' I cried. 'You will succeed. You will find him. I am sure of it.'

'Ah, *mon ami*, you mistake my emotion. It is this villainous sea that troubles me! The *mal de mer*—it is horrible suffering!'

'Oh!' I said, rather taken aback.

The first throb of the engines was felt, and Poirot groaned and closed his eyes.

'Major Norman has a map of Northern France if you would like to study it?'

Poirot shook his head impatiently.

'But no, but no! Leave me, my friend. See you, to think, the stomach and the brain must be in harmony. Laverguier has a method most excellent for averting the *mal de mer*. You breathe in—and out—slowly, so—turning the head from left to right and counting six between each breath.'

I left him to his gymnastic endeavours, and went on deck.

As we came slowly into Boulogne Harbour Poirot appeared, neat and smiling, and announced to me in a whisper that Laverguier's system had succeeded 'to a marvel!'

Japp's forefinger was still tracing imaginary routes on his map. 'Nonsense! The car started from Boulogne—

here they branched off. Now, my idea is that they transferred the Prime Minister to another car. See?'

'Well,' said the tall detective, 'I shall make for the seaports. Ten to one, they've smuggled him on board a ship.'

Japp shook his head. 'Too obvious. The order went out at once to close all the ports.'

The day was just breaking as we landed. Major Norman touched Poirot on the arm. 'There's a military car here waiting for you, sir.'

'Thank you, monsieur. But, for the moment, I do not propose to leave Boulogne.'

'What?'

'No, we will enter this hotel here, by the quay.'

He suited the action to the word, demanded and was accorded a private room. We three followed him, puzzled and uncomprehending.

He shot a quick glance at us. 'It is not so that the good detective should act, eh? I perceive your thought. He must be full of energy. He must rush to and fro. He should prostrate himself on the dusty road and seek the marks of tyres through a little glass. He must gather up the cigarette-end, the fallen match? That is your idea, is it not?'

His eyes challenged us. 'But I—Hercule Poirot—tell you that it is not so! The true clues are within—*here*!' He tapped his forehead. 'See you, I need not have left London. It would have been sufficient for me to sit quietly in my rooms there. All that matters is the little grey cells within. Secretly and silently they do their part, until suddenly I call for a map, and I lay my finger on a spot—so—and I say: the Prime Minister is *there*! And it

145

is so! With method and logic one can accomplish anything! This frantic rushing to France was a mistake—it is playing a child's game of hide-and-seek. But now, though it may be too late, I will set to work the right way, from within. Silence, my friends, I beg of you.'

And for five long hours the little man sat motionless, blinking his eyelids like a cat, his green eyes flickering and becoming steadily greener and greener. The Scotland Yard man was obviously contemptuous, Major Norman was bored and impatient, and I myself found the time passed with wearisome slowness.

Finally, I got up, and strolled as noiselessly as I could to the window. The matter was becoming a farce. I was secretly concerned for my friend. If he failed, I would have preferred him to fail in a less ridiculous manner. Out of the window I idly watched the daily leave boat, belching forth columns of smoke, as she lay alongside the quay.

Suddenly I was aroused by Poirot's voice close to my elbow.

'*Mes amis*, let us start!'

I turned. An extraordinary transformation had come over my friend. His eyes were flickering with excitement, his chest was swelled to the uttermost.

'I have been an imbecile, my friends! But I see daylight at last.'

Major Norman moved hastily to the door. 'I'll order the car.'

'There is no need. I shall not use it. Thank Heaven the wind has fallen.'

'Do you mean you are going to walk, sir?'

'No, my young friend. I am no St Peter. I prefer to cross the sea by boat.'

'To cross the *sea*?'

'Yes. To work with method, one must begin from the beginning. And the beginning of this affair was in England. Therefore, we return to England.'

At three o'clock, we stood once more upon Charing Cross platform. To all our expostulations, Poirot turned a deaf ear, and reiterated again and again that to start at the beginning was not a waste of time, but the only way. On the way over, he had conferred with Norman in a low voice, and the latter had despatched a sheaf of telegrams from Dover.

Owing to the special passes held by Norman, we got through everywhere in record time. In London, a large police car was waiting for us, with some plain-clothes men, one of whom handed a typewritten sheet of paper to my friend. He answered my inquiring glance.

'A list of the cottage hospitals within a certain radius west of London. I wired for it from Dover.'

We were whirled rapidly through the London streets. We were on the Bath Road. On we went, through Hammersmith, Chiswick and Brentford. I began to see our objective. Through Windsor and so on to Ascot. My heart gave a leap. Ascot was where Daniels had an aunt living. We were after *him*, then, not O'Murphy.

We duly stopped at the gate of a trim villa. Poirot jumped out and rang the bell. I saw a perplexed frown dimming the radiance of his face. Plainly, he was not satisfied. The bell was answered. He was ushered inside. In a few moments he reappeared, and climbed into the car with a short, sharp shake of his head. My hopes began to die down. It was past four now. Even if he found certain evidence incriminating Daniels, what would be the good of it, unless he could wring from someone the exact spot in France where they were holding the Prime Minister?

Our return progress towards London was an interrupted one. We deviated from the main road more than once, and occasionally stopped at a small building, which I had no difficulty in recognizing as a cottage hospital. Poirot only spent a few minutes at each, but at every halt his radiant assurance was more and more restored.

He whispered something to Norman, to which the latter replied:

'Yes, if you turn off to the left, you will find them waiting by the bridge.'

We turned up a side road, and in the failing light I discerned a second car, waiting by the side of the road. It contained two men in plain clothes. Poirot got down and spoke to them, and then we started off in a northerly direction, the other car following close behind.

We drove for some time, our objective being obviously one of the northern suburbs of London. Finally, we drove up to the front door of a tall house, standing a little back from the road in its own grounds.

Norman and I were left in the car. Poirot and one of the detectives went up to the door and rang. A neat parlourmaid opened it. The detective spoke.

'I am a police officer, and I have a warrant to search this house.'

The girl gave a little scream, and a tall, handsome woman of middle age appeared behind her in the hall.

'Shut the door, Edith. They are burglars, I expect.'

But Poirot swiftly inserted his foot in the door, and at the same moment blew a whistle. Instantly the other detectives ran up, and poured into the house, shutting the door behind them.

Norman and I spent about five minutes cursing our forced inactivity. Finally the door reopened, and the men emerged, escorting three prisoners—a woman and two men. The woman, and one of the men, were taken to the second car. The other man was placed in our car by Poirot himself.

'I must go with the others, my friend. But have great care of this gentleman. You do not know him, no? *Eh bien*, let me present to you, Monsieur O'Murphy!'

O'Murphy! I *gaped* at him open-mouthed as we started again. He was not handcuffed, but I did not fancy he would try to escape. He sat there staring in front of him as though dazed. Anyway, Norman and I would be more than a match for him.

To my surprise, we still kept a northerly route. We were not returning to London, then! I was much puzzled. Suddenly, as the car slowed down, I recognized that we were close to Hendon Aerodrome. Immediately I grasped Poirot's idea. He proposed to reach France by aeroplane.

It was a sporting idea, but, on the face of it, impracticable. A telegram would be far quicker. Time was everything. He must leave the personal glory of rescuing the Prime Minister to others.

As we drew up, Major Norman jumped out, and a plain-clothes man took his place. He conferred with Poirot for a few minutes, and then went off briskly.

I, too, jumped out, and caught Poirot by the arm.

'I congratulate you, old fellow! They have told you the hiding-place? But, look here, you must wire to France at once. You'll be too late if you go yourself.'

Poirot looked at me curiously for a minute or two.

'Unfortunately, my friend, there are some things that cannot be sent by telegram.'

At that moment Major Norman returned, accompanied by a young officer in the uniform of the Flying Corps.

'This is Captain Lyall, who will fly you over to France. He can start at once.'

'Wrap up warmly, sir,' said the young pilot. 'I can lend you a coat, if you like.'

Poirot was consulting his enormous watch. He murmured to himself: 'Yes, there is time—just time.' Then he looked up and bowed politely to the young officer. 'I thank you, monsieur. But it is not I who am your passenger. It is this gentleman here.'

He moved a little aside as he spoke, and a figure came forward out of the darkness. It was the second male prisoner who had gone in the other car, and as the light fell on his face, I gave a start of surprise.

It was the Prime Minister!

'For Heaven's sake, tell me all about it,' I cried impatiently, as Poirot, Norman and I motored back to London. 'How in the world did they manage to smuggle him back to England?'

'There was no need to smuggle him back,' replied Poirot dryly. 'The Prime Minister has never left England. He was kidnapped on his way from Windsor to London.'

'*What?*'

'I will make all clear. The Prime Minister was in his car, his secretary beside him. Suddenly a pad of chloroform is clapped on his face—'

'But by whom?'

'By the clever linguistic Captain Daniels. As soon as the Prime Minister is unconscious, Daniels picks up the speaking-tube, and directs O'Murphy to turn to the right, which the chauffeur, quite unsuspicious, does. A few yards down that unfrequented road a large car is standing, apparently broken down. Its driver signals to O'Murphy to stop. O'Murphy slows up. The stranger approaches. Daniels leans out of the window, and, probably with the aid of an instantaneous anaesthetic, such as ethylchloride, the chloroform trick is repeated. In a few seconds, the two helpless men are dragged out and transferred to the other car, and a pair of substitutes take their places.'

'Impossible!'

'*Pas du tout!* Have you not seen music-hall turns imitating celebrities with marvellous accuracy? Nothing is easier than to personate a public character. The Prime Minister of England is far easier to understudy than Mr John Smith of Clapham, say. As for O'Murphy's "double", no one was going to take much notice of him until after the departure of the Prime Minister, and by then he would have made himself scarce. He drives straight from Charing Cross to the meeting-place of his friends. He goes in as O'Murphy, he emerges as someone quite different. O'Murphy has disappeared, leaving a conveniently suspicious trail behind him.'

'But the man who personated the Prime Minister was seen by everyone!'

'He was not seen by anyone who knew him privately or intimately. And Daniels shielded him from contact with anyone as much as possible. Moreover, his face was bandaged up, and anything unusual in his manner would be put down to the fact that he was suffering from shock as a result of the attempt upon his life. Mr MacAdam has a weak throat, and always spares his voice as much as possible before any great speech. The deception was perfectly easy to keep up as far as France. There it would be impracticable and impossible—so the Prime Minister disappears. The police of this country hurry across the Channel, and no one bothers to go into the details of the first attack. To sustain the illusion that the abduction has taken place in France, Daniels is gagged and chloroformed in a convincing manner.'

'And the man who has enacted the part of the Prime Minister?'

'Rids himself of his disguise. He and the bogus chauffeur may be arrested as suspicious characters, but no one will dream of suspecting their real part in the drama, and they will eventually be released for lack of evidence.'

'And the real Prime Minister?'

'He and O'Murphy were driven straight to the house of "Mrs Everard", at Hampstead, Daniels' so-called "aunt". In reality, she is Frau Bertha Ebenthal, and the police have been looking for her for some time. It is a valuable little present that I have made them—to say nothing of Daniels! Ah, it was a clever plan, but he did not reckon on the cleverness of Hercule Poirot!'

I think my friend might well be excused his moment of vanity.

'When did you first begin to suspect the truth of the matter?'

'When I began to work the right way—from *within*! I could not make that shooting affair fit in—but when I saw that the net result of it was that *the Prime Minister went to France with his face bound up* I began to comprehend! And when I visited all the cottage hospitals between Windsor and London, and found that no one answering to my description had had his face bound up and dressed that morning, I was sure! After that, it was child's play for a mind like mine!'

The following morning, Poirot showed me a telegram he had just received. It had no place of origin, and was unsigned. It ran:

'In time.'

Later in the day the evening papers published an account of the Allied Conference. They laid particular stress on the magnificent ovation accorded to Mr David MacAdam, whose inspiring speech had produced a deep and lasting impression.

The Listerdale Mystery

Mrs St Vincent was adding up figures. Once or twice she sighed, and her hand stole to her aching forehead. She had always disliked arithmetic. It was unfortunate that nowadays her life should seem to be composed entirely of one particular kind of sum, the ceaseless adding together of small necessary items of expenditure making a total that never failed to surprise and alarm her.

Surely it couldn't come to *that!* She went back over the figures. She had made a trifling error in the pence, but otherwise the figures were correct.

Mrs St Vincent sighed again. Her headache by now was very bad indeed. She looked up as the door opened and her daughter Barbara came into the room. Barbara St Vincent was a very pretty girl, she had her mother's delicate features, and the same proud turn of the head, but her eyes were dark instead of blue, and she had a different mouth, a sulky red mouth not without attraction.

'Oh! Mother,' she cried. 'Still juggling with those horrid old accounts? Throw them all into the fire.'

'We must know where we are,' said Mrs St Vincent uncertainly.

The girl shrugged her shoulders.

'We're always in the same boat,' she said dryly. 'Damned hard up. Down to the last penny as usual.'

Mrs St Vincent sighed.

'I wish—' she began, and then stopped.

'I must find something to do,' said Barbara in hard tones. 'And find it quickly. After all, I have taken that shorthand and typing course. So have about one million other girls from all I can see! "What experience?" "None, but—" "Oh! thank you, good-morning. We'll let you know." But they never do! I must find some other kind of a job—*any* job.'

'Not yet, dear,' pleaded her mother. 'Wait a little longer.' Barbara went to the window and stood looking out with unseeing eyes that took no note of the dingy line of houses opposite.

'Sometimes,' she said slowly, 'I'm sorry Cousin Amy took me with her to Egypt last winter. Oh! I know I had fun— about the only fun I've ever had or am likely to have in my life. I *did* enjoy myself—enjoyed myself thoroughly. But it was very unsettling. I mean—coming back to *this*.'

She swept a hand round the room. Mrs St Vincent followed it with her eyes and winced. The room was typical of cheap furnished lodgings. A dusty aspidistra, showily ornamental furniture, a gaudy wallpaper faded in patches. There were signs that the personality of the tenants had struggled with that of the landlady; one or two pieces of good china, much cracked and mended, so that their saleable value was *nil*, a piece of embroidery thrown over the back of the sofa, a water colour sketch of a young girl in the fashion of twenty years ago; near enough still to Mrs St Vincent not to be mistaken.

'It wouldn't matter,' continued Barbara, 'if we'd never known anything else. But to think of Ansteys—'

She broke off, not trusting herself to speak of that dearly loved home which had belonged to the St Vincent family for centuries and which was now in the hands of strangers.

'If only father—hadn't speculated—and borrowed—'

'My dear,' said Mrs St Vincent, 'your father was never, in any sense of the word, a business man.'

She said it with a graceful kind of finality, and Barbara came over and gave her an aimless sort of kiss, as she murmured, 'Poor old Mums. I won't say anything.'

Mrs St Vincent took up her pen again, and bent over her desk. Barbara went back to the window. Presently the girl said:

'Mother. I heard from—from Jim Masterton this morning. He wants to come and see me.'

Mrs St Vincent laid down her pen and looked up sharply.

'Here?' she exclaimed.

'Well, we can't ask him to dinner at the Ritz very well,' sneered Barbara.

Her mother looked unhappy. Again she looked round the room with innate distaste.

'You're right,' said Barbara. 'It's a disgusting place. Genteel poverty! Sounds all right—a white-washed cottage, in the country, shabby chintzes of good design, bowls of roses, crown Derby tea service that you wash up yourself. That's what it's like in books. In real life, with a son starting on the bottom rung of office life, it means London. Frowsy landladies, dirty children on the stairs, fellow-lodgers who always seem to be foreigners, haddocks for breakfasts that aren't quite—quite and so on.'

'If only—' began Mrs St Vincent. 'But, really, I'm beginning to be afraid we can't afford even this room much longer.'

'That means a bed-sitting room—horror!—for you and me,' said Barbara. 'And a cupboard under the tiles for Rupert. And when Jim comes to call, I'll receive him in that dreadful room downstairs with tabbies all round the walls knitting, and staring at us, and coughing that dreadful kind of gulping cough they have!'

There was a pause.

'Barbara,' said Mrs St Vincent at last. 'Do you—I mean—would you—?'

She stopped, flushing a little.

'You needn't be delicate, Mother,' said Barbara. 'Nobody is nowadays. Marry Jim, I suppose you mean? I would like a shot if he asked me. But I'm so awfully afraid he won't.'

'Oh! Barbara, dear.'

'Well, it's one thing seeing me out there with Cousin Amy, moving (as they say in novelettes) in the best society. He *did* take a fancy to me. Now he'll come here and see me in *this*! And he's a funny creature, you know, fastidious and old-fashioned. I—I rather like him for that. It reminds me of Ansteys and the village—everything a hundred years behind the times, but so—so—oh! I don't know—so fragrant. Like lavender!'

She laughed, half-ashamed of her eagerness. Mrs St Vincent spoke with a kind of earnest simplicity.

'I should like you to marry Jim Masterton,' she said. 'He is—one of us. He is very well off, also, but that I don't mind about so much.'

'I do,' said Barbara. 'I'm sick of being hard up.'

'But, Barbara, it isn't—'

'Only for that? No. I do really. I—oh! Mother, can't you *see* I do?'

Mrs St Vincent looked very unhappy.

'I wish he could see you in your proper setting, darling,' she said wistfully.

'Oh, well!' said Barbara. 'Why worry? We might as well try and be cheerful about things. Sorry I've had such a grouch. Cheer up, darling.'

She bent over her mother, kissed her forehead lightly, and went out. Mrs St Vincent, relinquishing all attempts at finance, sat down on the uncomfortable sofa. Her thoughts ran round in circles like squirrels in a cage.

'One may say what one likes, appearances *do* put a man off. Not later—not if they were really engaged. He'd know then what a sweet, dear girl she is. But it's so easy for young people to take the tone of their surroundings. Rupert, now, he's quite different from what he used to be. Not that I want my children to be stuck up. That's not it a bit. But I should hate it if Rupert got engaged to that dreadful girl in the tobacconist's. I daresay she may be a very nice girl, really. But she's not our kind. It's all so difficult. Poor little Babs. If I could do anything—anything. But where's the money to come from? We've sold everything to give Rupert his start. We really can't even afford this.'

To distract herself Mrs St Vincent picked up the *Morning Post*, and glanced down the advertisements on the front page. Most of them she knew by heart. People who wanted capital, people who had capital and were anxious to dispose of it on note of hand alone, people who wanted to buy teeth (she always wondered why), people who wanted to sell furs and gowns and who had optimistic ideas on the subject of price.

Suddenly she stiffened to attention. Again and again she read the printed words.

'To gentlepeople only. Small house in Westminster, exquisitely furnished, offered to those who would really care for it. Rent purely nominal. No agents.'

A very ordinary advertisement. She had read many the same or—well, nearly the same. Nominal rent, that was where the trap lay.

Yet, since she was restless and anxious to escape from her thoughts she put on her hat straightaway, and took a convenient bus to the address given in the advertisement.

It proved to be that of a firm of house-agents. Not a new bustling firm—a rather decrepit, old-fashioned place. Rather timidly she produced the advertisement, which she had torn out, and asked for particulars.

The white-haired old gentleman who was attending to her stroked his chin thoughtfully.

'Perfectly. Yes, perfectly, madam. That house, the house mentioned in the advertisement is No 7 Cheviot Place. You would like an order?'

'I should like to know the rent first?' said Mrs St Vincent.

'Ah! the rent. The exact figure is not settled, but I can assure you that it is purely nominal.'

'Ideas of what is purely nominal can vary,' said Mrs St Vincent.

The old gentleman permitted himself to chuckle a little.

'Yes, that's an old trick—an old trick. But you can take my word for it, it isn't so in this case. Two or three guineas a week, perhaps, not more.'

Mrs St Vincent decided to have the order. Not, of course, that there was any real likelihood of her being able to afford the place. But, after all, she might just *see* it. There must be some grave disadvantage attaching to it, to be offered at such a price.

But her heart gave a little throb as she looked up at the outside of 7 Cheviot Place. A gem of a house. Queen Anne, and in perfect condition! A butler answered the door, he had grey hair and little side-whiskers, and the meditative calm of an archbishop. A kindly archbishop, Mrs St Vincent thought.

He accepted the order with a benevolent air.

'Certainly, madam. I will show you over. The house is ready for occupation.'

He went before her, opening doors, announcing rooms.

'The drawing-room, the white study, a powder closet through here, madam.'

It was perfect—a dream. The furniture all of the period, each piece with signs of wear, but polished with loving care. The loose rugs were of beautiful dim old colours. In each room were bowls of fresh flowers. The back of the house looked over the Green Park. The whole place radiated an old-world charm.

The tears came into Mrs St Vincent's eyes, and she fought them back with difficulty. So had Ansteys looked—Ansteys . . .

She wondered whether the butler had noticed her emotion. If so, he was too much the perfectly trained

161

servant to show it. She liked these old servants, one felt safe with them, at ease. They were like friends.

'It is a beautiful house,' she said softly. 'Very beautiful. I am glad to have seen it.'

'Is it for yourself alone, madam?'

'For myself and my son and daughter. But I'm afraid—'

She broke off. She wanted it so dreadfully—so dreadfully.

She felt instinctively that the butler understood. He did not look at her, as he said in a detached impersonal way:

'I happen to be aware, madam, that the owner requires above all, suitable tenants. The rent is of no importance to him. He wants the house to be tenanted by someone who will really care for and appreciate it.'

'I should appreciate it,' said Mrs St Vincent in a low voice.

She turned to go.

'Thank you for showing me over,' she said courteously. 'Not at all, madam.'

He stood in the doorway, very correct and upright as she walked away down the street. She thought to herself: 'He knows. He's sorry for me. He's one of the old lot too. He'd like *me* to have it—not a labour member, or a button manufacturer! We're dying out, our sort, but we hang together.'

In the end she decided not to go back to the agents. What was the good? She could afford the rent—but there were servants to be considered. There would have to be servants in a house like that.

The next morning a letter lay by her plate. It was from the house-agents. It offered her the tenancy of 7

Cheviot Place for six months at two guineas a week, and went on: 'You have, I presume, taken into consideration the fact that the servants are remaining at the landlord's expense? It is really a unique offer.'

It was. So startled was she by it, that she read the letter out. A fire of questions followed and she described her visit of yesterday.

'Secretive little Mums!' cried Barbara. 'Is it really so lovely?'

Rupert cleared his throat, and began a judicial cross-questioning.

'There's something behind all this. It's fishy if you ask me. Decidedly fishy.'

'So's my egg,' said Barbara wrinkling her nose. 'Ugh! Why should there be something behind it? That's just like you, Rupert, always making mysteries out of nothing. It's those dreadful detective stories you're always reading.'

'The rent's a joke,' said Rupert. 'In the city,' he added importantly, 'one gets wise to all sorts of queer things. I tell you, there's something very fishy about this business.'

'Nonsense,' said Barbara. 'House belongs to a man with lots of money, he's fond of it, and he wants it lived in by decent people whilst he's away. Something of that kind. Money's probably no object to him.'

'What did you say the address was?' asked Rupert of his mother.

'Seven Cheviot Place.'

'Whew!' He pushed back his chair. 'I say, this is exciting. That's the house Lord Listerdale disappeared from.'

'Are you sure?' asked Mrs St Vincent doubtfully.

'Positive. He's got a lot of other houses all over London, but this is the one he lived in. He walked out

163

of it one evening saying he was going to his club, and nobody ever saw him again. Supposed to have done a bunk to East Africa or somewhere like that, but nobody knows why. Depend upon it, he was murdered in that house. You say there's a lot of panelling?'

'Ye-es,' said Mrs St Vincent faintly: 'but—'

Rupert gave her no time. He went on with immense enthusiasm.

'Panelling! There you are. Sure to be a secret recess somewhere. Body's been stuffed in there and has been there ever since. Perhaps it was embalmed first.'

'Rupert, dear, don't talk nonsense,' said his mother.

'Don't be a double-dyed idiot,' said Barbara. 'You've been taking that peroxide blonde to the pictures too much.'

Rupert rose with dignity—such dignity as his lanky and awkward age allowed, and delivered a final ultimatum.

'You take that house, Mums. *I'll* ferret out the mystery. You see if I don't.'

Rupert departed hurriedly, in fear of being late at the office.

The eyes of the two women met.

'Could we, Mother?' murmured Barbara tremulously. 'Oh! if we could.'

'The servants,' said Mrs St Vincent pathetically, 'would *eat*, you know. I mean, of course, one would want them to—but that's the drawback. One can so easily—just do without things—when it's only oneself.'

She looked piteously at Barbara, and the girl nodded.

'We must think it over,' said the mother.

But in reality her mind was made up. She had seen the sparkle in the girl's eyes. She thought to herself: 'Jim

Masterton *must* see her in proper surroundings. This is a chance—a wonderful chance. I must take it.'

She sat down and wrote to the agents accepting their offer.

'Quentin, where did the lilies come from? I really can't buy expensive flowers.'

'They were sent up from King's Cheviot, madam. It has always been the custom here.'

The butler withdrew. Mrs St Vincent heaved a sigh of relief. What would she do without Quentin? He made everything so *easy*. She thought to herself, 'It's too good to last. I shall wake up soon, I know I shall, and find it's been all a dream. I'm so *happy* here—two months already, and it's passed like a flash.'

Life indeed had been astonishingly pleasant. Quentin, the butler, had displayed himself the autocrat of 7 Cheviot Place. 'If you will leave everything to me, madam,' he had said respectfully. 'You will find it the best way.'

Each week, he brought her the housekeeping books, their totals astonishingly low. There were only two other servants, a cook and a housemaid. They were pleasant in manner, and efficient in their duties, but it was Quentin who ran the house. Game and poultry appeared on the table sometimes, causing Mrs St Vincent solicitude. Quentin reassured her. Sent up from Lord Listerdale's country seat, King's Cheviot, or from his Yorkshire moor. 'It has always been the custom, madam.'

Privately Mrs St Vincent doubted whether the absent Lord Listerdale would agree with those words. She was inclined to suspect Quentin of usurping his master's authority. It was clear that he had taken a fancy to them, and that in his eyes nothing was too good for them.

Her curiosity aroused by Rupert's declaration, Mrs St Vincent had made a tentative reference to Lord Listerdale when she next interviewed the house-agent. The white-haired old gentleman had responded immediately.

Yes, Lord Listerdale was in East Africa, had been there for the last eighteen months.

'Our client is rather an eccentric man,' he had said, smiling broadly. 'He left London in a most unconventional manner, as you may perhaps remember? Not a word to anyone. The newspapers got hold of it. There were actually inquiries on foot at Scotland Yard. Luckily news was received from Lord Listerdale himself from East Africa. He invested his cousin, Colonel Carfax, with power of attorney. It is the latter who conducts all Lord Listerdale's affairs. Yes, rather eccentric, I fear. He has always been a great traveller in the wilds—it is quite on the cards that he may not return for years to England, though he is getting on in years.'

'Surely he is not so very old,' said Mrs St Vincent, with a sudden memory of a bluff, bearded face, rather like an Elizabethan sailor, which she had once noticed in an illustrated magazine.

'Middle-aged,' said the white-haired gentleman. 'Fifty-three, according to Debrett.'

This conversation Mrs St Vincent had retailed to Rupert with the intention of rebuking that young gentleman.

Rupert, however, was undismayed.

'It looks fishier than ever to me,' he had declared. 'Who's this Colonel Carfax? Probably comes into the title if anything happens to Listerdale. The letter from East Africa was probably forged. In three years, or whatever it is, this Carfax will presume death, and take the title. Meantime, he's got all the handling of the estate. *Very* fishy, I call it.'

He had condescended graciously to approve the house. In his leisure moments he was inclined to tap the panelling and make elaborate measurements for the possible location of a secret room, but little by little his interest in the mystery of Lord Listerdale abated. He was also less enthusiastic on the subject of the tobacconist's daughter. Atmosphere tells.

To Barbara the house had brought great satisfaction. Jim Masterton had come home, and was a frequent visitor. He and Mrs St Vincent got on splendidly together, and he said something to Barbara one day that startled her.

'This house is a wonderful setting for your mother, you know.'

'For *Mother*?'

'Yes. It was made for her! She belongs to it in an extraordinary way. You know there's something queer about this house altogether, something uncanny and haunting.'

'Don't get like Rupert,' Barbara implored him. 'He is convinced that the wicked Colonel Carfax murdered Lord Listerdale and hid his body under the floor.'

Masterton laughed.

'I admire Rupert's detective zeal. No, I didn't mean anything of *that* kind. But there's something in the air, some atmosphere that one doesn't quite understand.'

They had been three months in Cheviot Place when Barbara came to her mother with a radiant face.

'Jim and I—we're engaged. Yes—last night. Oh, Mother! It all seems like a fairy tale come true.'

'Oh, my dear! I'm so glad—so glad.'

Mother and daughter clasped each other close.

'You know Jim's almost as much in love with you as he is with me,' said Barbara at last, with a mischievous laugh.

Mrs St Vincent blushed very prettily.

'He is,' persisted the girl. 'You thought this house would make such a beautiful setting for me, and all the time it's really a setting for *you*. Rupert and I don't quite belong here. You do.'

'Don't talk nonsense, darling.'

'It's not nonsense. There's a flavour of enchanted castle about it, with you as an enchanted princess and Quentin as—as—oh! a benevolent magician.'

Mrs St Vincent laughed and admitted the last item.

Rupert received the news of his sister's engagement very calmly.

'I thought there was something of the kind in the wind,' he observed sapiently.

He and his mother were dining alone together; Barbara was out with Jim.

Quentin placed the port in front of him, and withdrew noiselessly.

'That's a rum old bird,' said Rupert, nodding towards the closed door. 'There's something odd about him, you know, something—'

'Not fishy?' interrupted Mrs St Vincent, with a faint smile.

'Why, Mother, how did you know what I was going to say?' demanded Rupert in all seriousness.

'It's rather a word of yours, darling. You think everything is fishy. I suppose you have an idea that it was Quentin who did away with Lord Listerdale and put him under the floor?'

'Behind the panelling,' corrected Rupert. 'You always get things a little bit wrong, Mother. No, I've inquired about that. Quentin was down at King's Cheviot at the time.'

Mrs St Vincent smiled at him, as she rose from the table and went up to the drawing-room. In some ways Rupert was a long time growing up.

Yet a sudden wonder swept over her for the first time as to Lord Listerdale's reasons for leaving England so abruptly. There must be something behind it, to account for that sudden decision. She was still thinking the matter over when Quentin came in with the coffee tray, and she spoke out impulsively.

'You have been with Lord Listerdale a long time, haven't you, Quentin?'

'Yes, madam; since I was a lad of twenty-one. That was in the late Lord's time. I started as third footman.'

'You must know Lord Listerdale very well. What kind of a man is he?'

The butler turned the tray a little, so that she could help herself to sugar more conveniently, as he replied in even unemotional tones:

'Lord Listerdale was a very selfish gentleman, madam: with no consideration for others.'

He removed the tray and bore it from the room. Mrs St Vincent sat with her coffee cup in her hand, and a puzzled frown on her face. Something struck her as odd in the speech apart from the views it expressed. In another minute it flashed home to her.

Quentin had used the word '*was*' not 'is'. But then, he must think—must believe—She pulled herself up. She was as bad as Rupert! But a very definite uneasiness assailed her. Afterwards she dated her first suspicions from that moment.

With Barbara's happiness and future assured, she had time to think her own thoughts, and against her will, they began to centre round the mystery of Lord Listerdale. What was the real story? Whatever it was Quentin knew something about it. Those had been odd words of his—'a very selfish gentleman—no consideration for others.' What lay behind them? He had spoken as a judge might speak, detachedly and impartially.

Was Quentin involved in Lord Listerdale's disappearance? Had he taken an active part in any tragedy there might have been? After all, ridiculous as Rupert's assumption had seemed at the time, that single letter with its power of attorney coming from East Africa was—well, open to suspicion.

But try as she would, she could not believe any real evil of Quentin. Quentin, she told herself over and over again, was *good*—she used the word as simply as a child might have done. Quentin was *good*. But he knew something!

She never spoke with him again of his master. The subject was apparently forgotten. Rupert and Barbara had other things to think of, and there were no further discussions.

It was towards the end of August that her vague surmises crystallized into realities. Rupert had gone for a fortnight's holiday with a friend who had a motor-cycle and trailer. It was some ten days after his departure that

Mrs St Vincent was startled to see him rush into the room where she sat writing.

'Rupert!' she exclaimed.

'I know, Mother. You didn't expect to see me for another three days. But something's happened. Anderson—my pal, you know—didn't much care where he went, so I suggested having a look in at King's Cheviot—'

'King's Cheviot? But why—?'

'You know perfectly well, Mother, that I've always scented something fishy about things here. Well, I had a look at the old place—it's let, you know—nothing there. Not that I actually expected to find anything—I was just nosing round, so to speak.'

Yes, she thought. Rupert was very like a dog at this moment. Hunting in circles for something vague and undefined, led by instinct, busy and happy.

'It was when we were passing through a village about eight or nine miles away that it happened—that I saw him, I mean.'

'Saw whom?'

'Quentin—just going into a little cottage. Something fishy here, I said to myself, and we stopped the bus, and I went back. I rapped on the door and he himself opened it.'

'But I don't understand. Quentin hasn't been away—'

'I'm coming to that, Mother. If you'd only listen, and not interrupt. It was Quentin, and it wasn't Quentin, if you know what I mean.'

Mrs St Vincent clearly did not know, so he elucidated matters further.

'It was Quentin all right, but it wasn't *our* Quentin. It was the real man.'

'Rupert!'

'You listen. I was taken in myself at first, and said: "It is Quentin, isn't it?" And the old johnny said: "Quite right, sir, that is my name. What can I do for you?" And then I saw that it wasn't our man, though it was precious like him, voice and all. I asked a few questions, and it all came out. The old chap hadn't an idea of anything fishy being on. He'd been butler to Lord Listerdale all right, and was retired on a pension and given this cottage just about the time that Lord Listerdale was supposed to have gone off to Africa. You see where that leads us. This man's an impostor—he's playing the part of Quentin for purposes of his own. My theory is that he came up to town that evening, pretending to be the butler from King's Cheviot, got an interview with Lord Listerdale, killed him and hid his body behind the panelling. It's an old house, there's sure to be a secret recess—'

'Oh, don't let's go into all that again,' interrupted Mrs St Vincent wildly.'I can't bear it. Why should he—that's what I want to know—why? *If* he did such a thing— which I don't believe for one minute, mind you—what was the *reason* for it all?'

'You're right,' said Rupert. 'Motive—that's important. Now I've made inquiries. Lord Listerdale had a lot of house property. In the last two days I've discovered that practically every one of these houses of his has been let in the last eighteen months to people like ourselves for a merely nominal rent—*and with the proviso that the servants should remain*. And in every case Quentin himself—the man calling himself Quentin, I mean—has been there for part of the time as butler. That looks as though there were something—jewels, or

172

papers—secreted in one of Lord Listerdale's houses, and the gang doesn't know which. I'm assuming a gang, but of course this fellow Quentin may be in it single-handed. There's a—'

Mrs St Vincent interrupted him with a certain amount of determination:

'Rupert! Do stop talking for one minute. You're making my head spin. Anyway, what you are saying is nonsense—about gangs and hidden papers.'

'There's another theory,' admitted Rupert. 'This Quentin may be someone that Lord Listerdale has injured. The real butler told me a long story about a man called Samuel Lowe—an under-gardener he was, and about the same height and build as Quentin himself. He'd got a grudge against Listerdale—'

Mrs St Vincent started.

'With no consideration for others.' The words came back to her mind in their passionless, measured accents. Inadequate words, but what might they not stand for?

In her absorption she hardly listened to Rupert. He made a rapid explanation of something that she did not take in, and went hurriedly from the room.

Then she woke up. Where had Rupert gone? What was he going to do? She had not caught his last words. Perhaps he was going for the police. In that case . . .

She rose abruptly and rang the bell. With his usual promptness, Quentin answered it.

'You rang, madam?'

'Yes. Come in, please, and shut the door.'

The butler obeyed, and Mrs St Vincent was silent a moment whilst she studied him with earnest eyes.

She thought: 'He's been kind to me—nobody knows

how kind. The children wouldn't understand. This wild story of Rupert's may be all nonsense—on the other hand, there may—yes, there may—be something in it. Why should one judge? One can't *know*. The rights and wrongs of it, I mean . . . And I'd stake my life—yes, I would!—on his being a good man.'

Flushed and tremulous, she spoke.

'Quentin, Mr Rupert has just got back. He has been down to King's Cheviot—to a village near there—'

She stopped, noticing the quick start he was not able to conceal.

'He has—seen someone,' she went on in measured accents.

She thought to herself: 'There—he's warned. At any rate, he's warned.'

After that first quick start, Quentin had resumed his unruffled demeanour, but his eyes were fixed on her face, watchful and keen, with something in them she had not seen there before. They were, for the first time, the eyes of a man and not of a servant.

He hesitated for a minute, then said in a voice which also had subtly changed:

'Why do you tell me this, Mrs St Vincent?'

Before she could answer, the door flew open and Rupert strode into the room. With him was a dignified middle-aged man with little side-whiskers and the air of a benevolent archbishop. *Quentin!*

'Here he is,' said Rupert. 'The real Quentin. I had him outside in the taxi. Now, Quentin, look at this man and tell me—is he Samuel Lowe?'

It was for Rupert a triumphant moment. But it was short-lived, almost at once he scented something wrong.

For while the real Quentin was looking abashed and highly uncomfortable the second Quentin was smiling, a broad smile of undisguised enjoyment.

He slapped his embarrassed duplicate on the back.

'It's all right, Quentin. Got to let the cat out of the bag some time, I suppose. You can tell 'em who I am.'

The dignified stranger drew himself up.

'This, sir,' he announced, in a reproachful tone, 'is my master, Lord Listerdale, sir.'

The next minute beheld many things. First, the complete collapse of the cocksure Rupert. Before he knew what was happening, his mouth still open from the shock of the discovery, he found himself being gently manœuvred towards the door, a friendly voice that was, and yet was not, familiar in his ear.

'It's quite all right, my boy. No bones broken. But I want a word with your mother. Very good work of yours, to ferret me out like this.'

He was outside on the landing gazing at the shut door. The real Quentin was standing by his side, a gentle stream of explanation flowing from his lips. Inside the room Lord Listerdale was fronting Mrs St Vincent.

'Let me explain—if I can! I've been a selfish devil all my life—the fact came home to me one day. I thought I'd try a little altruism for a change, and being a fantastic kind of fool, I started my career fantastically. I'd sent subscriptions to odd things, but I felt the need of doing something—well, something *personal*. I've been sorry always for the class that can't beg, that must suffer in silence—poor gentlefolk. I have a lot of house property. I conceived the idea of leasing these houses to people who—well, needed and appreciated them. Young couples with their way to make, widows with sons and daughters starting in the world. Quentin has been more than butler to me, he's a friend. With his consent and assistance I borrowed his personality. I've always had a talent for acting. The idea came to me on my way to the club one night, and I went straight off to talk it over with Quentin. When I found they were making a fuss about my disappearance, I arranged that a letter should come from me in East Africa. In it, I gave full instructions to my cousin, Maurice Carfax. And—well, that's the long and short of it.'

He broke off rather lamely, with an appealing glance at Mrs St Vincent. She stood very straight, and her eyes met his steadily.

'It was a kind plan,' she said. 'A very unusual one, and one that does you credit. I am—most grateful. But—of course, you understand that we cannot stay?'

'I expected that,' he said. 'Your pride won't let you accept what you'd probably style "charity".'

'Isn't that what it is?' she asked steadily.

'No,' he answered. 'Because I ask something in exchange.'

'Something?'

'Everything.' His voice rang out, the voice of one accustomed to dominate.

'When I was twenty-three,' he went on, 'I married the girl I loved. She died a year later. Since then I have been very lonely. I have wished very much I could find a certain lady—the lady of my dreams . . .'

'Am I that?' she asked, very low. 'I am so old—so faded.' He laughed.

176

'Old? You are younger than either of your children. Now I am old, if you like.'

But her laugh rang out in turn. A soft ripple of amusement.

'You? You are a boy still. A boy who loves to dress up.'

She held out her hands and he caught them in his.

The Case of the Caretaker

'Well,' demanded Doctor Haydock of his patient. 'And how goes it today?'

Miss Marple smiled at him wanly from pillows.

'I suppose, really, that I'm better,' she admitted, 'but I feel so terribly depressed. I can't help feeling how much better it would have been if I had died. After all, I'm an old woman. Nobody wants me or cares about me.'

Doctor Haydock interrupted with his usual brusqueness. 'Yes, yes, typical after-reaction of this type of flu. What you need is something to take you out of yourself. A mental tonic.'

Miss Marple sighed and shook her head.

'And what's more,' continued Doctor Haydock, 'I've brought my medicine with me!'

He tossed a long envelope on to the bed.

'Just the thing for you. The kind of puzzle that is right up your street.'

'A puzzle?' Miss Marple looked interested.

'Literary effort of mine,' said the doctor, blushing a little. 'Tried to make a regular story of it. "He said," "she said," "the girl thought," etc. Facts of the story are true.'

'But why a puzzle?' asked Miss Marple.

Doctor Haydock grinned. 'Because the interpretation is up to you. I want to see if you're as clever as you always make out.'

With that Parthian shot he departed.

Miss Marple picked up the manuscript and began to read.

'And where is the bride?' asked Miss Harmon genially.

The village was all agog to see the rich and beautiful young wife that Harry Laxton had brought back from abroad. There was a general indulgent feeling that Harry—wicked young scapegrace—had had all the luck. Everyone had always felt indulgent towards Harry. Even the owners of windows that had suffered from his indiscriminate use of a catapult had found their indignation dissipated by young Harry's abject expression of regret. He had broken windows, robbed orchards, poached rabbits, and later had run into debt, got entangled with the local tobacconist's daughter—been disentangled and sent off to Africa—and the village as represented by various ageing spinsters had murmured indulgently. 'Ah, well! Wild oats! He'll settle down!'

And now, sure enough, the prodigal had returned— not in affliction, but in triumph. Harry Laxton had 'made good' as the saying goes. He had pulled himself together, worked hard, and had finally met and successfully wooed a young Anglo-French girl who was the possessor of a considerable fortune.

Harry might have lived in London, or purchased an estate in some fashionable hunting county, but he preferred to come back to the part of the world that was home to him. And there, in the most romantic way, he purchased the derelict estate in the dower house of which he had passed his childhood.

Kingsdean House had been unoccupied for nearly seventy years. It had gradually fallen into decay and abandon. An elderly caretaker and his wife lived in the one habitable corner of it. It was a vast, unprepossessing grandiose mansion, the gardens overgrown with rank vegetation and the trees hemming it in like some gloomy enchanter's den.

The dower house was a pleasant, unpretentious house and had been let for a long term of years to Major Laxton, Harry's father. As a boy, Harry had roamed over the Kingsdean estate and knew every inch of the tangled woods, and the old house itself had always fascinated him.

Major Laxton had died some years ago, so it might have been thought that Harry would have had no ties to bring him back—nevertheless it was to the home of his boyhood that Harry brought his bride. The ruined old Kingsdean House was pulled down. An army of builders and contractors swooped down upon the place, and in almost a miraculously short space of time—so marvellously does wealth tell—the new house rose white and gleaming among the trees.

Next came a posse of gardeners and after them a procession of furniture vans.

The house was ready. Servants arrived. Lastly, a costly limousine deposited Harry and Mrs Harry at the front door.

The village rushed to call, and Mrs Price, who owned the largest house, and who considered herself to lead society in the place, sent out cards of invitation for a party 'to meet the bride'.

It was a great event. Several ladies had new frocks for the occasion. Everyone was excited, curious, anxious to see this fabulous creature. They said it was all so like a fairy story!

Miss Harmon, weather-beaten, hearty spinster, threw out her question as she squeezed her way through the crowded drawing-room door. Little Miss Brent, a thin, acidulated spinster, fluttered out information.

'Oh, my dear, quite charming. Such pretty manners. And quite young. Really, you know, it makes one feel quite envious to see someone who has everything like that. Good looks and money and breeding—most distinguished, nothing in the least common about her—and dear Harry so devoted!'

'Ah,' said Miss Harmon, 'it's early days yet!'

Miss Brent's thin nose quivered appreciatively. 'Oh, my dear, do you really think—'

'We all know what Harry is,' said Miss Harmon.

'We know what he was! But I expect now—'

'Ah,' said Miss Harmon, 'men are always the same. Once a gay deceiver, always a gay deceiver. I know them.'

'Dear, dear. Poor young thing.' Miss Brent looked much happier. 'Yes, I expect she'll have trouble with him. Someone ought really to warn her. I wonder if she's heard anything of the old story?'

'It seems so very unfair,' said Miss Brent, 'that she should know nothing. So awkward. Especially with only the one chemist's shop in the village.'

For the erstwhile tobacconist's daughter was now married to Mr Edge, the chemist.

'It would be so much nicer,' said Miss Brent, 'if Mrs Laxton were to deal with Boots in Much Benham.'

'I dare say,' said Miss Harmon, 'that Harry Laxton will suggest that himself.'

And again a significant look passed between them. 'But I certainly think,' said Miss Harmon, 'that she ought to know.'

'Beasts!' said Clarice Vane indignantly to her uncle, Doctor Haydock. 'Absolute beasts some people are.'

He looked at her curiously.

She was a tall, dark girl, handsome, warm-hearted and impulsive. Her big brown eyes were alight now with indignation as she said, 'All these cats—saying things—hinting things.'

'About Harry Laxton?'

'Yes, about his affair with the tobacconist's daughter.'

'Oh, that!' The doctor shrugged his shoulders. 'A great many young men have affairs of that kind.'

'Of course they do. And it's all over. So why harp on it? And bring it up years after? It's like ghouls feasting on dead bodies.'

'I dare say, my dear, it does seem like that to you. But you see, they have very little to talk about down here, and so I'm afraid they do tend to dwell upon past scandals. But I'm curious to know why it upsets you so much?'

Clarice Vane bit her lip and flushed. She said, in a curiously muffled voice. 'They—they look so happy. The Laxtons, I mean. They're young and in love, and it's all so lovely for them. I hate to think of it being spoiled by whispers and hints and innuendoes and general beastliness.'

'H'm. I see.'

Clarice went on. 'He was talking to me just now. He's so happy and eager and excited and—yes, thrilled—at having got his heart's desire and rebuilt Kingsdean. He's like a child about it all. And she— well, I don't suppose anything has ever gone wrong in her whole life. She's always had everything. You've seen her. What did you think of her?'

The doctor did not answer at once. For other people, Louise Laxton might be an object of envy. A spoiled darling of fortune. To him she had brought only the refrain of a popular song heard many years ago, Poor little rich girl—

A small, delicate figure, with flaxen hair curled rather stiffly round her face and big, wistful blue eyes.

Louise was drooping a little. The long stream of congratulations had tired her. She was hoping it might soon be time to go. Perhaps, even now, Harry might say so. She looked at him sideways. So tall and broad-shouldered with his eager pleasure in this horrible, dull party.

Poor little rich girl—

'Ooph!' It was a sigh of relief.

Harry turned to look at his wife amusedly. They were driving away from the party.

She said, 'Darling, what a frightful party!'

Harry laughed. 'Yes, pretty terrible. Never mind, my sweet. It had to be done, you know. All these old dears knew me when I lived here as a boy. They'd have been terribly disappointed not to have got a look at you close up.'

Louise made a grimace. She said, 'Shall we have to see a lot of them?'

'What? Oh, no. They'll come and make ceremonious calls with card cases, and you'll return the calls and then you needn't bother any more. You can have your own friends down or whatever you like.'

Louise said, after a minute or two, 'Isn't there anyone amusing living down here?'

'Oh, yes. There's the County, you know. Though you may find them a bit dull, too. Mostly interested in bulbs and dogs and horses. You'll ride, of course. You'll enjoy that. There's a horse over at Eglinton I'd like you to see. A beautiful animal, perfectly trained, no vice in him but plenty of spirit.'

The car slowed down to take the turn into the gates of Kingsdean. Harry wrenched the wheel and swore as a grotesque figure sprang up in the middle of the road and he only just managed to avoid it. It stood there, shaking a fist and shouting after them.

Louise clutched his arm. 'Who's that—that horrible old woman?'

Harry's brow was black. 'That's old Murgatroyd. She and her husband were caretakers in the old house. They were there for nearly thirty years.'

'Why does she shake her fist at you?'

Harry's face got red. 'She—well, she resented the house being pulled down. And she got the sack, of course. Her husband's been dead two years. They say she got a bit queer after he died.'

'Is she—she isn't—starving?'

Louise's ideas were vague and somewhat melodramatic. Riches prevented you coming into contact with reality.

Harry was outraged. 'Good Lord, Louise, what an idea! I pensioned her off, of course—and handsomely, too! Found her a new cottage and everything.'

Louise asked, bewildered, 'Then why does she mind?'

Harry was frowning, his brows drawn together. 'Oh, how should I know? Craziness! She loved the house.'

'But it was a ruin, wasn't it?'

'Of course it was—crumbling to pieces—roof leaking—more or less unsafe. All the same I suppose it meant something to her. She'd been there a long time. Oh, I don't know! The old devil's cracked, I think.'

Louise said uneasily, 'She—I think she cursed us. Oh, Harry, I wish she hadn't.'

It seemed to Louise that her new home was tainted and poisoned by the malevolent figure of one crazy old woman. When she went out in the car, when she rode, when she walked out with the dogs, there was always the same figure waiting. Crouched down on herself, a battered hat over wisps of iron-grey hair, and the slow muttering of imprecations.

Louise came to believe that Harry was right—the old woman was mad. Nevertheless that did not make things easier. Mrs Murgatroyd never actually came to the house, nor did she use definite threats, nor offer violence. Her squatting figure remained always just outside the gates. To appeal to the police would have been useless and, in any case, Harry Laxton was averse to that course of action. It would, he said, arouse local sympathy for the old brute. He took the matter more easily than Louise did.

'Don't worry about it, darling. She'll get tired of this silly cursing business. Probably she's only trying it on.'

'She isn't, Harry. She—she hates us! I can feel it. She—she's ill-wishing us.'

'She's not a witch, darling, although she may look like one! Don't be morbid about it all.'

Louise was silent. Now that the first excitement of settling in was over, she felt curiously lonely and at a loose end. She had been used to life in London and the Riviera. She had no knowledge of or taste for English country life. She was ignorant of gardening, except for the final act of 'doing the flowers'. She did not really care for dogs. She was bored by such neighbours as she met. She enjoyed riding best, sometimes with Harry, sometimes, when he was busy about the estate, by herself. She hacked through the woods and lanes, enjoying the easy paces of the beautiful horse that Harry had bought for her. Yet even Prince Hal, most sensitive of chestnut steeds, was wont to shy and snort as he carried his mistress past the huddled figure of a malevolent old woman.

One day Louise took her courage in both hands. She was out walking. She had passed Mrs Murgatroyd, pretending not to notice her, but suddenly she swerved back and went right up to her. She said, a little breathlessly, 'What is it? What's the matter? What do you want?'

187

The old woman blinked at her. She had a cunning, dark gypsy face, with wisps of iron-grey hair, and bleared, suspicious eyes. Louise wondered if she drank.

She spoke in a whining and yet threatening voice. 'What do I want, you ask? What, indeed! That which has been took away from me. Who turned me out of Kingsdean House? I'd lived there, girl and woman, for near on forty years. It was a black deed to turn me out and it's black bad luck it'll bring to you and him!'

Louise said, 'You've got a very nice cottage and—'

She broke off. The old woman's arms flew up. She screamed, 'What's the good of that to me? It's my own place I want and my own fire as I sat beside all them years. And as for you and him, I'm telling you there will be no happiness for you in your new fine house. It's the black sorrow will be upon you! Sorrow and death and my curse. May your fair face rot.'

Louise turned away and broke into a little stumbling run. She thought, I must get away from here! We must sell the house! We must go away.

At the moment, such a solution seemed easy to her. But Harry's utter incomprehension took her back. He exclaimed, 'Leave here? Sell the house? Because of a crazy old woman's threats? You must be mad.'

'No, I'm not. But she—she frightens me, I know something will happen.'

Harry Laxton said grimly, 'Leave Mrs Murgatroyd to me. I'll settle her!'

A friendship had sprung up between Clarice Vane and young Mrs Laxton. The two girls were much of an age, though dissimilar both in character and in tastes.

In Clarice's company, Louise found reassurance. Clarice was so self-reliant, so sure of herself. Louise mentioned the matter of Mrs Murgatroyd and her threats, but Clarice seemed to regard the matter as more annoying than frightening.

'It's so stupid, that sort of thing,' she said. 'And really very annoying for you.'

'You know, Clarice, I—I feel quite frightened sometimes. My heart gives the most awful jumps.'

'Nonsense, you mustn't let a silly thing like that get you down. She'll soon tire of it.'

She was silent for a minute or two. Clarice said, 'What's the matter?'

Louise paused for a minute, then her answer came with a rush. 'I hate this place! I hate being here. The woods and this house, and the awful silence at night, and the queer noise owls make. Oh, and the people and everything.'

'The people. What people?'

'The people in the village. Those prying, gossiping old maids.'

Clarice said sharply, 'What have they been saying?'

'I don't know. Nothing particular. But they've got nasty minds. When you've talked to them you feel you wouldn't trust anybody—not anybody at all.'

Clarice said harshly, 'Forget them. They've nothing to do but gossip. And most of the muck they talk they just invent.'

Louise said, 'I wish we'd never come here. But Harry adores it so.' Her voice softened.

Clarice thought, how she adores him. She said abruptly, 'I must go now.'

'I'll send you back in the car. Come again soon.'

Clarice nodded. Louise felt comforted by her new friend's visit. Harry was pleased to find her more cheerful and from then on urged her to have Clarice often to the house.

Then one day he said, 'Good news for you, darling.'

'Oh, what?'

'I've fixed the Murgatroyd. She's got a son in America, you know. Well, I've arranged for her to go out and join him. I'll pay her passage.'

'Oh, Harry, how wonderful. I believe I might get to like Kingsdean after all.'

'Get to like it? Why, it's the most wonderful place in the world!'

Louise gave a little shiver. She could not rid herself of her superstitious fear so easily.

If the ladies of St Mary Mead had hoped for the pleasure of imparting information about her husband's past to the bride, this pleasure was denied them by Harry Laxton's own prompt action.

Miss Harmon and Clarice Vane were both in Mr Edge's shop, the one buying mothballs and the other a packet of boracic, when Harry Laxton and his wife came in.

After greeting the two ladies, Harry turned to the counter and was just demanding a toothbrush when he stopped in mid-speech and exclaimed heartily, 'Well, well, just see who's here! Bella, I do declare.'

Mrs Edge, who had hurried out from the back parlour to attend to the congestion of business, beamed back cheerfully at him, showing her big white teeth. She had been a dark, handsome girl and was still a reasonably handsome woman, though she had put on weight, and the lines of her face had coarsened; but her large brown eyes were full of warmth as she answered, 'Bella, it is, Mr Harry, and pleased to see you after all these years.'

Harry turned to his wife. 'Bella's an old flame of mine, Louise,' he said. 'Head-over-heels in love with her, wasn't I, Bella?'

'That's what you say,' said Mrs Edge.

Louise laughed. She said, 'My husband's very happy seeing all his old friends again.'

'Ah,' said Mrs Edge, 'we haven't forgotten you, Mr Harry. Seems like a fairy tale to think of you married and building up a new house instead of that ruined old Kingsdean House.'

'You look very well and blooming,' said Harry, and Mrs Edge laughed and said there was nothing wrong with her and what about that toothbrush?

Clarice, watching the baffled look on Miss Harmon's face, said to herself exultantly, Oh, well done, Harry. You've spiked their guns.

Doctor Haydock said abruptly to his niece, 'What's all this nonsense about old Mrs Murgatroyd hanging about Kingsdean and shaking her fist and cursing the new regime?'

'It isn't nonsense. It's quite true. It's upset Louise a good deal.'

'Tell her she needn't worry—when the Murgatroyds were caretakers they never stopped grumbling about the place—they only stayed because Murgatroyd drank and couldn't get another job.'

'I'll tell her,' said Clarice doubtfully, 'but I don't think she'll believe you. The old woman fairly screams with rage.'

'Always used to be fond of Harry as a boy. I can't understand it.'

Clarice said, 'Oh, well—they'll be rid of her soon. Harry's paying her passage to America.'

Three days later, Louise was thrown from her horse and killed.

Two men in a baker's van were witnesses of the accident. They saw Louise ride out of the gates, saw the old woman spring up and stand in the road waving her arms and shouting, saw the horse start, swerve, and then bolt madly down the road, flinging Louise Laxton over his head.

One of them stood over the unconscious figure, not knowing what to do, while the other rushed to the house to get help.

Harry Laxton came running out, his face ghastly. They took off a door of the van and carried her on it to the house. She died without regaining consciousness and before the doctor arrived.

(End of Doctor Haydock's manuscript.)

When Doctor Haydock arrived the following day, he was pleased to note that there was a pink flush in Miss Marple's cheek and decidedly more animation in her manner.

'Well,' he said, 'what's the verdict?'

'What's the problem, Doctor Haydock?' countered Miss Marple.

'Oh, my dear lady, do I have to tell you that?'

'I suppose,' said Miss Marple, 'that it's the curious conduct of the caretaker. Why did she behave in that very odd way? People do mind being turned out of their old homes. But it wasn't her home. In fact, she used to complain and grumble while she was there. Yes, it certainly looks very fishy. What became of her, by the way?'

'Did a bunk to Liverpool. The accident scared her. Thought she'd wait there for her boat.'

'All very convenient for somebody,' said Miss Marple. 'Yes, I think the "Problem of the Caretaker's Conduct" can be solved easily enough. Bribery, was it not?'

'That's your solution?'

'Well, if it wasn't natural for her to behave in that way, she must have been "putting on an act" as people say, and that means that somebody paid her to do what she did.'

'And you know who that somebody was?'

'Oh, I think so. Money again, I'm afraid. And I've always noticed that gentlemen always tend to admire the same type.'

'Now I'm out of my depth.'

'No, no, it all hangs together. Harry Laxton admired Bella Edge, a dark, vivacious type. Your niece Clarice was the same. But the poor little wife was quite a different type—fair-haired and clinging—not his type at all. So he must have married her for her money. And murdered her for her money, too!'

'You use the word "murder"?'

'Well, he sounds the right type. Attractive to women and quite unscrupulous. I suppose he wanted to keep his

193

wife's money and marry your niece. He may have been seen talking to Mrs Edge. But I don't fancy he was attached to her any more. Though I dare say he made the poor woman think he was, for ends of his own. He soon had her well under his thumb, I fancy.'

'How exactly did he murder her, do you think?'

Miss Marple stared ahead of her for some minutes with dreamy blue eyes.

'It was very well timed—with the baker's van as witness. They could see the old woman and, of course, they'd put down the horse's fright to that. But I should imagine, myself, that an air gun, or perhaps a catapult. Yes, just as the horse came through the gates. The horse bolted, of course, and Mrs Laxton was thrown.'

She paused, frowning.

'The fall might have killed her. But he couldn't be sure of that. And he seems the sort of man who would lay his plans carefully and leave nothing to chance. After all, Mrs Edge could get him something suitable without her husband knowing. Otherwise, why would Harry bother with her? Yes, I think he had some powerful drug handy, that could be administered before you arrived. After all, if a woman is thrown from her horse and has serious injuries and dies without recovering consciousness, well—a doctor wouldn't normally be suspicious, would he? He'd put it down to shock or something.'

Doctor Haydock nodded.

'Why did you suspect?' asked Miss Marple.

'It wasn't any particular cleverness on my part,' said Doctor Haydock. 'It was just the trite, well-known fact that a murderer is so pleased with his cleverness that he doesn't take proper precautions. I was just saying a few consolatory words to the bereaved husband—and feeling damned sorry for the fellow, too—when he flung himself down on the settee to do a bit of play-acting and a hypodermic syringe fell out of his pocket.

'He snatched it up and looked so scared that I began to think. Harry Laxton didn't drug; he was in perfect health; what was he doing with a hypodermic syringe? I did the autopsy with a view to certain possibilities. I found strophanthin. The rest was easy. There was strophanthin in Laxton's possession, and Bella Edge, questioned by the police, broke down and admitted to having got it for him. And finally old Mrs Murgatroyd confessed that it was Harry Laxton who had put her up to the cursing stunt.'

'And your niece got over it?'

'Yes, she was attracted by the fellow, but it hadn't gone far.'

The doctor picked up his manuscript.

'Full marks to you, Miss Marple—and full marks to me for my prescription. You're looking almost yourself again.'

The Lonely God

He stood on a shelf in the British Museum, alone and forlorn amongst a company of obviously more important deities. Ranged round the four walls, these greater personages all seemed to display an overwhelming sense of their own superiority. The pedestal of each was duly inscribed with the land and race that had been proud to possess him. There was no doubt of their position; they were divinities of importance and recognized as such.

Only the little god in the corner was aloof and remote from their company. Roughly hewn out of grey stone, his features almost totally obliterated by time and exposure, he sat there in isolation, his elbows on his knees, and his head buried in his hands; a lonely little god in a strange country.

There was no inscription to tell the land whence he came. He was indeed lost, without honour or renown, a pathetic little figure very far from home. No one noticed him, no one stopped to look at him. Why should they? He was so insignificant, a block of grey stone in a corner. On either side of him were two Mexican gods worn smooth with age, placid idols with folded hands, and cruel mouths curved in a smile that showed openly their contempt of humanity. There was also a rotund, violently self-assertive little god, with a clenched fist, who evidently suffered from a swollen sense of his own importance, but passers-by stopped to give him a glance sometimes, even if it was only to laugh at the contrast of his absurd pomposity with the smiling indifference of his Mexican companions.

And the little lost god sat on there hopelessly, his head in his hands, as he had sat year in and year out, till one day the impossible happened, and he found—a worshipper.

'Any letters for me?'

The hall porter removed a packet of letters from a pigeon-hole, gave a cursory glance through them, and said in a wooden voice:

'Nothing for you, sir.'

Frank Oliver sighed as he walked out of the club again. There was no particular reason why there should have been anything for him. Very few people wrote to him. Ever since he had returned from Burma in the spring, he had become conscious of a growing and increasing loneliness.

Frank Oliver was a man just over forty, and the last eighteen years of his life had been spent in various parts of the globe, with brief furloughs in England. Now that he had retired and come home to live for good, he realized for the first time how very much alone in the world he was.

True, there was his sister Greta, married to a Yorkshire clergyman, very busy with parochial duties and the bringing up of a family of small children. Greta was naturally very fond of her only brother, but equally naturally she had very little time to give him. Then there was his old friend Tom Hurley. Tom was married to a nice, bright, cheerful girl, very energetic and practical, of whom Frank was secretly afraid. She told him brightly that he must not be a crabbed old bachelor, and was always producing 'nice girls'. Frank Oliver found that he never had anything to say to these 'nice girls'; they persevered with him for a while, then gave him up as hopeless.

And yet he was not really unsociable. He had a great longing for companionship and sympathy, and ever since he had been back in England he had become aware of a growing discouragement. He had been away too long, he was out of tune with the times. He spent long, aimless days wandering about, wondering what on earth he was to do with himself next.

It was on one of these days that he strolled into the British Museum. He was interested in Asiatic curiosities, and so it was that he chanced upon the lonely god. Its charm held him at once. Here was something vaguely akin to himself; here, too, was someone lost and astray in a strange land. He became in the habit of paying frequent visits to the Museum, just to glance in on the little grey stone figure, in its obscure place on the high shelf.

'Rough luck on the little chap,' he thought to himself. 'Probably had a lot of fuss made about him once, kowtowing and offerings and all the rest of it.'

He had begun to feel such a proprietary right in his little friend (it really almost amounted to a sense of actual ownership) that he was inclined to be resentful when he found that the little god had made a second conquest. *He* had discovered the lonely god; nobody else, he felt, had a right to interfere.

But after the first flash of indignation, he was forced to smile at himself. For this second worshipper was such a little bit of a thing, such a ridiculous, pathetic creature, in a shabby black coat and skirt that had seen its best days. She was young, a little over twenty he should judge, with fair hair and blue eyes, and a wistful droop to her mouth.

Her hat especially appealed to his chivalry. She had evidently trimmed it herself, and it made such a brave attempt to be smart that its failure was pathetic. She was obviously a lady, though a poverty-stricken one, and he immediately decided in his own mind that she was a governess and alone in the world.

He soon found out that her days for visiting the god were Tuesdays and Fridays, and she always arrived at ten o'clock, as soon as the Museum was open. At first he disliked her intrusion, but little by little it began to form one of the principal interests of his monotonous life. Indeed, the fellow devotee was fast ousting the object of devotion from his position of pre-eminence. The days that he did not see the 'Little Lonely Lady', as he called her to himself, were blank.

Perhaps she, too, was equally interested in him, though she endeavoured to conceal the fact with studious unconcern. But little by little a sense of fellowship was slowly growing between them, though as yet they had exchanged no spoken word. The truth of the matter was, the man was too shy! He argued to himself that very likely she had not even noticed him (some inner sense gave the lie to that instantly), that she would consider it a great impertinence, and, finally, that he had not the least idea what to say.

But Fate, or the little god, was kind and sent him an inspiration—or what he regarded as such. With infinite delight in his own cunning, he purchased a woman's handkerchief, a frail little affair of cambric and lace which he almost feared to touch, and, thus armed, he followed her as she departed and stopped her in the Egyptian room.

'Excuse me, but is this yours?' He tried to speak with airy unconcern, and signally failed.

The Lonely Lady took it, and made a pretence of examining it with minute care.

'No, it is not mine.' She handed it back, and added, with what he felt guiltily was a suspicious glance: 'It's quite a new one. The price is still on it.'

But he was unwilling to admit that he had been found out. He started on an over-plausible flow of explanation.

'You see, I picked it up under that big case. It was just by the farthest leg of it.' He derived great relief from this detailed account. 'So, as you had been standing there, I thought it must be yours and came after you with it.'

She said again: 'No, it isn't mine,' and added, as if with a sense of ungraciousness, 'thank you.'

The conversation came to an awkward standstill. The girl stood there, pink and embarrassed, evidently uncertain how to retreat with dignity.

He made a desperate effort to take advantage of his opportunity.

'I—I didn't know there was anyone else in London who cared for our little lonely god till you came.'

She answered eagerly, forgetting her reserve:

'Do *you* call him that too?'

Apparently, if she had noticed his pronoun, she did not resent it. She had been startled into sympathy, and his quiet 'Of course!' seemed the most natural rejoinder in the world.

Again there was a silence, but this time it was a silence born of understanding.

It was the Lonely Lady who broke it in a sudden remembrance of the conventionalities.

She drew herself up to her full height, and with an almost ridiculous assumption of dignity for so small a person, she observed in chilling accents:

'I must be going now. Good morning.' And with a slight, stiff inclination of her head, she walked away, holding herself very erect.

By all acknowledged standards Frank Oliver ought to have felt rebuffed, but it is a regrettable sign of his rapid advance in depravity that he merely murmured to himself: 'Little darling!'

He was soon to repent of his temerity, however. For ten days his little lady never came near the Museum. He was in despair! He had frightened her away! She would never come back! He was a brute, a villain! He would never see her again!

In his distress he haunted the British Museum all day long. She might merely have changed her time of coming. He soon began to know the adjacent rooms by heart, and he contracted a lasting hatred of mummies. The guardian policeman observed him with suspicion when he spent three hours poring over Assyrian hieroglyphics, and the contemplation of endless vases of all ages nearly drove him mad with boredom.

But one day his patience was rewarded. She came again, rather pinker than usual, and trying hard to appear self-possessed.

He greeted her with cheerful friendliness.

'Good morning. It is ages since you've been here.'

'Good morning.'

She let the words slip out with icy frigidity, and coldly ignored the end part of his sentence.

But he was desperate.

'Look here!' He stood confronting her with pleading eyes that reminded her irresistibly of a large, faithful dog. 'Won't you be friends? I'm all alone in London— all alone in the world, and I believe you are, too. We ought to be friends. Besides, our little god has introduced us.'

She looked up half doubtfully, but there was a faint smile quivering at the corners of her mouth.

'Has he?'

'Of course!'

It was the second time he had used this extremely positive form of assurance, and now, as before, it did not fail of its effect, for after a minute or two the girl said, in that slightly royal manner of hers:

'Very well.'

'That's splendid,' he replied gruffly, but there was something in his voice as he said it that made the girl glance at him swiftly, with a sharp impulse of pity.

And so the queer friendship began. Twice a week they met, at the shrine of a little heathen idol. At first they confined their conversation solely to him. He was, as it were, at once a palliation of, and an excuse for, their friendship. The question of his origin was widely discussed. The man insisted on attributing to him the most bloodthirsty characteristics. He depicted him as the terror and dread of his native land, insatiable for human sacrifice, and bowed down to by his people in fear and trembling. In the contrast between his former greatness and his present insignificance there lay, according to the man, all the pathos of the situation.

The Lonely Lady would have none of this theory. He was essentially a kind little god, she insisted. She doubted whether he had ever been very powerful. If he had been so, she argued, he would not now be lost and friendless, and, anyway, he was a dear little god, and she loved him, and she hated to think of him sitting there day after day with all those other horrid, supercilious things jeering at him, because you could see they did! After this vehement outburst the little lady was quite out of breath.

That topic exhausted, they naturally began to talk of themselves. He found out that his surmise was correct. She was a nursery governess to a family of children who lived at Hampstead. He conceived an instant dislike of these children; of Ted, who was five and really not *naughty*, only mischievous; of the twins who *were* rather trying, and of Molly, who wouldn't do anything she was told, but was such a dear you couldn't be cross with her!

'Those children bully you,' he said grimly and accusingly to her.

'They do not,' she retorted with spirit. 'I am extremely stern with them.'

'Oh! Ye gods!' he laughed. But she made him apologize humbly for his scepticism.

She was an orphan she told him, quite alone in the world.

Gradually he told her something of his own life: of his official life, which had been painstaking and mildly successful; and of his unofficial pastime, which was the spoiling of yards of canvas.

'Of course, I don't know anything about it,' he explained. 'But I have always felt I could paint something some day. I can sketch pretty decently, but I'd like to do a real picture of something. A chap who knew once told me that my technique wasn't bad.'

She was interested, pressed for details.

'I am sure you paint awfully well.' He shook his head.

'No, I've begun several things lately and chucked them up in despair. I always thought that, when I had the time, it would be plain sailing. I have been storing up that idea for years, but now, like everything else, I suppose, I've left it too late.'

'Nothing's too late—ever,' said the little lady, with the vehement earnestness of the very young.

He smiled down on her. 'You think not, child? It's too late for some things for me.'

And the little lady laughed at him and nicknamed him Methuselah.

They were beginning to feel curiously at home in the British Museum. The solid and sympathetic policeman who patrolled the galleries was a man of tact, and on the appearance of the couple he usually found that his onerous duties of guardianship were urgently needed in the adjoining Assyrian room.

One day the man took a bold step. He invited her out to tea!

At first she demurred.

'I have no time. I am not free. I can come some mornings because the children have French lessons.'

'Nonsense,' said the man. 'You could manage one day. Kill off an aunt or a second cousin or something, but *come*. We'll go to a little ABC shop near here, and have buns for tea! I know you must love buns!'

'Yes, the penny kind with currants!'

'And a lovely glaze on top—'

'They are such plump, dear things—'

'There is something,' Frank Oliver said solemnly, 'infinitely comforting about a bun!'

So it was arranged, and the little governess came, wearing quite an expensive hothouse rose in her belt in honour of the occasion.

He had noticed that, of late, she had a strained, worried look, and it was more apparent than ever this afternoon as she poured out the tea at the little marble-topped table.

'Children been bothering you?' he asked solicitously.

She shook her head. She had seemed curiously disinclined to talk about the children lately.

'*They're* all right. I never mind them.'

'Don't you?'

His sympathetic tone seemed to distress her unwarrantably.

'Oh, no. It was never that. But—but, indeed, I was lonely. I was indeed!' Her tone was almost pleading.

He said quickly, touched: 'Yes, yes, child, I know—I know.'

After a minute's pause he remarked in a cheerful tone: 'Do you know, you haven't even asked my name yet?'

She held up a protesting hand.

'Please, I don't want to know it. And don't ask mine. Let us be just two lonely people who've come together and made friends. It makes it so much more wonderful—and—and different.'

He said slowly and thoughtfully: 'Very well. In an otherwise lonely world we'll be two people who have just each other.'

It was a little different from her way of putting it, and she seemed to find it difficult to go on with the conversation. Instead, she bent lower and lower over her plate, till only the crown of her hat was visible.

'That's rather a nice hat,' he said by way of restoring her equanimity.

'I trimmed it myself,' she informed him proudly.

'I thought so the moment I saw it,' he answered, saying the wrong thing with cheerful ignorance.

'I'm afraid it is not as fashionable as I meant it to be!'

'I think it's a perfectly lovely hat,' he said loyally.

Again constraint settled down upon them. Frank Oliver broke the silence bravely.

'Little Lady, I didn't mean to tell you yet, but I can't help it. I love you. I want you. I loved you from the first moment I saw you standing there in your little black suit. Dearest, if two lonely people were together—why—there would be no more loneliness. And I'd work, oh! how I'd work! I'd paint you. I could, I know I could. Oh! my little girl, I can't live without you. I can't indeed—'

His little lady was looking at him very steadily. But what she said was quite the last thing he expected her to say. Very quietly and distinctly she said: 'You *bought* that handkerchief!'

207

He was amazed at this proof of feminine perspicacity, and still more amazed at her remembering it against him now. Surely, after this lapse of time, it might have been forgiven him.

'Yes, I did,' he acknowledged humbly. 'I wanted an excuse to speak to you. Are you very angry?' He waited meekly for her words of condemnation.

'I think it was sweet of you!' cried the little lady with vehemence. 'Just sweet of you!' Her voice ended uncertainly.

Frank Oliver went on in his gruff tone:

'Tell me, child, is it impossible? I know I'm an ugly, rough old fellow . . .'

The Lonely Lady interrupted him.

'No, you're not! I wouldn't have you different, not in any way. I love you just as you are, do you understand? Not because I'm sorry for you, not because I'm alone in the world and want someone to be fond of me and take care of me—but because you're just—*you*. Now do you understand?'

'Is it true?' he asked half in a whisper.

And she answered steadily: 'Yes, it's true—' The wonder of it overpowered them.

At last he said whimsically: 'So we've fallen upon heaven, dearest!'

'In an ABC shop,' she answered in a voice that held tears and laughter.

But terrestrial heavens are short-lived. The little lady started up with an exclamation.

'I'd no idea how late it was! I must go at once.'

'I'll see you home.'

'No, no, *no!*'

He was forced to yield to her insistence, and merely accompanied her as far as the Tube station.

'Goodbye, dearest.' She clung to his hand with an intensity that he remembered afterwards.

'Only goodbye till tomorrow,' he answered cheerfully. 'Ten o'clock as usual, and we'll tell each other our names and our histories, and be frightfully practical and prosaic.'

'Goodbye to—heaven, though,' she whispered.

'It will be with us always, sweetheart!'

She smiled back at him, but with that same sad appeal that disquieted him and which he could not fathom. Then the relentless lift dragged her down out of sight.

He was strangely disturbed by those last words of hers, but he put them resolutely out of his mind and substituted radiant anticipations of tomorrow in their stead.

At ten o'clock he was there, in the accustomed place. For the first time he noticed how malevolently the other idols looked down upon him. It almost seemed as if they were possessed of some secret evil knowledge affecting him, over which they were gloating. He was uneasily aware of their dislike.

The little lady was late. Why didn't she come? The atmosphere of this place was getting on his nerves. Never had his own little friend (*their* god) seemed so hopelessly impotent as today. A helpless lump of stone, hugging his own despair!

His cogitations were interrupted by a small, sharp-faced boy who had stepped up to him, and was earnestly scrutinizing him from head to foot. Apparently satisfied with the result of his observations, he held out a letter.

'For me?'

It had no superscription. He took it, and the sharp boy decamped with extraordinary rapidity.

Frank Oliver read the letter slowly and unbelievingly. It was quite short.

Dearest,

I can never marry you. Please forget that I ever came into your life at all, and try to forgive me if I have hurt you. Don't try to find me, because it will be no good. It is really 'goodbye'.

The Lonely Lady

There was a postscript which had evidently been scribbled at the last moment:

I do love you. I do indeed.

And that little impulsive postscript was all the comfort he had in the weeks that followed. Needless to say, he disobeyed her injunction 'not to try to find her', but all in vain. She had vanished completely, and he had no clue to trace her by. He advertised despairingly, imploring her in veiled terms at least to explain the mystery, but blank silence rewarded his efforts. She was gone, never to return.

And then it was that for the first time in his life he really began to paint. His technique had always been good. Now craftsmanship and inspiration went hand in hand.

The picture that made his name and brought him renown was accepted and hung in the Academy, and was accounted to be *the* picture of the year, no less for the exquisite treatment of the subject than for the masterly workmanship and technique. A certain amount of mystery, too, rendered it more interesting to the general outside public.

His inspiration had come quite by chance. A fairy story in a magazine had taken a hold on his imagination.

It was the story of a fortunate Princess who had always had everything she wanted. Did she express a wish? It was instantly gratified. A desire? It was granted. She had a devoted father and mother, great riches, beautiful clothes and jewels, slaves to wait upon her and fulfil her lightest whim, laughing maidens to bear her company, all that the heart of a Princess could desire. The handsomest and richest Princes paid her court and sued in vain for her hand, and were willing to kill any number of dragons to prove their devotion. And yet, the loneliness of the Princess was greater than that of the poorest beggar in the land.

He read no more. The ultimate fate of the Princess interested him not at all. A picture had risen up before him of the pleasure-laden Princess with the sad, solitary soul, surfeited with happiness, suffocated with luxury, starving in the Palace of Plenty.

He began painting with furious energy. The fierce joy of creation possessed him.

He represented the Princess surrounded by her court, reclining on a divan. A riot of Eastern colour pervaded the picture. The Princess wore a marvellous gown of strange-coloured embroideries; her golden hair fell round her, and on her head was a heavy jewelled circlet. Her maidens surrounded her, and Princes knelt at her

211

feet bearing rich gifts. The whole scene was one of luxury and richness.

But the face of the Princess was turned away; she was oblivious of the laughter and mirth around her. Her gaze was fixed on a dark and shadowy corner where stood a seemingly incongruous object: a little grey stone idol with its head buried in its hands in a quaint abandonment of despair.

Was it so incongruous? The eyes of the young Princess rested on it with a strange sympathy, as though a dawning sense of her own isolation drew her glance irresistibly. They were akin, these two. The world was at her feet—yet she was alone: a Lonely Princess looking at a lonely little god.

All London talked of this picture, and Greta wrote a few hurried words of congratulation from Yorkshire, and Tom Hurley's wife besought Frank Oliver to 'come for a weekend and meet a really delightful girl, a great admirer of your work'. Frank Oliver laughed once sardonically, and threw the letter into the fire. Success had come—but what was the use of it? He only wanted one thing—that little lonely lady who had gone out of his life for ever.

It was Ascot Cup Day, and the policeman on duty in a certain section of the British Museum rubbed his eyes and wondered if he were dreaming, for one does not expect to see there an Ascot vision, in a lace frock and a marvellous hat, a veritable nymph as imagined by a Parisian genius. The policeman stared in rapturous admiration.

The lonely god was not perhaps so surprised. He may

212

have been in his way a powerful little god; at any rate, here was one worshipper brought back to the fold.

The Little Lonely Lady was staring up at him, and her lips moved in a rapid whisper.

'Dear little god, oh! dear little god, please help me! Oh, please do help me!'

Perhaps the little god was flattered. Perhaps, if he was indeed the ferocious, unappeasable deity Frank Oliver had imagined him, the long weary years and the march of civilization had softened his cold, stone heart. Perhaps the Lonely Lady had been right all along and he was really a kind little god. Perhaps it was merely a coincidence. However that may be, it was at that very moment that Frank Oliver walked slowly and sadly through the door of the Assyrian room.

He raised his head and saw the Parisian nymph.

In another moment his arm was round her, and she was stammering out rapid, broken words.

'I was so lonely—*you* know, you must have read that story I wrote; you couldn't have painted that picture unless you had, and unless you had understood. The Princess was I; I had everything, and yet I was lonely beyond words. One day I was going to a fortune-teller's, and I borrowed my maid's clothes. I came in here on the way and saw you looking at the little god. That's how it all began. I pretended—oh! it was hateful of me, and I went on pretending, and afterwards I didn't dare confess that I had told you such dreadful lies. I thought you would be disgusted at the way I had deceived you. I couldn't bear you to find out, so I went away. Then I wrote that story, and yesterday I saw your picture. It *was* your picture, wasn't it?'

213

Only the gods really know the word 'ingratitude'. It is to be presumed that the lonely little god knew the black ingratitude of human nature. As a divinity he had unique opportunities of observing it, yet in the hour of trial he who had had sacrifices innumerable offered to him, made sacrifice in his turn. He sacrificed his only two worshippers in a strange land, and it showed him to be a great little god in his way, since he sacrificed all that he had.

Through the chinks in his fingers he watched them go, hand in hand, without a backward glance, two happy people who had found heaven and had no need of him any longer.

What was he, after all, but a very lonely little god in a strange land?

The Sign in the Sky

The Judge was finishing his charge to the jury.

'Now, gentlemen, I have almost finished what I want to say to you. There is evidence for you to consider as to whether this case is plainly made out against this man so that you may say he is guilty of the murder of Vivien Barnaby. You have had the evidence of the servants as to the time the shot was fired. They have one and all agreed upon it. You have had the evidence of the letter written to the defendant by Vivien Barnaby on the morning of that same day, Friday, September 13th—a letter which the defence has not attempted to deny. You have had evidence that the prisoner first denied having been at Deering Hill, and later, after evidence had been given by the police, admitted he had. You will draw your own conclusions from that denial. This is not a case of direct evidence. You will have to come to your own conclusions on the subject of motive—of means, of opportunity. The contention of the defence is that some person unknown entered the music room after the defendant had left it, and shot Vivien Barnaby with the gun which, by strange forgetfulness, the defendant had left behind him. You have heard the defendant's story of the reason it took him half an hour to get home. If you disbelieve the defendant's story and are satisfied, beyond any reasonable doubt, that the defendant did, upon Friday, September 13th, discharge his gun at close quarters to Vivien Barnaby's head with intent to kill her, then, gentlemen, your verdict must be Guilty. If, on the other hand, you have any reasonable doubt, it is your duty to acquit the prisoner. I will now ask you to retire to your room and consider and let me know when you have arrived at a conclusion.'

The jury were absent a little under half an hour. They returned the verdict that to everyone had seemed a foregone conclusion, the verdict of 'Guilty'.

Mr Satterthwaite left the court after hearing the verdict, with a thoughtful frown on his face.

A mere murder trial as such did not attract him. He was of too fastidious a temperament to find interest in the sordid details of the average crime. But the Wylde case had been different. Young Martin Wylde was what is termed a gentleman—and the victim, Sir George Barnaby's young wife, had been personally known to the elderly gentleman.

He was thinking of all this as he walked up Holborn, and then plunged into a tangle of mean streets leading in the direction of Soho. In one of these streets there was a small restaurant, known only to the few, of whom Mr Satterthwaite was one. It was not cheap—it was, on the contrary, exceedingly expensive, since it catered exclusively for the palate of the jaded *gourmet*. It was quiet—no strains of jazz were allowed to disturb the hushed atmosphere—it was rather dark, waiters appeared soft-footed out of the twilight, bearing silver dishes with the air of participating in some holy rite. The name of the restaurant was Arlecchino.

Still thoughtful, Mr Satterthwaite turned into the Arlecchino and made for his favourite table in a recess in the far corner. Owing to the twilight before mentioned, it was not until he was quite close to it that he saw it was already occupied by a tall dark man who sat with his face in shadow, and with a play of colour from a stained window turning his sober garb into a kind of riotous motley.

Mr Satterthwaite would have turned back, but just at that moment the stranger moved slightly and the other recognized him.

'God bless my soul,' said Mr Satterthwaite, who was given to old-fashioned expressions. 'Why, it's Mr Quin!'

Three times before he had met Mr Quin, and each time the meeting had resulted in something a little out of the ordinary. A strange person, this Mr Quin, with a knack of showing you the things you had known all along in a totally different light.

At once Mr Satterthwaite felt excited—pleasurably excited. His role was that of the looker-on, and he knew it, but sometimes when in the company of Mr Quin he had the illusion of being an actor—and the principal actor at that.

'This is very pleasant,' he said, beaming all over his dried-up little face. 'Very pleasant indeed. You've no objection to my joining you, I hope?'

'I shall be delighted,' said Mr Quin. 'As you see, I have not yet begun my meal.'

A deferential head waiter hovered up out of the shadows. Mr Satterthwaite, as befitted a man with a seasoned palate, gave his whole mind to the task of selection. In a few minutes, the head waiter, a slight smile of approbation on his lips, retired, and a young satellite began his ministrations. Mr Satterthwaite turned to Mr Quin.

'I have just come from the Old Bailey,' he began. 'A sad business, I thought.'

'He was found guilty?' said Mr Quin.

'Yes, the jury were out only half an hour.'

Mr Quin bowed his head.

'An inevitable result—on the evidence,' he said.

'And yet,' began Mr Satterthwaite—and stopped.

Mr Quin finished the sentence for him.

'And yet your sympathies were with the accused? Is that what you were going to say?'

'I suppose it was. Martin Wylde is a nice-looking young fellow—one can hardly believe it of him. All the same, there have been a good many nice-looking young fellows lately who have turned out to be murderers of a particularly cold-blooded and repellent type.'

'Too many,' said Mr Quin quietly.

'I beg your pardon?' said Mr Satterthwaite, slightly startled.

'Too many for Martin Wylde. There has been a tendency from the beginning to regard this as just one more of a series of the same type of crime—a man seeking to free himself from one woman in order to marry another.'

'Well,' said Mr Satterthwaite doubtfully. 'On the evidence—'

'Ah!' said Mr Quin quickly. 'I am afraid I have not followed all the evidence.'

Mr Satterthwaite's self-confidence came back to him

with a rush. He felt a sudden sense of power. He was tempted to be consciously dramatic.

'Let me try and show it to you. I have met the Barnabys, you understand. I know the peculiar circumstances. With me, you will come behind the scenes—you will see the thing from inside.'

Mr Quin leant forward with his quick encouraging smile.

'If anyone can show me that, it will be Mr Satterthwaite,' he murmured.

Mr Satterthwaite gripped the table with both hands. He was uplifted, carried out of himself. For the moment, he was an artist pure and simple—an artist whose medium was words.

Swiftly, with a dozen broad strokes, he etched in the picture of life at Deering Hill. Sir George Barnaby, elderly, obese, purse-proud. A man perpetually fussing over the little things of life. A man who wound up his clocks every Friday afternoon, and who paid his own house-keeping books every Tuesday morning, and who always saw to the locking of his own front door every night. A careful man.

And from Sir George he went on to Lady Barnaby. Here his touch was gentler, but none the less sure. He had seen her but once, but his impression of her was definite and lasting. A vivid defiant creature—pitifully young. A trapped child, that was how he described her.

'She hated him, you understand? She had married him before she knew what she was doing. And now—'

She was desperate—that was how he put it. Turning this way and that. She had no money of her own, she was entirely dependent on this elderly husband. But all the same she was a creature at bay—still unsure of her own powers, with a beauty that was as yet more promise than actuality. And she was greedy. Mr Satterthwaite affirmed that definitely. Side by side with defiance there ran a greedy streak—a clasping and a clutching at life.

'I never met Martin Wylde,' continued Mr Satterthwaite. 'But I heard of him. He lived less than a mile away. Farming, that was his line. And she took an interest in farming—or pretended to. If you ask me, it was pretending. I think that she saw in him her only way of escape—and she grabbed at him, greedily, like a child might have done. Well, there could only be one end to that. We know what that end was, because the letters were read out in court. He kept her letters—she didn't keep his, but from the text of hers one can see that he was cooling off. He admits as much. There was the other girl. She also lived in the village of Deering Vale. Her father was the doctor there. You saw her in court, perhaps? No, I remember, you were not there, you said. I shall have to describe her to you. A fair girl—very fair. Gentle. Perhaps—yes, perhaps a tiny bit stupid. But very restful, you know. And loyal. Above all, loyal.'

He looked at Mr Quin for encouragement, and Mr Quin gave it to him by a slow appreciative smile. Mr Satterthwaite went on.

'You heard that last letter read—you must have seen it, in the papers, I mean. The one written on the morning of Friday, September 13th. It was full of desperate reproaches and vague threats, and it ended by begging Martin Wylde to come to Deering Hill that same evening at six o'clock. "*I will leave the side door open for*

220

you, so that no one need know you have been here. I shall be in the music room." It was sent by hand.'

Mr Satterthwaite paused for a minute or two.

'When he was first arrested, you remember, Martin Wylde denied that he had been to the house at all that evening. His statement was that he had taken his gun and gone out shooting in the woods. But when the police brought forward their evidence, that statement broke down. They had found his finger-prints, you remember, both on the wood of the side door and on one of the two cocktail glasses on the table in the music room. He admitted then that he had come to see Lady Barnaby, that they had had a stormy interview, but that it had ended in his having managed to soothe her down. He swore that he left his gun outside leaning against the wall near the door, and that he left Lady Barnaby alive and well, the time being then a minute or two after a quarter past six. He went straight home, he says. But evidence was called to show that he did not reach his farm until a quarter to seven, and as I have just mentioned, it is barely a mile away. It would not take half an hour to get there. He forgot all about his gun, he declares. Not a very likely statement—and yet—'

'And yet?' queried Mr Quin.

'Well,' said Mr Satterthwaite slowly, 'it's a possible one, isn't it? Counsel ridiculed the supposition, of course, but I think he was wrong. You see, I've known a good many young men, and these emotional scenes upset them very much—especially the dark, nervous type like Martin Wylde. Women now, can go through a scene like that and feel positively better for it afterwards, with all their wits about them. It acts like a safety valve for them, steadies their nerves down and all that. But I can see Martin Wylde going away with his head in a whirl, sick and miserable, and without a thought of the gun he had left leaning up against the wall.'

He was silent for some minutes before he went on.

'Not that it matters. For the next part is only too clear, unfortunately. It was exactly twenty minutes past six when the shot was heard. All the servants heard it, the cook, the kitchen-maid, the butler, the housemaid and Lady Barnaby's own maid. They came rushing to the music room. She was lying huddled over the arm of her chair. The gun had been discharged close to the back of her head, so that the shot hadn't a chance to scatter. At least two of them penetrated the brain.'

He paused again and Mr Quin asked casually:

'The servants gave evidence, I suppose?'

Mr Satterthwaite nodded.

'Yes. The butler got there a second or two before the others, but their evidence was practically a repetition of each other's.'

'So they *all* gave evidence,' said Mr Quin musingly. 'There were no exceptions?'

'Now I remember it,' said Mr Satterthwaite, 'the housemaid was only called at the inquest. She's gone to Canada since, I believe.'

'I see,' said Mr Quin.

There was a silence, and somehow the air of the little restaurant seemed to be charged with an uneasy feeling. Mr Satterthwaite felt suddenly as though he were on the defensive.

'Why shouldn't she?' he said abruptly.

'Why should she?' said Mr Quin with a very slight shrug of the shoulders.

Somehow, the question annoyed Mr Satterthwaite. He wanted to shy away from it—to get back on familiar ground.

'There couldn't be much doubt who fired the shot. As a matter of fact the servants seemed to have lost their heads a bit. There was no one in the house to take charge. It was some minutes before anyone thought of ringing up the police, and when they did so they found that the telephone was out of order.'

'Oh!' said Mr Quin. 'The telephone was out of order.'

'It was,' said Mr Satterthwaite—and was struck suddenly by the feeling that he had said something tremendously important. 'It might, of course, have been done on purpose,' he said slowly. 'But there seems no point in that. Death was practically instantaneous.'

Mr Quin said nothing, and Mr Satterthwaite felt that his explanation was unsatisfactory.

'There was absolutely no one to suspect but young Wylde,' he went on. 'By his own account, even, he was only out of the house three minutes before the shot was fired. And who else could have fired it? Sir George was at a bridge party a few houses away. He left there at half-past six and was met just outside the gate by a servant bringing him the news. The last rubber finished at half-past six exactly—no doubt about that. Then there was Sir George's secretary, Henry Thompson. He was in London that day, and actually at a business meeting at the moment the shot was fired. Finally, there is Sylvia Dale, who after all, had a perfectly good motive, impossible as it seems that she should have had anything to do with such a crime. She was at the station of Deering Vale seeing a friend off by the 6.28 train. That lets her out. Then the servants. What earthly motive could any one of them have? Besides they all arrived on the spot practically simultaneously. No, it must have been Martin Wylde.'

But he said it in a dissatisfied kind of voice.

They went on with their lunch. Mr Quin was not in a talkative mood, and Mr Satterthwaite had said all he had to say. But the silence was not a barren one. It was filled with the growing dissatisfaction of Mr Satterthwaite, heightened and fostered in some strange way by the mere acquiescence of the other man.

Mr Satterthwaite suddenly put down his knife and fork with a clatter.

'Supposing that that young man is really innocent,' he said. 'He's going to be hanged.'

He looked very startled and upset about it. And still Mr Quin said nothing.

'It's not as though—' began Mr Satterthwaite, and stopped. 'Why shouldn't the woman go to Canada?' he ended inconsequently.

Mr Quin shook his head.

'I don't even know what part of Canada she went to,' continued Mr Satterthwaite peevishly.

'Could you find out?' suggested the other.

'I suppose I could. The butler, now. He'd know. Or possibly Thompson, the secretary.'

He paused again. When he resumed speech, his voice sounded almost pleading.

'It's not as though it were anything to do with me?'

'That a young man is going to be hanged in a little over three weeks?'

'Well, yes—if you put it that way, I suppose. Yes, I see what you mean. Life and death. And that poor girl, too. It's not that I'm hard-headed—but, after all—what good will it do? Isn't the whole thing rather fantastic? Even if I found out where the woman's gone in Canada—why, it would probably mean that I should have to go out there myself.'

Mr Satterthwaite looked seriously upset.

'And I was thinking of going to the Riviera next week,' he said pathetically.

And his glance towards Mr Quin said as plainly as it could be said, 'Do let me off, won't you?'

'You have never been to Canada?'

'Never.'

'A very interesting country.'

Mr Satterthwaite looked at him undecidedly.

'You think I ought to go?'

Mr Quin leaned back in his chair and lighted a cigarette. Between puffs of smoke, he spoke deliberately.

'You are, I believe, a rich man, Mr Satterthwaite. Not a millionaire, but a man able to indulge a hobby without counting the expense. You have looked on at the dramas of other people. Have you never contemplated stepping in and playing a part? Have you never seen yourself for a minute as the arbiter of other people's destinies—standing in the centre of the stage with life and death in your hands?'

Mr Satterthwaite leant forward. The old eagerness surged over him.

'You mean—if I go on this wild-goose chase to Canada—?'

Mr Quin smiled.

225

'Oh! it was your suggestion, going to Canada, not mine,' he said lightly.

'You can't put me off like that,' said Mr Satterthwaite earnestly. 'Whenever I have come across you—' He stopped.

'Well?'

'There is something about you I do not understand. Perhaps I never shall. The last time I met you—'

'On Midsummer's Eve.'

Mr Satterthwaite was startled, as though the words held a clue that he did not quite understand.

'Was it Midsummer's Eve?' he asked confusedly.

'Yes. But let us not dwell on that. It is unimportant, is it not?'

'Since you say so,' said Mr Satterthwaite courteously. He felt that elusive clue slipping through his fingers. 'When I come back from Canada'—he paused a little awkwardly—'I—I—should much like to see you again.'

'I am afraid I have no fixed address for the moment,' said Mr Quin regretfully. 'But I often come to this place. If you also frequent it, we shall no doubt meet before very long.'

They parted pleasantly.

Mr Satterthwaite was very excited. He hurried round to Cook's and inquired about boat sailings. Then he rang up Deering Hill. The voice of a butler, suave and deferential, answered him.

'My name is Satterthwaite. I am speaking for a—er— firm of solicitors. I wished to make a few inquiries about a young woman who was recently housemaid in your establishment.'

'Would that be Louisa, sir? Louisa Bullard?'

'That is the name,' said Mr Satterthwaite, very pleased to be told it.

'I regret she is not in this country, sir. She went to Canada six months ago.'

'Can you give me her present address?'

The butler was afraid he couldn't. It was a place in the mountains she had gone to—a Scotch name—ah! Banff, that was it. Some of the other young women in the house had been expecting to hear from her, but she had never written or given them any address.

Mr Satterthwaite thanked him and rang off. He was still undaunted. The adventurous spirit was strong in his breast. He would go to Banff. If this Louisa Bullard was there, he would track her down somehow or other.

To his own surprise, he enjoyed the trip greatly. It was many years since he had taken a long sea voyage. The Riviera, Le Touquet and Deauville, and Scotland had been his usual round. The feeling that he was setting off on an impossible mission added a secret zest to his journey. What an utter fool these fellow travellers of his would think him did they but know the object of his quest! But then—they were not acquainted with Mr Quin.

In Banff he found his objective easily attained. Louisa Bullard was employed in the large hotel there. Twelve hours after his arrival he was standing face to face with her.

She was a woman of about thirty-five, anaemic looking, but with a strong frame. She had pale brown hair inclined to curl, and a pair of honest brown eyes. She was, he thought, slightly stupid, but very trustworthy.

She accepted quite readily his statement that he had

been asked to collect a few further facts from her about the tragedy at Deering Hill.

'I saw in the paper that Mr Martin Wylde had been convicted, sir. Very sad, it is, too.'

She seemed, however, to have no doubt as to his guilt.

'A nice young gentleman gone wrong. But though I wouldn't speak ill of the dead, it was her ladyship what led him on. Wouldn't leave him alone, she wouldn't. Well, they've both got their punishment. There's a text used to hang on my wall when I was a child, "God is not mocked," and it's very true. I knew something was going to happen that very evening—and sure enough it did.'

'How was that?' said Mr Satterthwaite.

'I was in my room, sir, changing my dress, and I happened to glance out of the window. There was a train going along, and the white smoke of it rose up in the air, and if you'll believe me it formed itself into the sign of a gigantic hand. A great white hand against the crimson of the sky. The fingers were crooked like, as though they were reaching out for something. It fair gave me a turn. "Did you ever now?" I said to myself. "That's a sign of something coming"—and sure enough at that very minute I heard the shot. "It's come," I said to myself, and I rushed downstairs and joined Carrie and the others who were in the hall, and we went into the music room and there she was, shot through the head—and the blood and everything. Horrible! I spoke up, I did, and told Sir George how I'd seen the sign beforehand, but he didn't seem to think much of it. An unlucky day, that was, I'd felt it in my bones from early in the morning. Friday, and the 13th—what could you expect?'

She rambled on. Mr Satterthwaite was patient. Again and again he took her back to the crime, questioning her closely. In the end he was forced to confess defeat. Louisa Bullard had told all she knew, and her story was perfectly simple and straightforward.

Yet he did discover one fact of importance. The post in question had been suggested to her by Mr Thompson, Sir George's secretary. The wages attached were so large that she was tempted, and accepted the job, although it involved her leaving England very hurriedly. A Mr Denman had made all the arrangements this end and had also warned her not to write to her fellow servants in England, as this might 'get her into trouble with the immigration authorities', which statement she had accepted in blind faith.

The amount of wages, casually mentioned by her, was indeed so large that Mr Satterthwaite was startled. After some hesitation he made up his mind to approach this Mr Denman.

He found very little difficulty in inducing Mr Denman to tell all he knew. The latter had come across Thompson in London and Thompson had done him a good turn. The secretary had written to him in September saying that for personal reasons Sir George was anxious to get this girl out of England. Could he find her a job? A sum of money had been sent to raise the wages to a high figure.

'Usual trouble, I guess,' said Mr Denman, leaning back nonchalantly in his chair. 'Seems a nice quiet girl, too.'

Mr Satterthwaite did not agree that this was the usual trouble. Louisa Bullard, he was sure, was not a cast-off fancy of Sir George Barnaby's. For some reason it had been vital to get her out of England. But why? And who was at the bottom of it? Sir George himself, working through Thompson? Or the latter working on his own initiative, and dragging in his employer's name?

Still pondering over these questions, Mr Satterthwaite made the return journey. He was cast down and despondent. His journey had done no good.

Smarting under a sense of failure, he made his way to the *Arlecchino* the day after his return. He hardly expected to be successful the first time, but to his satisfaction the familiar figure was sitting at the table in the recess, and the dark face of Mr Harley Quin smiled a welcome.

'Well,' said Mr Satterthwaite as he helped himself to a pat of butter, 'you sent me on a nice wild-goose chase.'

Mr Quin raised his eyebrows.

'I sent you?' he objected. 'It was your own idea entirely.'

'Whosoever idea it was, it's not succeeded. Louisa Bullard has nothing to tell.'

Thereupon Mr Satterthwaite related the details of his conversation with the housemaid and then went on to his interview with Mr Denman. Mr Quin listened in silence.

'In one sense, I was justified,' continued Mr Satterthwaite. 'She was deliberately got out of the way. But why? I can't see it.'

'No?' said Mr Quin, and his voice was, as ever, provocative.

Mr Satterthwaite flushed.

'I dare say you think I might have questioned her

more adroitly. I can assure you that I took her over the story again and again. It was not my fault that I did not get what we want.'

'Are you sure,' said Mr Quin, 'that you did not get what you want?'

Mr Satterthwaite looked up at him in astonishment, and met that sad, mocking gaze he knew so well.

The little man shook his head, slightly bewildered.

There was a silence, and then Mr Quin said, with a total change of manner:

'You gave me a wonderful picture the other day of the people in this business. In a few words you made them stand out as clearly as though they were etched. I wish you would do something of that kind for the place—you left that in shadow.'

Mr Satterthwaite was flattered.

'The place? Deering Hill? Well, it's a very ordinary sort of house nowadays. Red brick, you know, and bay windows. Quite hideous outside, but very comfortable inside. Not a very large house. About two acres of ground. They're all much the same, those houses round the links. Built for rich men to live in. The inside of the house is reminiscent of a hotel—the bedrooms are like hotel suites. Baths and hot and cold basins in all the bed-rooms and a good many gilded electric-light fittings. All wonderfully comfortable, but not very country-like. You can tell that Deering Vale is only nineteen miles from London.'

Mr Quin listened attentively.

'The train service is bad, I have heard,' he remarked.

'Oh! I don't know about that,' said Mr Satterthwaite, warming to his subject. 'I was down there for a bit last summer. I found it quite convenient for town. Of course the trains only go every hour. Forty-eight minutes past the hour from Waterloo—up to 10.48.'

'And how long does it take to Deering Vale?'

'Just about three quarters of an hour. Twenty-eight minutes past the hour at Deering Vale.'

'Of course,' said Mr Quin with a gesture of vexation. 'I should have remembered. Miss Dale saw someone off by the 6.28 that evening, didn't she?'

Mr Satterthwaite did not reply for a minute or two. His mind had gone back with a rush to his unsolved problem. Presently he said:

'I wish you would tell me what you meant just now when you asked me if I was sure I had not got what I wanted?'

It sounded rather complicated, put that way, but Mr Quin made no pretence of not understanding.

'I just wondered if you weren't being a little too exacting. After all, you found out that Louisa Bullard was deliberately got out of the country. That being so, there must be a reason. And the reason must lie in what she said to you.'

'Well,' said Mr Satterthwaite argumentatively. 'What did she say? If she'd given evidence at the trial, what could she have said?'

'She might have told what she saw,' said Mr Quin.

'What did she see?'

'A sign in the sky.'

Mr Satterthwaite stared at him.

'Are you thinking of *that* nonsense? That superstitious notion of its being the hand of God?'

'Perhaps,' said Mr Quin, 'for all you and I know it may have been the hand of God, you know.'

The other was clearly puzzled at the gravity of his manner.

'Nonsense,' he said. 'She said herself it was the smoke of the train.'

'An up train or a down train, I wonder?' murmured Mr Quin.

'Hardly an up train. They go at ten minutes to the hour. It must have been a down train—the 6.28—no, that won't do. She said the shot came immediately afterwards, and we know the shot was fired at twenty minutes past six. The train couldn't have been ten minutes early.'

'Hardly, on that line,' agreed Mr Quin.

Mr Satterthwaite was staring ahead of him.

'Perhaps a goods train,' he murmured. 'But surely, if so—'

'There would have been no need to get her out of England. I agree,' said Mr Quin.

Mr Satterthwaite gazed at him, fascinated.

'The 6.28,' he said slowly. 'But if so, if the shot was fired then, why did everyone say it was earlier?'

'Obvious,' said Mr Quin. 'The clocks must have been wrong.'

'All of them?' said Mr Satterthwaite doubtfully. 'That's a pretty tall coincidence, you know.'

'I wasn't thinking of it as a coincidence,' said the other. 'I was thinking it was Friday.'

'Friday?' said Mr Satterthwaite.

'You did tell me, you know, that Sir George always wound the clocks on a Friday afternoon,' said Mr Quin apologetically.

'He put them back ten minutes,' said Mr Satterthwaite, almost in a whisper, so awed was he by the discoveries he

233

was making. 'Then he went out to bridge. I think he must have opened the note from his wife to Martin Wylde that morning—yes, decidedly he opened it. He left his bridge party at 6.30, found Martin's gun standing by the side door, and went in and shot her from behind. Then he went out again, threw the gun into the bushes where it was found later, and was apparently just coming out of the neighbour's gate when someone came running to fetch him. But the telephone—what about the telephone? Ah! yes, I see. He disconnected it so that a summons could not be sent to the police that way—they might have noted the time it was received. And Wylde's story works out now. The real time he left was five and twenty minutes past six. Walking slowly, he would reach home about a quarter to seven. Yes, I see it all. Louisa was the only danger with her endless talk about her superstitious fancies. Someone might realize the significance of the train and then—goodbye to that excellent *alibi*.'

'Wonderful,' commented Mr Quin.

Mr Satterthwaite turned to him, flushed with success.

'The only thing is—how to proceed now?'

'I should suggest Sylvia Dale,' said Mr Quin.

Mr Satterthwaite looked doubtful.

'I mentioned to you,' he said, 'she seemed to me a little—er—stupid.'

'She has a father and brothers who will take the necessary steps.'

'That is true,' said Mr Satterthwaite, relieved.

A very short time afterwards he was sitting with the girl telling her the story. She listened attentively. She put no questions to him but when he had done she rose.

'I must have a taxi—at once.'

'My dear child, what are you going to do?'

'I am going to Sir George Barnaby.'

'Impossible. Absolutely the wrong procedure. Allow me to—'

He twittered on by her side. But he produced no impression. Sylvia Dale was intent on her own plans. She allowed him to go with her in the taxi, but to all his remonstrances she addressed a deaf ear. She left him in the taxi while she went into Sir George's city office.

It was half an hour later when she came out. She looked exhausted, her fair beauty drooping like a waterless flower. Mr Satterthwaite received her with concern.

'I've won,' she murmured, as she leant back with half-closed eyes.

'What?' He was startled. 'What did you do? What did you say?'

She sat up a little.

'I told him that Louisa Bullard had been to the police with her story. I told him that the police had made inquiries and that he had been seen going into his own grounds and out again a few minutes after half-past six. I told him that the game was up. He—he went to pieces. I told him that there was still time for him to get away, that the police weren't coming for another hour to arrest him. I told him that if he'd sign a confession that he'd killed Vivien I'd do nothing, but that if he didn't I'd scream and tell the whole building the truth. He was so panicky that he didn't know what he was doing. He signed the paper without realizing what he was doing.'

She thrust it into his hands.

'Take it—take it. You know what to do with it so that they'll set Martin free.'

'He actually signed it,' cried Mr Satterthwaite, amazed.

'He is a little stupid, you know,' said Sylvia Dale. 'So am I,' she added as an afterthought. 'That's why I know how stupid people behave. We get rattled, you know, and then we do the wrong thing and are sorry afterwards.'

She shivered and Mr Satterthwaite patted her hand.

'You need something to pull you together,' he said. 'Come, we are close to a very favourite resort of mine— the *Arlecchino*. Have you ever been there?'

She shook her head.

Mr Satterthwaite stopped the taxi and took the girl into the little restaurant. He made his way to the table in the recess, his heart beating hopefully. But the table was empty.

Sylvia Dale saw the disappointment in his face.

'What is it?' she asked.

'Nothing,' said Mr Satterthwaite. 'That is, I half expected to see a friend of mine here. It doesn't matter. Some day, I expect, I shall see him again . . .'

The Adventure of the Cheap Flat

So far, in the cases which I have recorded, Poirot's investigations have started from the central fact, whether murder or robbery, and have proceeded from thence by a process of logical deduction to the final triumphant unravelling. In the events I am now about to chronicle a remarkable chain of circumstances led from the apparently trivial incidents which first attracted Poirot's attention to the sinister happenings which completed a most unusual case.

I had been spending the evening with an old friend of mine, Gerald Parker. There had been, perhaps, about half a dozen people there besides my host and myself, and the talk fell, as it was bound to do sooner or later wherever Parker found himself, on the subject of house-hunting in London. Houses and flats were Parker's special hobby. Since the end of the War, he had occupied at least half a dozen different flats and maisonettes. No sooner was he settled anywhere than he would light unexpectedly upon a new find, and would forthwith depart bag and baggage. His moves were nearly always accomplished at a slight pecuniary gain, for he

237

had a shrewd business head, but it was sheer love of the sport that actuated him, and not a desire to make money at it. We listened to Parker for some time with the respect of the novice for the expert. Then it was our turn, and a perfect babel of tongues was let loose. Finally the floor was left to Mrs Robinson, a charming little bride who was there with her husband. I had never met them before, as Robinson was only a recent acquaintance of Parker's.

'Talking of flats,' she said, 'have you heard of our piece of luck, Mr Parker? We've got a flat—at last! In Montagu Mansions.'

'Well,' said Parker, 'I've always said there are plenty of flats—at a price!'

'Yes, but this isn't at a price. It's dirt cheap. Eighty pounds a year!'

'But—but Montagu Mansions is just off Knightsbridge, isn't it? Big handsome building. Or are you talking of a poor relation of the same name stuck in the slums somewhere?'

'No, it's the Knightsbridge one. That's what makes it so wonderful.'

'Wonderful is the word! It's a blinking miracle. But there must be a catch somewhere. Big premium, I suppose?'

'No premium!'

'No prem—oh, hold my head, somebody!' groaned Parker.

'But we've got to buy the furniture,' continued Mrs Robinson.

'Ah!' Parker bristled up. 'I knew there was a catch!'

'For fifty pounds. And it's beautifully furnished!'

'I give it up,' said Parker. 'The present occupants must be lunatics with a taste for philanthropy.'

Mrs Robinson was looking a little troubled. A little pucker appeared between her dainty brows.

'It *is* queer, isn't it? You don't think that—that—the place is *haunted*?'

'Never heard of a haunted flat,' declared Parker decisively.

'N-o.' Mrs Robinson appeared far from convinced. 'But there were several things about it all that struck me as—well, queer.'

'For instance—' I suggested.

'Ah,' said Parker, 'our criminal expert's attention is aroused! Unburden yourself to him, Mrs Robinson. Hastings is a great unraveller of mysteries.'

I laughed, embarrassed, but not wholly displeased with the role thrust upon me.

'Oh, not really queer, Captain Hastings, but when we went to the agents, Stosser and Paul—we hadn't tried them before because they only have the expensive Mayfair flats, but we thought at any rate it would do no harm—everything they offered us was four and five hundred a year, or else huge premiums, and then, just as we were going, they mentioned that they had a flat at eighty, but that they doubted if it would be any good our going there, because it had been on their books some time and they had sent so many people to see it that it was almost sure to be taken—"snapped up" as the clerk put it—only people were so tiresome in not letting them know, and then they went on sending, and people get annoyed at being sent to a place that had, perhaps, been let some time.'

Mrs Robinson paused for some much needed breath, and then continued:

'We thanked him, and said that we quite understood it would probably be no good, but that we should like an order all the same—just in case. And we went there straight away in a taxi, for, after all, you never know. No. 4 was on the second floor, and just as we were waiting for the lift, Elsie Ferguson— she's a friend of mine, Captain Hastings, and they are looking for a flat too—came hurrying down the stairs. "Ahead of you for once, my dear," she said. "But it's no good. It's already let." That seemed to finish it, but—well, as John said, the place was very cheap, we could afford to give more, and perhaps if we offered a premium. A horrid thing to do, of course, and I feel quite ashamed of telling you, but you know what flat-hunting is.'

I assured her that I was well aware that in the struggle for house-room the baser side of human nature frequently triumphed over the higher, and that the well-known rule of dog eat dog always applied.

'So we went up and, would you believe it, the flat wasn't let at all. We were shown over it by the maid, and then we saw the mistress, and the thing was settled then and there. Immediate possession and fifty pounds for the furniture. We signed the agreement next day, and we are to move in tomorrow!' Mrs Robinson paused triumphantly.

'And what about Mrs Ferguson?' asked Parker. 'Let's have your deductions, Hastings.'

'"Obvious, my dear Watson,"' I quoted lightly. 'She went to the wrong flat.'

'Oh, Captain Hastings, how clever of you!' cried Mrs Robinson admiringly.

I rather wished Poirot had been there. Sometimes I have the feeling that he rather underestimates my capabilities.

The whole thing was rather amusing, and I propounded the thing as a mock problem to Poirot on the following morning. He seemed interested, and questioned me rather narrowly as to the rents of flats in various localities.

'A curious story,' he said thoughtfully. 'Excuse me, Hastings, I must take a short stroll.'

When he returned, about an hour later, his eyes were gleaming with a peculiar excitement. He laid his stick on the table, and brushed the nap of his hat with his usual tender care before he spoke.

'It is as well, *mon ami*, that we have no affairs of moment on hand. We can devote ourselves wholly to the present investigation.'

'What investigation are you talking about?'

'The remarkable cheapness of your friend, Mrs Robinson's, new flat.'

'Poirot, you are not serious!'

'I am most serious. Figure to yourself, my friend, that the real rent of those flats is £350. I have just ascertained that from the landlord's agents. And yet this particular flat is being sublet at eighty pounds! Why?'

'There must be something wrong with it. Perhaps it is haunted, as Mrs Robinson suggested.'

Poirot shook his head in a dissatisfied manner.

'Then again how curious it is that her friend tells her

the flat is let, and, when she goes up, behold, it is not so at all!'

'But surely you agree with me that the other woman must have gone to the wrong flat. That is the only possible solution.'

'You may or may not be right on that point, Hastings. The fact still remains that numerous other applicants were sent to see it, and yet, in spite of its remarkable cheapness, it was still in the market when Mrs Robinson arrived.'

'That shows that there *must* be something wrong about it.'

'Mrs Robinson did not seem to notice anything amiss. Very curious, is it not? Did she impress you as being a truthful woman, Hastings?'

'She was a delightful creature!'

'*Évidemment*! since she renders you incapable of replying to my question. Describe her to me, then.'

'Well, she's tall and fair; her hair's really a beautiful shade of auburn—'

'Always you have had a penchant for auburn hair!' murmured Poirot. 'But continue.'

'Blue eyes and a very nice complexion and—well, that's all, I think,' I concluded lamely.

'And her husband?'

'Oh, he's quite a nice fellow—nothing startling.'

'Dark or fair?'

'I don't know—betwixt and between, and just an ordinary sort of face.'

Poirot nodded.

'Yes, there are hundreds of these average men—and anyway, you bring more sympathy and appreciation to your description of women. Do you know anything about these people? Does Parker know them well?'

'They are just recent acquaintances, I believe. But surely, Poirot, you don't think for an instant—'

Poirot raised his hand.

'*Tout doucement, mon ami.* Have I said that I think anything? All I say is—it is a curious story. And there is nothing to throw light upon it; except perhaps the lady's name, eh, Hastings?'

'Her name is Stella,' I said stiffly, 'but I don't see—'

Poirot interrupted me with a tremendous chuckle. Something seemed to be amusing him vastly.

'And Stella means a star, does it not? Famous!'

'What on earth—?'

'And stars give light! *Voilà!* Calm yourself, Hastings. Do not put on that air of injured dignity. Come, we will go to Montagu Mansions and make a few inquiries.'

I accompanied him, nothing loath. The Mansions were a handsome block of buildings in excellent repair. A uniformed porter was sunning himself on the threshold, and it was to him that Poirot addressed himself.

'Pardon, but could you tell me if a Mr and Mrs Robinson reside here?'

The porter was a man of few words and apparently of a sour or suspicious disposition. He hardly looked at us and grunted out:

'No. 4. Second floor.'

'I thank you. Can you tell me how long they have been here?'

'Six months.'

I started forward in amazement, conscious as I did so of Poirot's malicious grin.

'Impossible,' I cried. 'You must be making a mistake.'

'Six months.'

'Are you sure? The lady I mean is tall and fair with reddish gold hair and—'

'That's 'er,' said the porter. 'Come in the Michaelmas quarter, they did. Just six months ago.'

He appeared to lose interest in us and retreated slowly up the hall. I followed Poirot outside.

'*Eh bien*, Hastings?' my friend demanded slyly. 'Are you so sure now that delightful women always speak the truth?'

I did not reply.

Poirot had steered his way into Brompton Road before I asked him what he was going to do and where we were going.

'To the house agents, Hastings. I have a great desire to have a flat in Montagu Mansions. If I am not mistaken, several interesting things will take place there before long.'

We were fortunate in our quest. No. 8, on the fourth floor, was to be let furnished at ten guineas a week. Poirot promptly took it for a month. Outside in the street again, he silenced my protests:

'But I make money nowadays! Why should I not indulge a whim? By the way, Hastings, have you a revolver?'

'Yes—somewhere,' I answered, slightly thrilled. 'Do you think—'

'That you will need it? It is quite possible. The idea pleases you, I see. Always the spectacular and romantic appeals to you.'

The following day saw us installed in our temporary home. The flat was pleasantly furnished. It occupied the same position in the building as that of the Robinsons, but was two floors higher.

The day after our installation was a Sunday. In the afternoon, Poirot left the front door ajar, and summoned me hastily as a bang reverberated from somewhere below.

'Look over the banisters. Are those your friends? Do not let them see you.'

I craned my neck over the staircase.

'That's them,' I declared in an ungrammatical whisper.

'Good. Wait awhile.'

About half an hour later, a young woman emerged in brilliant and varied clothing. With a sigh of satisfaction, Poirot tiptoed back into the flat.

'*C'est ça.* After the master and mistress, the maid. The flat should now be empty.'

'What are we going to do?' I asked uneasily.

Poirot had trotted briskly into the scullery and was hauling at the rope of the coal-lift.

'We are about to descend after the method of the dustbins,' he explained cheerfully. 'No one will observe us. The Sunday concert, the Sunday "afternoon out", and finally the Sunday nap after the Sunday dinner of England—*le rosbif*—all these will distract attention from the doings of Hercule Poirot. Come, my friend.'

He stepped into the rough wooden contrivance and I followed him gingerly.

'Are we going to break into the flat?' I asked dubiously.

Poirot's answer was not too reassuring:

'Not precisely today,' he replied.

Pulling on the rope, we descended slowly till we reached the second floor. Poirot uttered an exclamation

245

of satisfaction as he perceived that the wooden door into the scullery was open.

'You observe? Never do they bolt these doors in the daytime. And yet anyone could mount or descend as we have done. At night, yes—though not always then—and it is against that that we are going to make provision.'

He had drawn some tools from his pocket as he spoke, and at once set deftly to work, his object being to arrange the bolt so that it could be pulled back from the lift. The operation only occupied about three minutes. Then Poirot returned the tools to his pocket, and we reascended once more to our own domain.

On Monday Poirot was out all day, but when he returned in the evening he flung himself into his chair with a sigh of satisfaction.

'Hastings, shall I recount to you a little history? A story after your own heart and which will remind you of your favourite cinema?'

'Go ahead,' I laughed. 'I presume that it is a true story, not one of your efforts of fancy.'

'It is true enough. Inspector Japp of Scotland Yard will vouch for its accuracy, since it was through his kind offices that it came to my ears. Listen, Hastings. A little over six months ago some important Naval plans were stolen from an American Government department. They showed the position of some of the most important Harbour defences, and would be worth a considerable sum to any foreign Government—that of Japan, for example. Suspicion fell upon a young man named Luigi Valdarno, an Italian by birth, who was employed in a minor capacity in the Department and who was missing at the same time as the papers. Whether Luigi Valdarno was the thief or not, he was found two days later on the East Side in New York, shot dead. The papers were not on him. Now for some time past Luigi Valdarno had been going about with a Miss Elsa Hardt, a young concert singer who had recently appeared and who lived with a brother in an apartment in Washington. Nothing was known of the antecedents of Miss Elsa Hardt, and she disappeared suddenly about the time of Valdarno's death. There are reasons for believing that she was in reality an accomplished international spy who has done much nefarious work under various aliases. The American Secret Service, while doing their best to trace her, also kept an eye upon certain insignificant Japanese gentlemen living in Washington. They felt pretty certain that, when Elsa Hardt had covered her tracks sufficiently, she would approach the gentlemen in question. One of them left suddenly for England a fortnight ago. On the face of it, therefore, it would seem that Elsa Hardt is in England.' Poirot paused, and then added softly: 'The official description of Elsa Hardt is: Height 5 ft 7, eyes blue, hair auburn, fair complexion, nose straight, no special distinguishing marks.'

'Mrs Robinson!' I gasped.

'Well, there is a chance of it, anyhow,' amended Poirot. 'Also I learn that a swarthy man, a foreigner of some kind, was inquiring about the occupants of No. 4 only this morning. Therefore, *mon ami*, I fear that you must forswear your beauty sleep tonight, and join me in my all-night vigil in the flat below—armed with that excellent revolver of yours, *bien entendu!*'

'Rather,' I cried with enthusiasm. 'When shall we start?'

'The hour of midnight is both solemn and suitable, I fancy. Nothing is likely to occur before then.'

At twelve o'clock precisely, we crept cautiously into the coal–lift and lowered ourselves to the second floor. Under Poirot's manipulation, the wooden door quickly swung inwards, and we climbed into the flat. From the scullery we passed into the kitchen where we established ourselves comfortably in two chairs with the door into the hall ajar.

'Now we have but to wait,' said Poirot contentedly, closing his eyes.

To me, the waiting appeared endless. I was terrified of going to sleep. Just when it seemed to me that I had been there about eight hours—and had, as I found out afterwards, in reality been exactly one hour and twenty minutes—a faint scratching sound came to my ears. Poirot's hand touched mine. I rose, and together we moved carefully in the direction of the hall. The noise came from there. Poirot placed his lips to my ear.

'Outside the front door. They are cutting out the lock. When I give the word, not before, fall upon him from behind and hold him fast. Be careful, he will have a knife.'

Presently there was a rending sound, and a little circle of light appeared through the door. It was extinguished immediately and then the door was slowly opened. Poirot and I flattened ourselves against the wall. I heard a man's breathing as he passed us. Then he flashed on his torch, and as he did so, Poirot hissed in my ear:

'*Allez.*'

We sprang together, Poirot with a quick movement enveloped the intruder's head with a light woollen scarf whilst I pinioned his arms. The whole affair was quick and noiseless. I twisted a dagger from his hand, and as Poirot brought down the scarf from his eyes, whilst keeping it wound tightly round his mouth, I jerked up my revolver where he could see it and understand that resistance was useless. As he ceased to struggle Poirot put his mouth close to his ear and began to whisper rapidly. After a minute the man nodded. Then enjoining silence with a movement of the hand, Poirot led the way out of the flat and down the stairs. Our captive followed, and I brought up the rear with the revolver. When we were out in the street, Poirot turned to me.

'There is a taxi waiting just round the corner. Give me the revolver. We shall not need it now.'

'But if this fellow tries to escape?'

Poirot smiled.

'He will not.'

I returned in a minute with the waiting taxi. The scarf had been unwound from the stranger's face, and I gave a start of surprise.

'He's not a Jap,' I ejaculated in a whisper to Poirot.

'Observation was always your strong point, Hastings! Nothing escapes you. No, the man is not a Jap. He is an Italian.'

We got into the taxi, and Poirot gave the driver an address in St John's Wood. I was by now completely fogged. I did not like to ask Poirot where we were going in front of our captive, and strove in vain to obtain some light upon the proceedings.

We alighted at the door of a small house standing back from the road. A returning wayfarer, slightly drunk, was lurching along the pavement and almost collided with Poirot, who said something sharply to him which I did not catch. All three of us went up the steps of the house. Poirot rang the bell and motioned us to stand a little aside. There was no answer and he rang again and then seized the knocker which he plied for some minutes vigorously.

A light appeared suddenly above the fanlight, and the door was opened cautiously a little way.

'What the devil do you want?' a man's voice demanded harshly.

'I want the doctor. My wife is taken ill.'

'There's no doctor here.'

The man prepared to shut the door, but Poirot thrust his foot in adroitly. He became suddenly a perfect caricature of an infuriated Frenchman.

'What you say, there is no doctor? I will have the law of you. You must come! I will stay here and ring and knock all night.'

'My dear sir—' The door was opened again, the man, clad in a dressing-gown and slippers, stepped forward to pacify Poirot with an uneasy glance round.

'I will call the police.'

Poirot prepared to descend the steps.

'No, don't do that for Heaven's sake!' The man dashed after him.

With a neat push Poirot sent him staggering down the steps. In another minute all three of us were inside the door and it was pushed to and bolted.

'Quick—in here.' Poirot led the way into the nearest room, switching on the light as he did so. 'And you—behind the curtain.'

'*Si, Signor*,' said the Italian and slid rapidly behind the full folds of rose-coloured velvet which draped the embrasure of the window.

Not a minute too soon. Just as he disappeared from view a woman rushed into the room. She was tall with reddish hair and held a scarlet kimono round her slender form.

'Where is my husband?' she cried, with a quick frightened glance. 'Who are you?'

Poirot stepped forward with a bow.

'It is to be hoped your husband will not suffer from a chill. I observed that he had slippers on his feet, and that his dressing-gown was a warm one.'

'Who are you? What are you doing in my house?'

'It is true that none of us have the pleasure of your acquaintance, madame. It is especially to be regretted as one of our number has come specially from New York in order to meet you.'

The curtains parted and the Italian stepped out. To my horror I observed that he was brandishing my revolver, which Poirot must doubtless have put down through inadvertence in the cab.

The woman gave a piercing scream and turned to fly, but Poirot was standing in front of the closed door.

'Let me by,' she shrieked. 'He will murder me.'

'Who was it dat croaked Luigi Valdarno?' asked the Italian hoarsely, brandishing the weapon, and sweeping each one of us with it. We dared not move.

'My God, Poirot, this is awful. What shall we do?' I cried.

'You will oblige me by refraining from talking so much, Hastings. I can assure you that our friend will not shoot until I give the word.'

'Youse sure o' dat, eh?' said the Italian, leering unpleasantly.

It was more than I was, but the woman turned to Poirot like a flash.

'What is it you want?'

Poirot bowed.

'I do not think it is necessary to insult Miss Elsa Hardt's intelligence by telling her.'

With a swift movement, the woman snatched up a big black velvet cat which served as a cover for the telephone.

'They are stitched in the lining of that.'

'Clever,' murmured Poirot appreciatively. He stood aside from the door. 'Good evening, madame. I will detain your friend from New York whilst you make your getaway.'

'Whatta fool!' roared the big Italian, and raising the revolver he fired point-blank at the woman's retreating figure just as I flung myself upon him.

But the weapon merely clicked harmlessly and Poirot's voice rose in mild reproof.

'Never will you trust your old friend, Hastings. I do not care for my friends to carry loaded pistols about with them and never would I permit a mere acquaintance to do so. No, no, *mon ami.*' This to the Italian who was swearing hoarsely. Poirot continued to address him in a tone of mild reproof: 'See now, what I have done for you. I have saved you from being hanged. And do not think that our beautiful lady will escape. No, no, the house is watched, back and front. Straight into the arms of the police they will go. Is not that a beautiful and consoling thought? Yes, you may leave the room now.

But be careful—be very careful. I—Ah, he is gone! And my friend Hastings looks at me with eyes of reproach. But it's all so simple! It was clear, from the first, that out of several hundred, probably, applicants for No. 4 Montagu Mansions, only the Robinsons were considered suitable. Why? What was there that singled them out from the rest—at practically a glance. Their appearance? Possibly, but it was not so unusual. Their name, then!'

'But there's nothing unusual about the name of Robinson,' I cried. 'It's quite a common name.'

'Ah! *Sapristi*, but exactly! That was the point. Elsa Hardt and her husband, or brother or whatever he really is, come from New York, and take a flat in the name of Mr and Mrs Robinson. Suddenly they learn that one of these secret societies, the Mafia, or the Camorra, to which doubtless Luigi Valdarno belonged, is on their track. What do they do? They hit on a scheme of transparent simplicity. Evidently they knew that their pursuers were not personally acquainted with either of them. What, then, can be simpler? They offer the flat at an absurdly low rental. Of the thousands of young couples in London looking for flats, there cannot fail to be several Robinsons. It is only a matter of waiting. If you will look at the name of Robinson in the telephone directory, you will realize that a fair-haired Mrs Robinson was pretty sure to come along sooner or later. Then what will happen? The avenger arrives. He knows the name, he knows the address. He strikes! All is over, vengeance is satisfied, and Miss Elsa Hardt has escaped by the skin of her teeth once more. By the way, Hastings, you must present me to the real Mrs Robinson— that delightful and truthful creature! What will they think when they find their flat has been broken into! We must hurry back. Ah, that sounds like Japp and his friends arriving.'

A mighty tattoo sounded on the knocker.

'How do you know this address?' I asked as I followed Poirot out into the hall. 'Oh, of course, you had the first Mrs Robinson followed when she left the other flat.'

'*A la bonne heure*, Hastings. You use your grey cells at last. Now for a little surprise for Japp.'

Softly unbolting the door, he stuck the cat's head round the edge and ejaculated a piercing 'Miaow'.

The Scotland Yard inspector, who was standing outside with another man, jumped in spite of himself.

'Oh, it's only Monsieur Poirot at one of his little jokes!' he exclaimed, as Poirot's head followed that of the cat. 'Let us in, moosior.'

'You have our friends safe and sound?'

'Yes, we've got the birds all right. But they hadn't got the goods with them.'

'I see. So you come to search. Well, I am about to depart with Hastings, but I should like to give you a little lecture upon the history and habits of the domestic cat.'

'For the Lord's sake, have you gone completely balmy?'

'The cat,' declaimed Poirot, 'was worshipped by the ancient Egyptians. It is still regarded as a symbol of good luck if a black cat crosses your path. This cat crossed your path tonight, Japp. To speak of the interior of any animal or any person is not, I know, considered polite in England. But the interior of this cat is perfectly delicate. I refer to the lining.'

With a sudden grunt, the second man seized the cat from Poirot's hand.

'Oh, I forgot to introduce you,' said Japp. 'Mr Poirot, this is Mr Burt of the United States Secret Service.'

The American's trained fingers had felt what he was looking for. He held out his hand, and for a moment speech failed him. Then he rose to the occasion.

'Pleased to meet you,' said Mr Burt.

BIBLIOGRAPHY

Agatha Christie's short stories typically appeared first in magazines and then in her short story books, which tended to be different collections in the UK and the US. This list attempts to catalogue the first publication of each of the stories included in this collection, and gives alternative story titles when used.

Introduction

Excerpted from *An Autobiography* © 1977 Agatha Christie Limited.

The Affair at the Victory Ball

© Agatha Christie Ltd 1923. First published in the UK in *The Sketch* No. 1571, 7 March 1923 and in the US in the *Blue Book Magazine* Vol. 37, No. 5, September 1923. Reprinted in *Poirot's Early Cases* (UK, 1974).

The Tuesday Night Club

© Agatha Christie Limited 1927. First published in the UK in *The Royal Magazine*, No. 350, December 1927 and in the US in *Detective Story Magazine*, Vol. 101, N. 5, 2 June 1928 as 'The Solving Six'. Reprinted in *Poirot's Early Cases* (UK, 1974).

The Case of the Discontented Soldier

© Agatha Christie Limited 1932. First published in the US in *Cosmopolitan*, No. 554, August 1932 as 'The Soldier Who Wanted Danger'. First published in the UK in *Woman's Pictorial*, No. 614, 15 October 1932 as 'Adventure – By Request'. Reprinted in *Parker Pyne Investigates* (UK, 1934).

The Adventure of the Clapham Cook

© Agatha Christie Limited 1923. First published in the UK in *The Sketch* No. 1607, 14 November 1923 and in the US in the *Blue Book Magazine* Vol.41, No. 5, September 1925. Reprinted in *Poirot's Early Cases* (UK, 1974).

The Case of the Caretaker

© Agatha Christie Limited 1942. First published in the UK in *Strand Magazine*, No. 613, January 1942 and in the US in the *Chicago Sunday Tribune*, 5 July 1942. Reprinted in the UK in *Miss Marple's Final Cases and Two Other Stories* (1979).

A Fairy in the Flat

© Agatha Christie Limited 1924. First published as 'Publicity' in *The Sketch*, 24 September 1924, and reprinted in *Partners in Crime* (US and UK, 1929) in which the story became the first two chapters: 'A Fairy in the Flat' and 'A Pot of Tea'.

The Kidnapped Prime Minister

© Agatha Christie Limited 1923. First published in the UK in *The Sketch* No. 1578, 25 April 1923 and in the US in the *Blue Book Magazine* Vol. 39, No. 3, July 1924 under the title 'The Kidnapped Premier'.

The Listerdale Mystery

© Agatha Christie Limited 1925. First published in the UK in *The Grand Magazine*, No. 250, December 1925 as 'The Benevolent Butler'. Reprinted in *The Listerdale Mystery* (UK, 1934).

Traitor Hands (The Witness for the Prosecution)

© Agatha Christie Limited 1925. First published in the US in *Flynn's Weekly*, 31 January 1925. Reprinted in *The Hound of Death* (UK, 1933) as 'The Witness for the Prosecution'.

The Lonely God

© Agatha Christie Limited 1926. First published in the UK in *The Royal Magazine*, Issue 333, July 1926. Reprinted in *While the Light Lasts and Other Stories* (UK, 1997).

The Sign in the Sky

© Agatha Christie Limited 1925. First published in the UK in *The Grand Magazine*, No. 245, July 1925 and in the US in *The Police Magazine*, June 1925.

The Adventure of the Cheap Flat

© Agatha Christie Limited 1923. First published in the UK in *The Sketch* No. 1580, 9 May 1923 and in the US in the *Blue Book Magazine* Vol. 39, No. 1, May 1924. Reprinted in *Poirot Investigates* (UK, 1924).

ALSO AVAILABLE

With spring comes April showers and blossoming
fields – but wickedness is never far from the surface.
With the turning of the year, Hercule Poirot, Jane
Marple, Tommy and Tuppence and many more of
Agatha Christie's unforgettable creations tangle with
a season of sinister schemes and perilous crimes.

'Without a doubt, the greatest
mystery writer of all time'

RAGNAR JÓNASSON

ALSO AVAILABLE

Summertime – as the temperature rises, so does the potential for evil. From Cornwall to the French Riviera, whether against a background of Delphic temples or English country houses, Agatha Christie's most famous characters solve even the most devilish of conundrums as the summer sun beats down. Pull up a deckchair and enjoy plot twists and red herrings galore from the bestselling fiction writer of all time.

'Agatha Christie is the gateway drug to crime fiction both for readers and for writers'

VAL McDERMID